THE ANATOMY OF LOSS

THE ANATOMY OF LOSS

A novel

ARJUN RAJ GAIND

BLOOMSBURY
NEW DELHI • LONDON • OXFORD • NEW YORK • SYDNEY

BLOOMSBURY INDIA
Bloomsbury Publishing India Pvt. Ltd
Second Floor, LSC Building No. 4, DDA Complex, Pocket C – 6 & 7,
Vasant Kunj, New Delhi, 110070

BLOOMSBURY, BLOOMSBURY INDIA and the Diana logo
are trademarks of Bloomsbury Publishing Plc

First published in India 2022
This edition published 2022

ISBN: PB: 978-93-54355-02-8; eBook: 978-93-54355-04-2
2 4 6 8 10 9 7 5 3 1

Typeset in Bembo Std by Manipal Technologies Limited
Printed and bound in India by Replika Press Pvt. Ltd.

For my Masumeh, who gave me the strength
to believe again

When I stand before thee at the day's end, thou shalt see my scars and know that I had my wounds and also my healing.

—**Rabindranath Tagore**, *Stray Birds*

One writes of scars healed, a loose parallel to the pathology of the skin, but there is no such thing in the life of an individual. There are open wounds, shrunk sometimes to the size of a pin-prick but wounds still. The marks of suffering are more comparable to the loss of a finger, or of the sight of an eye. We may not miss them, either, for one minute in a year, but if we should there is nothing to be done about it.

—**F. Scott Fitzgerald**, *Tender Is the Night*

AUTHOR'S NOTE

In the name of melodrama and nostalgia—the two ingredients without which no Punjabi story is complete—I have taken a few small factual liberties in the telling of this tale. The first and most glaring, of course, is my interpretation of the lyrics to the song sung by Nani outside the police station. The tragic saga of Heer–Ranjha in oral form has been performed since time immemorial in Punjab. The version I have chosen to use is the quissa written by the incomparable Waris Shah. There are many extant renditions of this marvellous folk song, most famously the one sung by Lata Mangeshkar, although personally I am somewhat partial to the version performed by Asa Singh Mastana. I have tried to keep my translation of the lyrics as accurate as possible. However, some purists out there may point out that my efforts are far from perfect, and I apologise for any linguistic inconsistencies on my part.

The other liberty I have taken is in my interpretation of the Mool Mantra. Generally, these twelve words, so holy to all Sikhs, are translated as one of two versions: either the one as interpreted by Eleanor Nesbitt or the other by Pashaura Singh. However, I have chosen to use a slightly different interpretation, more specifically the one my own grandfather recited to me when I was a boy and I asked him what these wonderful words meant. It is slightly removed from the exact translation but I believe it conveys, in a very clear manner, the sense of harmony and unwavering faith that is at the very core of the Sikh system of belief.

I

For as long as I could remember, my grandfather had always had a beard.

And what a beard it was—a shiny silver mane that made him seem majestic somehow, almost leonine! Personally, I confess, I had always found it odd that Nana would choose to cultivate such a monumental profusion of facial hair. After all, the rest of his head was almost entirely bare, tonsured like a monk's pate, and the ornate, almost Chaldean flourish of his whiskers made his appearance seem unusual, even a little eccentric.

Nonetheless, no matter how peculiar it may have looked, Nana was terribly proud of that beard of his. Every morning, I remember, he made a habit of grooming it with a fine-tooth comb made of ivory until it jutted forth from his chin like the barnacled prow of an ancient ship. And each night, he oiled its opulent facade with a pungent mixture of Silvikrin and coconut oil before wrapping it lovingly with a silk swaddling cloth to make sure that it lost none of its bushy shapeliness as he slept.

Why sometimes, as I watched him primp and prune and pluck, I would be overcome with envy that I didn't have any facial hair myself.

I was just eight years old at the time, but for some inexplicable reason, there was nothing more important to me than having a beard like my grandfather's. I cannot describe the countless hours I spent hunched in front of the bathroom mirror, waiting, hoping, praying for that first pubescent follicle to appear on my chin and signal to the world that I was a man at last. I did peculiar things to try and compel my facial hair to grow. Time and again, I shaved twice, sometimes even thrice, a day with a rusty old Wilkinson razor I found in a drawer, scraping away at my cheeks until they were so raw and red that Nani had to slather them with Lacto Calamine lotion. And though it's embarrassing to admit now, once I even went to bed after caking my face with a thick layer of rich Doab mud, hoping that the ripe loam of Punjab would somehow cause a sprinkling of hair to sprout overnight like magical grass.

As for my grandmother, she could not have felt more differently about Nana's beard.

For as long as I could recall, Nani had waged a secret war against this most prickly of opponents—a silent, subtle campaign to compel my grandfather to shave.

Often, his little comb would disappear, just when he wanted it the most, and from time to time, tiny hair would appear, as subtle little hints, in his lunch. Also, every single day, almost as if by magic, he would chance upon a never-ending succession of razor blades in the strangest of places—between the pages of the newspaper, inside the pocket of a freshly ironed shirt as he dressed and, once, even in the palm of his hand when he awakened from a nap on the living room divan.

It was a battle that had been raging for decades, long before I was even conceived.

'My cheeks are sensitive, Gobind,' my grandmother would often gripe. 'One of these days, I will not permit you to kiss me any more.'

'If you forbid me to kiss you,' Nana would reply with an impish smile, 'I will find another woman to be the queen of my heart because no woman in Punjab can resist a makhna with a beard as fine as mine.'

'Ha,' Nani would scoff when she heard this threat. 'As if anyone would have a flatulent old fool like you.'

Regardless of how often Nani nagged him, Nana always refused to shave even a solitary follicle. In fact, as he would often object to Nani, it was his birthright, no, his moral duty, to have a beard since he was a Bedi, which meant that in his veins flowed the blood of Nanak himself, the founder of the Sikh religion.

At that point, I was much too immature to understand the significance of our bloodline, too naïve to apprehend how indivisible a role religion played in Punjab, second only to family. When you are a child, faith, identity and spirituality are all abstracts, as immaterial as clouds. You are expected to believe in things without ever bothering to question them. You are supposed to accept, not investigate.

Of course, it didn't help that neither of my parents was particularly religious. My father, who was a Kashmiri Pandit, refused to go to the temple, not even for Diwali puja. If there really was a God, he would often say, where the hell was he hiding when the Abdullahs chased us out of Srinagar? As for my mother, the only time I had seen her pray was when she was cooking—reciting the japji under her breath when she fried an egg, probably hoping that this catechism would keep the yolk from splitting apart.

Both my grandparents were equally agnostic. Nana liked to call himself a theological non-cognitivist, whatever that was, and Nani, well, she never spoke of her beliefs at all, always finding some way to change the subject when it ever came up, preferring instead to speak of the weather or something equally mundane.

Still, in spite of my secular upbringing, Nana's claim managed to get me thinking. If he was a Bedi, what did that make me? Was I one too? Was Guru Nanak's blood running through my veins as well? Did that make me special in some way? Did it make me holy?

How could I find the answers to these questions? How could I possibly tell? I decided to ask our cook, who was quite appropriately called Cookie. She was an ancient sardarni, with buck teeth from smiling too much and flabby arms that wobbled when she moved, like Weikfield jelly. I knew she was very religious because she had once boasted proudly that she had committed the whole of the Granth Sahib to memory and was able to repeat it without taking a breath.

'Cookie,' I asked her, 'how can you tell if you are Sikh?'

'It's easy,' she told me, breathless and sweaty from pounding spices in a stone mortar with a pestle the size of my leg. 'There is a saying my mother taught me: "*sir vadey sardara dey, per vadey gavara dey*".' She pointed at my sneakers. 'All you have to do is check your feet. If they are bigger than your head, then you are definitely not a sardar.'

It was a perplexing and rather ridiculous answer, but I decided to test it out. Finding a quiet corner, I removed my PT shoes and tried my best to bring my foot up to my face so I could see which was larger. Sadly, I was much too chubby to manage such a feat of gymnastic flexibility, and after a few minutes of huffing and puffing, I gave up with a despairing groan.

Instead, I turned to the one other person I thought might have an answer for me.

I found my grandmother sitting on her favourite rocking chair, knitting yet another of her innumerable sweaters. In many ways, she was the precise opposite of my grandfather. While he was brash and loud, almost bumptious, Nani was quiet, calm and placid, except for her fingers, which never seemed to stay still, not even for a moment.

'Nani,' I asked, 'I need to know. Am I Hindu or am I Sikh?'

I could tell my question took her by surprise because, just for a heartbeat, the knitting needles stopped clacking. She did not reply at first, watching me pensively, but then, after a long interlude, her knitting resumed and she said, 'You can be anything you want, my beautiful boy. It is up to you to decide.'

This was certainly not the answer I was looking for. It left me only more confused, and I was about to tell her that she had been of no help at all when she shook her head.

'Did you know, my love, that I am Muslim?'

This revelation caused my jaw to drop, quite literally. Was she trying to be funny? Was this a bad joke? How could Nani be Muslim, of all things? It just did not make a whit of sense. Everybody knew that, in Punjab, Muslims were the enemy. They were the ones who had killed the ninth Guru, Tegh Bahadur, and murdered thousands during Partition.

I studied my grandmother intently, trying to deduce if there was something odd about her, something peculiar that I had failed to notice before, but she was the same delicate creature she had always been, as frail as a sparrow. I had never met a Muslim person before, but from all that I had heard, they were supposed to be different from us. How could Nani possibly be one of them, I found myself thinking, when she was so gentle, so kind and so beautiful? Surely, she was lying. But why?

She must have sensed the depth of my bewilderment because she gave me a gentle smile.

'It's true, my jaan. I was raised in an orthodox family; why, I even had to wear a burkha when I was your age, covering everything but my eyes. I met your grandfather in college and we fell in love, even though he was Sikh and I was Muslim. His father forbade him from marrying me. He insisted that if Gobind took me as his wife, he would be betraying his misl and tainting the purity of his bloodline.'

She sighed, a plaintive exclamation of breath.

'But your grandfather did not care. He loved me, you see, and would not forsake me, not even when his father disowned him. Can you imagine that, puttar?' Her eyes shone—I could not be sure if it was sorrow or exultation. 'He gave up everything for me; his family, his wealth, his faith. What could be a greater act of love than that?'

'That is the only answer I can give you, my beloved little sparrow. Love is the truth. Love is the only real god worth worshipping. Everything else is just words, little more than hyperbole.'

It was a beautiful, touching sentiment, but unfortunately, it only served to deepen the budding existential crisis that I found myself gripped by. If anything, Nani's words had left me with even more questions. What was I really? Was I Hindu, like my father's family? Was I Sikh, like Nana, or was I Muslim, like Nani?

It did not take me long to realise that there was only one person who could sort me out and that was my grandfather.

A long time ago, Nana had been a very important man, a professor sahib, a famous poet and storyteller, but he had long since retired from that life.

Now, he spent most of his time in his cluttered study, drinking cup after cup of Darjeeling tea and reading book after book after book. In fact, I don't think I ever actually saw him without a book of some sort clutched in his bony hands, not once in all those years I spent at his farm.

Nana worshipped books and they surrounded him like squat, square-faced companions. They lined the walls of the bungalow, so numerous that he had long since run out of shelf space and piles of books had accumulated on the cracked stone floor into haphazard towers of musty volumes whose dusty pages made me sneeze each time I cracked open their covers.

He would spend hours, sometimes days, sitting in his favourite easy chair, leafing through one of his books with a tiny, contented smile on his shaggy face. Sometimes, without even realising it, he would tear one corner from the page he was reading and roll it up into a tiny ball, which he would then pop into his mouth absent-mindedly. Nana would chew on this fragment of paper silently as long as he was reading until all that remained was a sour wet pulp, which he spat out into a spittoon like a stream of black tobacco. In fact, as I watched him, it would seem to me that he was eating words, the way most people eat snacks, as if he was absorbing them and making them a part of his own broad body.

Normally, I had strict instructions not to disturb him when he was in his study. That was what Nani called his imagination time, and I was always afraid that if I intruded, I would disturb some arcane ritual, as if Nana was like Dr Strange, hallucinating reality out of nothingness, knitting it with a pencil the way Nani wove her sweaters out of filaments of wool.

This one time though, caution lost out to curiosity.

'Do you believe in God, Nana?' I exclaimed, marching into his sanctum brashly.

I don't know if it was me or this question that surprised him more. His consternation at being disturbed lasted only a moment, before metamorphosing into an amused smile, his eyes dancing with delight as he contemplated my inquiry.

'Sometimes, especially when it rains, I do believe in God,' he replied, pursing his lips. 'Other times, I find it difficult to believe that an all-powerful deity would create something quite as irritating as humankind.'

Putting down his book, he gave me his undivided attention.

'Why do you ask, puttar? Why this sudden interest in ecclesiastical matters?'

'I'm so confused, Nana,' I said, and it all came gushing out—the depths of the dilemma that was consuming me.

Nana listened patiently while I poured my heart out, waiting until I was done before he sniffed, and said, 'Have you ever wondered, puttar, why there are no lions in Punjab?'

This abrupt change in direction left me quite discombobulated. What on earth was he talking about? What did lions have to do with anything? Was Nana making fun of me?

As it turned out, he wasn't. It was the beginning of one of his legendary stories, and as Nana sat back, taking a deep breath, I settled down on the floor at his feet, cradling my chin on my knees.

'Once upon a time,' he explained, 'Punjab was teeming with lions. You could find them everywhere, around every corner and in every garden, inside cupboards and beneath beds, and even in the trees, like birds, fast asleep atop the branches.'

This made me laugh. He was being mad on purpose, of course. Lions in trees, hah, that was impossible. Even I knew that.

Still, I decided to play along.

'What happened to them, Nana? Where did all the lions go?'

'Well, it so happened that one day, when Nanak was a young man, he was walking home when the meanest, biggest lion in Punjab sprang out from behind a bush and roared at him.'

'Grawwr,' Nana growled, imitating the lion so perfectly I nearly jumped out of my skin, 'I am going to eat you, boy.'

'Now, most people would have screamed and tried to run away, but even as a boy, Nanak was very special. Instead of panicking, he gave the lion a kind-hearted smile and said, "Why would you want to do that, my friend?"

'"Why?" The lion echoed, bewildered by such a calm reaction. After all, his fangs were as long as scimitars, and he was accustomed to inspiring nothing but fear. "Why? Because I am famished, of course, and you look very edible."

'Nanak laughed. "Do you realise, my friend, that if you eat me, then you eat all my sorrows and my woes and my problems as well? Surely that will give you some serious indigestion."

'This declaration left the lion even more confused. This was the first time he had encountered prey that dared to talk back to him, and frankly, when he gave it some thought, he realised that what Nanak had said to him made complete sense, and the last thing he wanted was an aching tummy.

'Frowning, he said, "If I do not eat you, boy, then how am I to fill my stomach?"

'"Well," Nanak said, "if you are really that hungry, you could share my lunch."

'Unwrapping his bundle, he offered the lion his food, which was a rough farmer's meal, just sarson da saag and makki di roti, but it had been cooked by his mother with a lot of love and as a result, smelled so heavenly that it made the lion's mouth water.

'Even though he was a staunch non-vegetarian, the lion decided, why not give it a try? Rather reluctantly, he took one tiny bite. Much to his surprise, it tasted fantastic, and so he took another bite and then two and finally gulped it all down.

'When everything was gone, he sat back and let out a satisfied belch, noticing that he had left Nanak nothing but crumbs.

'"Oh no," he purred, "what have I done? Forgive me, my friend, for you will go hungry now."

'"That's fine," Nanak replied with a smile. "I may be hungry but at least I am still alive."

'When he heard that, the lion gave a vast laugh.

'"I like you," he declared. "You are both generous and wise. I think that from this day on, I shall be your chela, your follower, as shall my sons and their sons after them."

'With that declaration, he stood up on his hind legs, pulled back his mane and tied it firmly into a topknot.

'"From this day onwards," he announced, "I shall be known as Sher Singh and I will be your most faithful follower."'

Nana grinned and patted my head.

'And that, my boy, is why there are no lions in Punjab—because they have all risen up on their hind legs and become Sikhs. And that is also why we call ourselves Singh—because once, when the world was young, we were all lions.'

It was a pretty wonderful story. If I shut my eyes, I could imagine that lion standing upright and tottering about like a baby taking its first steps. I could see him pulling back his mane to leave his face bare, except for a beard, of course, that was every bit as bushy as my grandfather's. In fact, that was what he looked like in my mind's eye, just like Nana, exactly as imperious and as proud.

'Do you understand what I am trying to say, puttar?' Nana said. 'Don't look for answers out there. If there is a god—' Leaning forward, he tapped my chest with one blunt knuckle, '—he is in here, inside you.'

'Remember, it does not matter if you decide to worship the Granth or the Koran or the Gita. They are all paths that lead to the same destination. All that matters is that *you* be brave enough to choose what you want to believe for yourself. Ignore what anyone else tells you is right or wrong, and just follow your heart because that is what it truly means to be Punjabi.'

I thought about it. It made so much sense—such simple, elegant eloquence—that I could not help but nod in agreement.

'I have made up my mind, Nana,' I said. 'When I grow up, I am going to be a Sikh because I want a beard exactly like yours.'

This announcement made Nana chuckle.

'Well,' he responded, 'I suppose that is as good a reason as any to be a Sikh.'

'Will it take very long, Nana? When will my beard begin to grow?'

Stifling a grin, my grandfather kissed me lightly on my forehead. The stiff coir of his moustache tickled my skin and I sighed, gripped by that effortless happiness that only a child can comprehend.

'Soon, puttar,' he said softly.

'Soon, when you are ready to be a man.'

2

Each year, during the torpid months of October and November, when Bombay became too humid to endure and all the schools closed for Diwali vacations, my parents would pack me off to Nana and Nani's farm, which was located just a few kilometres west of Amritsar.

I adored Punjab. I loved the pale calm of its temperate weather, the rustic charm of the yellow wheat fields and the ripe smell of sugar cane that languished listlessly in the thick air, like a sweet white mist. I revelled in the bare desolation of the landscape around the farm, uncluttered by the urban sprawl of city life, nothing but acres and acres of empty green space where I was free to wander and explore. It was such a pleasant change from Bombay—so different from the tall prison complex of skyscrapers within which I ordinarily resided, hemmed in on every side by miles of drab concrete and glass.

And, of course, more than anything else, I treasured every moment spent with my grandparents in the tiny colonial-era bungalow that was their home, tucked away behind a copse of acacia trees. To me, it was a self-contained universe, with its faded sepia photographs and chintz curtains and yellowing damask tablecloths, a safe haven where the present merged with the past, and the future, if only for a few moments, seemed to stand perfectly still.

At least until 1984.

That year, my parents very nearly made up their minds not to send me to Amritsar at all. After all, only three months had passed since the debacle of Operation Blue Star and the atmosphere in Punjab was still very, very tense.

Still, somehow Nana had prevailed upon my father to let me visit in spite of the chaos. He had insisted that I would be perfectly safe since the farm was much too isolated to see any real trouble. Also, he reminded my father that Nani had not been keeping well at all; the arthritis in her knees was bothering her more and more, and she could barely walk, much less endure the hardship of a long train journey to Bombay.

As a result, regardless of the turmoil in Punjab, I went to visit my grandparents as usual. Just as Nana promised, everything seemed quite peaceful, as if nothing bad had happened at all. To tell the truth, I did not understand what the hullabaloo was all about really. At first, when my grandparents' friends came over for tea and chattered on and on about Blue Star this and Blue Star that, I thought that they were talking about something that had fallen from space—a chunk of some faraway constellation as cerulean as the sea.

Strangely enough, as I look back now, I think that was the best holiday I spent with my grandparents.

That year, despite all the upheavals surrounding us, somehow their cottage managed to be even lovelier, even more idyllic, like the eye in the midst of a raging cyclone.

Because the weather had been warm, almost sultry, Nani allowed me, rather grudgingly, to sleep out on the verandah each night, with the stars glittering above me and the cicadas clicking in the bushes nearby like tiny castanets. That was the year Nana taught me how to shoot clay pigeons with a .22 and how to swim freestyle and how to play chess, and I actually even managed to beat him once or twice, much to my unending glee.

Sadly, what none of us had realised was that this tranquillity was merely temporary, the calm before the breaking of a terrible storm.

It was just after noon, I remember, when we found out what had happened.

We were ensconced in the living room, enjoying a quiet respite after a heavy lunch of aloo parathas and salted buttermilk. Nana was sitting in his favourite chair and reading an old issue of the *Illustrated Weekly*, Nani knitting one of her endless scarves and listening to a medley of Hindi film tunes on the transistor radio, while I sprawled on the floor with my G.I. Joes.

That was the precise moment the All India Radio broadcaster interrupted the scheduled broadcast to announce that Prime Minister Indira Gandhi had been assassinated.

Gasping with surprise, Nani sat up straight, going rigid with shock. Her knitting needles slipped from her fingers and fell to the floor, tinkling gently like tiny bells. As for my grandfather, he put down his magazine and leaned forward calmly to turn up the volume until the newscaster's buzzing words reverberated through the room, echoing slightly, as if they were made of glass.

We listened in stunned silence as the news trickled in.

The announcer's voice was unsteady, hissing with tension as he described what had happened earlier that morning in New Delhi. He explained that Mrs Gandhi had been on her way back to the prime minister's residence at 1, Safdarjung Road that morning when she was shot down by two of her own bodyguards.

Hesitantly, he paused before revealing the identity of the assassins. They were both Sikhs, he said, and the shooting seemed to be in retaliation for Operation Blue Star, which Mrs Gandhi had instigated a few months previously.

'Oh! God,' Nani moaned, clapping one horrified hand to her mouth. 'What have they done…? What have those fools done…?'

Gasping, she started to cry, keening softly, like a trapped bird. A soft trickle of tears brimmed from her eyes, becoming dribbles of dark mascara, which left jagged stains on her crinkled cheeks.

Still, Nana didn't say a word. His face remained entirely expressionless as if it had been carved from granite. As Nani's sobbing grew louder, more insistent, he made no move to console her. Instead, he just sat there, rooted to his chair like a statue, listening intently while the announcer droned on.

I don't know how long we sat there. I lost track of time. The news grew more and more horrifying. A huge mob had surrounded the All India Institute of Medical Sciences, where Mrs Gandhi's body had been taken, chanting the slogan '*khoon ka badla khoon*' (seek blood for blood). Already, buses had been stopped and numerous Sikhs pulled out and assaulted. Their turbans had been torn from their heads, and vehicles driven by sardars, including the President's motorcade, had been pelted with stones.

Then, we heard the words we had all been dreading, just as the cool hours of the early evening arrived.

The first fatality had occurred—a nameless casualty described only as an elderly Sikh man who had been doused with kerosene and set aflame by an angry crowd.

This was just too much for me to take. Terrified, I rushed to Nani. She swallowed me into her thin arms, hugging me close to her chest so desperately I could feel her heart pulsing through the rack of her ribs as furious as a hummingbird's wings.

'Enough! Switch it off, Gobind! Can't you see it's scaring the boy?'

With a frown, Nana obeyed. Stretching out a hand, he flicked the radio off. Abruptly, the announcer's crackling voice clicked into oblivion. Without it, suddenly the room seemed too quiet, empty, somehow macabre. My ears refused to stop hissing, ringing slightly, and I can't explain it, I felt somehow dizzy like I was going to fall over.

I saw this same knife-edge of panic mirrored on my grandmother's face.

'What is going to happen to us, Gobind?' Nani gulped. Her voice was taut, so brittle it echoed. She was shivering as if she was cold, and I hugged her even more tightly to try and keep her warm.

Even then Nana refused to speak. It unnerved me to see him like that. This was the longest I had known him to be silent. It felt unnatural, like he had somehow lost his voice, become stricken by mysterious laryngitis.

Instead of answering Nani's timorous inquiry, he stood up and retreated to the bathroom, shutting its thick door behind him with a dull, almost final, thump.

After his brusque departure, at first, I didn't move at all. Nani continued to hold me close until I could barely breathe. My nostrils filled with her smell—that sad, sour scent of roses mingled with despair.

'I am okay now, Nani,' I said. 'You can let go of me.'

She only did so very reluctantly, which made me wonder if I had been holding on to her or had it been the other way around. Her eyes were streaked and red. Forlornly, she made a great show of inspecting me, as if she wanted to make sure that I was still the same grandson I had been a few moments ago. I struggled and pulled away when she spat on one corner of her cotton chunni and carefully wiped my face clean where her tears had left smears.

'Go and play with your toys,' she said. 'I am going to make us all some dinner. Everything will feel better after a piping hot meal, just you wait and see.'

I tried to do as she ordered, retreating to the far corner of the room to entertain myself with my collection of G.I. Joe action figures, but suddenly, they seemed so trivial to me, so very plastic. Disappointed, I piled them in an untidy heap and sat limply on the floor, fidgeting uncomfortably, waiting impatiently for Nana to come back, but he was still closeted in the bathroom, doing God only knows what in there.

Finally, my boredom won out and I followed Nani into the kitchen. She was binding atta to make parathas, mixing flour and water in a massive brass plate called a prath with furious intensity, like she was trying to wrestle away all her nervous energy.

'Why did they shoot her, Nani?' I inquired, drawing a spiral in the loose flour with one curious finger.

This question brought her efforts to a halt. Her shoulders slumped, and she stopped pounding away at the atta to let out a solemn sigh.

'When you are older, son, I will explain it to you,' she murmured. 'That is the thing about hatred, puttar. In the end, all it begets is more hatred, no matter how noble the cause.'

Even though she was facing away from me, I could see her reflection distorted in the window in front of her as the wan creases that scarred her forehead grew deeper and more pronounced with grief. Nani shook her head exactly three times. The first was disbelief, the second futility and the last a helpless anguish that wracked through her body, not unlike the trembling of an epileptic. I could not help but think that she looked more fragile than I had ever seen her, like she was about to break apart and crack open into a thousand shards.

She was scared, I realised. Nani was terrified. It surprised me, and I confess, I was more than a little taken aback. She was a grown-up, and grown-ups were not supposed to be scared of anything, were they? Was it because she was a girl? Was that why she looked so worried, so petrified?

My confusion only lasted a moment before being replaced by concern and the need to comfort her. But what could I say? What words could possibly suffice? The truth was that I was equally terrified. My stomach was so queasy that I wanted to vomit. My legs felt weak and infirm, and it was taking all my willpower not to start bawling like a baby.

But to my surprise, something strange happened inside me. When I compared my own fear to the despair evident on my grandmother's face, suddenly my agitation seemed negligible, almost unimportant. I don't quite know how, but the realisation that she needed me somehow gave me newfound strength.

No, I thought to myself, biting down on my lip and blinking back the flush of heat that had been threatening to brim from my eyes. I will not break down. After all, a real man would never allow himself to weep, or feel scared, would he, especially not a man who wanted to grow up and have a beard like Nana's?

Nervously, I swallowed, striving to control the trembling in my chest.

'Don't worry, Nani,' I whispered to my grandmother, trying my best to hide my uneasiness and to sound as fearless as I possibly could. 'I'll take care of you. I won't let anyone hurt you, I promise.'

Nani smiled wanly when she heard the pompous bravado of my words. Abandoning the atta, she glanced back at me over her shoulder, one sad eye shining through a silver curtain of hair.

'Oh, my boy,' she sighed. Her voice brimmed with affection. 'My dear sweet boy. You are such a brave little boy.'

She smiled tenderly and reached out to pat my head with one arthritis-gnarled hand before she realised it was covered with flour and let it just hang there between us, fingers and knuckles curled into what seemed like a question mark.

'No, not a boy,' she whispered sweetly, slightly, brightly. 'A man. That's what you are. My brave little man.'

When I heard those words, in spite of the bitter quinine of anxiety souring my mouth, my heart swelled with a frenzy of pride. Almost instinctively, my fingers shot to my face, searching to see if any hair had begun to sprout.

And then, unbelievably, I found something—the first velvety bristle above my upper lip, so soft yet so tangible.

It felt just like cotton wool.

3

Almost two hours passed before Nana emerged from the bathroom.

Or rather, a stranger who bore a slight resemblance to my grandfather appeared—a pale, beardless ghost with pinched cheeks as white as porcelain and a chin as bare as a plain of virgin snow.

Astonished, I gaped at this apparition, quite unable to contain my amazement. It couldn't be Nana, I thought, staggering. Surely, this was an impostor and a poor one at that, so hairless and plain.

Bewildered, I studied this … this pretender's features carefully, barely able to recognise him.

This man, he was not commanding or imperious like my grandfather had been, no. Instead, he looked so ordinary, so small faced, so utterly common.

At first, I couldn't help but dislike him a little because he was brooding and strange and old. The bleakness of his visage scared me—the dull intensity that knotted his brows and the severity of his perpendicular gash of a mouth. His face was grey and dotted with liver spots, his cheeks sunken and hollow. But then, I saw his eyes, those familiar grey sorrow-flecked eyes, and I knew that it was my Nana after all, the same man I knew and loved so well.

Nani was busy on the telephone talking to one of our neighbours. When my grandfather entered the room, she paused momentarily to glance up at him. Curiously enough, she did not react at all as I had expected when she set eyes upon Nana's newly shorn avatar. I was sure she would clap her hands together with pleasure, perhaps even whoop with glee, because the naked pallor of Nana's face meant that she had finally triumphed, that she was rid of her old nemesis at long last.

But rather than exclaiming with delight, Nani remained impassive, entirely unaffected by this sudden metamorphosis in Nana's appearance. She didn't smile or laugh or even blink.

Instead, if anything, as she stared at him, sad dismay drifted across the sallow angles of her face, a shadowy gloom not unlike the penumbra of an eclipse.

Putting down the telephone receiver, she creaked to her feet and gathered up her purse from the antique side table that flanked the door. I saw that her hands were shivering, quivering with unsteadiness.

'I am going to go next door to see Mrs Suri for some time,' she said softly. 'She is very worried about her son.'

Her voice wavered, quavering, as full of trembling as her fingers. She watched Nana sadly, waiting for him to meet her eyes. But Nana didn't or couldn't, I could not tell which. Evasively, he nodded in her direction with an awkward, almost embarrassed grin and crossed the room to sink back into the cushioned embrace of his chair. Calmly, as if nothing at all had changed, he leaned forward and switched on the radio.

The All India Radio announcer's voice flooded through the room once again. It was a different person this time, a woman, her voice oscillating not just from the sketchy reception but also from hysteria. Breathlessly, she went on to describe that the situation in Delhi was worsening, that the number of attacks on Sikhs was growing steadily and that a curfew was about to be declared.

Nani groaned when she heard that, an appalled encore of breath. Her face blanched with horror. For one dreadful moment, I was certain that she was going to faint. But somehow she managed to stay upright. As unsteadily as a toddler, she turned and staggered out of the room. I watched her go before turning to glance at Nana, hoping that he would follow her and calm her down, but he stayed motionless, his mouth pursed with unease as his gaze remained fixed on the wire mesh of the radio.

I could not help but gawk at him, unable to tear my eyes away from the sheer newness of his countenance, its new sheerness. Up close, the transformation was quite astounding. I had never really noticed how gaunt his cheeks were before—how hollow and concave. And his jaw, it was weak and infirm, not robust as I had always imagined it to be beneath the elaborate maquillage of his beard. This was not the sort of jawline one found on the face of a warrior—not at all. This was an accountant's chin or a merchant's jowl, petulant and selfish and full of self-pity.

I went up and tapped him gently on his shoulder to garner his attention. Almost numbly, he leaned forward and clicked off the radio, cutting off the announcer in mid-sentence. Once more, a lonely hush engulfed us, a morbid noiselessness that seemed to augment every minor sound, transforming the khat-khat of the fan and the rattle of the wind against the windowpanes and the chattering of crickets out in the garden and the distant thunder of passing lorries into a strange, almost violent, cacophony of the mundane.

'Nana,' I whispered apprehensively, trying very hard not to sound worried even though the sepulchre of my grandfather's mood was beginning to alarm me more than a little.

'Yes, puttar,' he mumbled as he twisted to face me.

'Can I ask you a question…?'

'Of course!' He tried to smile, but all that he could muster was an uneasy rictus, more grimace than grin. 'I enjoy questions, you know that.'

'Why did you shave your beard?'

His brow clouded when he heard this query.

'It isn't just a beard,' he started to say. 'It's a symbol—'

He stopped midway.

'In the days to come,' he tried again after a minute, 'there will be those who will see any man with a beard and assume he is a Sikh and feel the need to extract revenge…'

Once again, his voice tapered away mid-sentence. Nana bit his lip. He looked very frustrated as if he was struggling to find an answer. That surprised me. I had never seen him quite this hesitant. Ordinarily, Nana wielded words like a swordsman flourishing a rapier, but now, he seemed uncharacteristically tongue-tied.

'If you must know,' he said at last, 'I did it for your Nani. I thought it would cheer her up.' He offered me a slight smile. 'She was a great admirer of Mrs Gandhi, you see. She even met her once and shook her hand.'

'Besides, it's only a beard,' he said. 'Underneath, I am still the same man.'

If the old Nana had said that to me, I would have believed him without a question. But this new Nana, his voice rang hollow and try as I might, I couldn't tell if he was saying what he was saying to reassure me or if he was trying to convince himself.

4

In the aftermath of Mrs Gandhi's death, the situation in Amritsar went from bad to worse very quickly.

For the next three days, we didn't dare leave the farm. Even though Punjab was far away from Delhi, a curfew had been declared here as well. It was rumoured that the police and the CRPF were arresting anyone who ventured forth after dark.

For seventy-two long hours, we huddled by the radio, listening worriedly as the climax of this horrible drama unfolded, a tragic denouement of violence and hate.

We heard of riots in Delhi, where unruly mobs led by furious Congress-wallahs were roving the streets, attacking Sikhs with iron rods and swords and hacking off their hair and beards. We heard that men with turbans were being dragged from their homes and murdered and women beaten and raped and that Sikh houses were being burnt down in the middle of the night by blood-thirsty gangs. We heard that the army had been deployed, that Sikh men were starting to disappear by the dozen, and that crowds of wailing wives and daughters had begun to gather outside police stations, screaming for their missing husbands and brothers and sons.

On the afternoon of the fourth day after Mrs Gandhi's death, I guess things had begun to calm down a little because Nani's friends came over to visit her.

There were three of them. I don't remember their names, but I used to call them the three witches because that was what they looked like—those cackling old ladies from Nana's favourite play. The only difference was they dressed like typical sardarnis, wearing chunnis on their heads with matching floral salwar-kameez outfits and identical white hi-top sneakers like it was some kind of uniform.

There was the tall one; I called her Hai Ni because she was immense, almost seven feet tall with hands as big as my head. She had the oddest habit. Before she began a sentence, she always said the phrase 'Hai ni' as though it was her own personal mantra. Then, there was the short dark one; I used to call her Moley because she had an immense mole on her chin from which three lank black hair hung like a peculiar little flower. And the last one I called Moti because she was so immensely round that she looked like a shiny white pearl that had somehow sprouted arms and legs.

It was a weekly ritual. Every Wednesday afternoon, they would drop by for what they called a satsang, a prayer meeting, and Nani would make them tea, cup after brimming cup, which disappeared down their parched gullets like water. Along with the tea, she would serve home-made jam biscuits and tiny bite-sized cucumber and chutney sandwiches, and then she and her friends would chit-chat for hours as they played mah-jong, laughing and slapping down the tiles with delight each time one of them recounted a particularly salacious piece of gossip.

I had made myself a little hiding place in the parlour where one of the bookshelves didn't quite meet the unpainted brick of the wall—a few empty feet of space where I had put down a cushion to make a cosy little cul-de-sac where I could sit and read the musty Modesty

Blaise novels I swiped from Nana's library. It was also the perfect place for me to lurk unobtrusively and pry on the grown-ups while they chatted and conversed about matters that were deemed to be too risqué for my immature ears. I particularly liked to hide there and eavesdrop when Nani's friends came over because they talked about the funniest things, like which shopkeeper was adding chuna to his flour and who was adulterating their milk with water and whose nephew was having an affair with whose sister and who was engaged to marry whose son and whose husband was secretly a drunkard.

It never ceased to amuse me as they harped on and on about the latest rumours fluttering around the village. Even though I had no inkling who these people they were talking about were, it always made me giggle softly when they narrated these spicy bits of tittle-tattle because of the dramatic way they rolled their eyes and hemmed and hawed and clucked their tongues and shook their heads, looking like a trio of demented hens.

That morning, however, their mood seemed unusually subdued. While Nani scuttled to make them tea, Hai Ni, Moley and Moti settled on the sofa in the living room. They did not gossip or smile or lay out the mah-jong tiles. Instead, they sat and stared at each other solemnly, more like they were at a funeral than a tea party.

Once Nani came and joined them, it was Moti who started, by leaning forward and whispering in a sepulchral voice, 'Oh ji, Mrs Singh, have you heard what happened in Dilli after that churail was killed? I heard from Mrs Kapoor who has a niece who lives in Defence Colony that a mob of Congressiyas murdered a whole colony of sardars in Sultanpuri, and that the police watched and did nothing even as the streets ran red with blood.'

Next, it was Moley's turn, her jowls wobbling with abject despair, making her mole dance, its tripartite clump of hair shivering like an insect's feelers.

'Arre, the atrocities they are committing in the name of that woman! Her family should be ashamed to show their faces in public. Why, I heard that in Rewari, they are stripping women naked and raping them in front of their husbands and sons and that they burnt down a gurudwara. Pigs.'

Finally, Hai Ni sighed and shook her head sadly.

'Hai ni, what is the world coming to? What is happening to our country, I ask you? Once India was such a great place to live, but now, we have become worse than animals, hai ni!'

Choking back a gasp, I cowered in my nook and listened with mounting alarm as they continued to recount tale after sordid tale of horror. I could barely believe what they were saying. It couldn't be true … so much death, so much carnage and mayhem. What was happening out there? It was almost too much for my childish ears to take. Until then, I had thought myself quite immune to violence, inured to it by a steady diet of Sylvester Stallone and Arnold Schwarzenegger movies, but now, I found myself nauseated, sick to the pit of my stomach.

And then Hai Ni looked at Nani seriously and said, 'Hai ni, just you see, they will come for us soon. They will not rest until every one of us is dead as well and Punjab is a graveyard.'

When I heard those words, I shuddered involuntarily, and before I knew it, I fell out of my hiding place, tumbling forward with a dull thump.

As I sprawled there on my hands and knees, the trio turned, smiling with surprise. And then, like a pack of hyenas, they were on me, pinching my cheeks with their hard, callused fingers and petting at my hair.

'Hai ni, what a handsome boy he is now!'

'No-no, not a boy. He is a man; a proper little man, henh, you little sweety?'

'So like his father he looks, na? Tell me, my jaan, how old are you now? I should introduce you to my Amanpreet. What a handsome couple you two would make!'

These insipid, almost parasitic, affections made me want to gag. As they buzzed around me, coochie-cooing, I felt my nausea growing, deepening into a panic that threatened to overwhelm me.

'Leave me alone,' I screeched. 'Don't touch me.'

My stridency stunned them. They recoiled, startled by such vehemence from someone so young.

Quickly, before they could recover, I dashed away as fast as I could.

I ran straight to find my grandfather. He was sitting out in the garden, slouched over on a rattan easy chair, poring over a dusty map that was mouldy at the edges and tattered with mildew.

Before he could say a word, I rushed up to him and threw myself into his arms, much to his surprise.

'What's wrong, puttar?' he asked, holding me delicately as if he was worried that I would break.

I held on to him as tightly as I could, desperate for the security of his proximity, locking my arms around his waist until he gasped with pain when my elbows dug into his kidneys.

'Nani's friends, they are saying that the Congress will come and kill us all. Is it true, Nana? Are they going to kill us?'

Nana didn't reply. Instead, he looked down at me solemnly. His unfamiliar, shaven visage was wracked by deep emotion, but I could not tell if it was fear or shame flitting across his features.

'I'm scared, Nana,' I mewled.

'Don't be scared,' he whispered, gently caressing my cheek with the heel of one hard palm. 'They can't hurt us. We Punjabis are invulnerable like Superman.'

With a grunt, he reached forward and lifted me off my feet and swept me through the air in a parody of flight.

Freed from the encumbrance of gravity, it was like my fears fell away. Elated, I laughed, and Nana folded me into his arms. Gratefully, I nestled into his chest, cradling my head against his shoulder. Even without the flourish of his beard, he still smelt of pomade and cough drops, just like he always had, and I inhaled a deep lungful of this scent. It made me feel reassured somehow, immeasurably safe.

'Come on,' he said with a knowing smile, 'I know just what will cheer you up.'

He carried me back indoors to his study, which was my favourite room in the whole house. My bedroom was right above it, and there were nights when I would hear him in there while I tried to sleep, click-clacking away on his old typewriter late into the night. It was an immensely comforting sound—that sibilant twang the keys made as he hammered at them with great gusto and the ringing clang that echoed each time he arrived at the end of a sentence and had to slap at the carriage lever to scroll down a line.

To my nascent ears, that staccato harmony of tap-tap-clang seemed to confirm that the world still made sense, a marvellously simple rhythm that had always served to calm me down, no matter how restless I felt.

Nana put me down on the chair in front of his cluttered writing desk. Happily, I reached out with one finger and tapped at one of the typewriter keys forcefully. A clacking sound rang through the room with an indignant peal that made me grin.

Meanwhile, he knelt down on one knee and began to rummage through a small cupboard until he found a sheet of stiff pink chart paper, which he held up with a triumphant smile.

'What are you doing, Nana?' I said, watching him curiously.

'You'll see,' he said. 'Now go out into the garden and fetch me a bamboo stick about as long as your arm, but not too thick, okay?'

'Why, Nana?' I asked, bewildered. 'What on earth do you need a bamboo for?'

'Just do as I say,' he replied insistently, 'or you'll ruin the surprise.'

Grumbling, I complied. I stamped out the postern door to the garden behind the farmhouse. There was a tall clump of bamboo there, growing in one corner of the yard. Circling it, I searched through its dense matting of foliage until I spied a long greyish branch as thick as a pipe hanging just above head height.

Jumping up, I tried to grab it with one outstretched hand—once, twice, thrice until the tips of my fingers closed around its knotted bole. Grimacing with effort, I bent it towards me so that I could get a firmer grip with both hands. Straining with every ounce of my strength, I pulled until at last, it snapped apart with a soft crack.

After sawing through the last fibrous tendrils with a sharp-edged piece of stone, I took it back to Nana in the study, dragging it behind me like a broom, its leafy branches leaving wavy, muddy ripples in my wake.

'Will this do?' I asked, dumping it on the floor in front of him.

Nana picked up the stick and examined it critically, stripping away the leaves until he had a slender knobbed culm of bamboo.

'Yes,' he said, 'this will do perfectly.'

Folding the bamboo over his knee, he carefully snapped it in two so that he was left holding a pair of roughly equal-sized pieces, each about twelve inches long. Then, he opened a drawer and rummaged through it, extracting a large pair of scissors and a mammoth green ball of twine, so huge that it was almost as large as my head.

Putting the twine, scissors and chart paper on the floor, he sat down next to them, folding his legs with some difficulty before turning to me.

'Come, puttar,' he declared with a broad grin, 'I am going to teach you how to make a kite.'

That announcement made me forget my irritation at having been made to go foraging in the garden in an instant. Sinking next to him, I leaned forward to watch as he notched each bamboo stick at the centre so that they fitted into each other tidily to make a simple X-frame, which he lashed together with a few small twists of twine.

It was the first time I had seen a kite being made. I observed every move eagerly, trying to commit each step to memory.

'Would you like to glue the sticks together?' Nana asked.

'Could I?' I said, excited.

Grinning, Nana held up a tube of Araldite, offering it to me. I snatched it from his grasp impatiently and proceeded to slather glue onto the branches until they were firmly bonded together. Unfortunately, I also ended up pasting my thumb and index finger to each other in the process, much to Nana's amusement, and he had to fetch a bottle of nail polish remover, which he dripped over my hand with a twist of cotton wool.

While I sat there, waiting for the glue to dissolve and for my thumb and finger to come unstuck, Nana moved on to the next part of the task.

Fascinated, I watched as he spread the chart paper flat and picked up the scissors.

'What do you think it should be?' he said, turning to me, peering expectantly over the rims of his glasses.

'A lion,' I replied without a hint of hesitation, 'with a mane and a beard.'

'Very well,' Nana said with a nod.

As I watched, he began to trim out a shape from the thick chart paper. The scissors glinted as he deftly manipulated their sharp blades back and forth until gradually a design began to emerge—a lion's face complete with a curly, leonine mane caught in a mid snarl.

As Nana worked, he explained, 'When I was a boy, we had a kite festival every year to celebrate the festival of Basant. It commemorated the coming of spring, and there would be a big mela in the village with jugglers and dancers and soda-bottle vendors and, best of all, horseback rides.

'We would all make kites then, and there would be a kite flying competition on the village maidan, and the best kite would win a prize of eight annas.'

'How much is eight annas, Nana?'

'Not a lot,' he replied with a laugh. 'About half a rupee.'

'That's nothing,' I said, 'not even enough to buy a Campa-Cola.'

Nana shook his head. 'Not now perhaps, but back then, when I was a boy, eight annas was a fortune. Those days, you could buy ten ice cream cones with that, but that was not the reason why I loved the kite festival.'

He sighed, a nostalgic gasp.

'It felt so good to see something you made with your own hands up there in the air. It was beautiful, puttar, to see the sky filled with a hundred flickering paper animals dancing and shivering with the wind. And best of all, we would all sing as the kites flew, a thousand voices in cadence until the very wind was ripe with music, praying for a good harvest.'

In a low voice, he began to hum, singing gently:

O sweet spring,
Make my wishes come true.
Don't break my heart
Until winter comes again.

He stopped abruptly—his mood faltered, his brow darkening with despair.

'After Partition,' he whispered, 'we stopped flying kites. What was the point…? After all that happened, what spring could be beautiful again?'

He paused and looked at me sadly. 'You know, I haven't flown a kite since that day, almost forty years ago. Not once.'

Vacantly, I stared at him, not quite sure how to respond. Nana must have sensed my puzzlement because he smiled sadly and shrugged.

'Forgive me, I am being maudlin again. Do me a favour and fetch me the paintbox from the second drawer in my desk.'

Rising to my feet, I obliged, rummaging around until I found a battered tin biscuit box filled with bottles of poster paint and a bundle of old dry brushes, which I handed over to him.

Nana opened a bottle of ochre paint and began to paint the face of the kite a bright bronze.

'Here,' he said, handing me a thick brush after dipping it in bright hansa yellow. 'You paint the eyes.'

Biting my lip, I took the brush and began to colour the lion's eyeballs carefully, making them a livid shade of amber.

'That's perfect,' Nana declared. With a flourish, he added one final dab of paint and held up the kite for me to approve. 'Well, what do you think?'

When its painted face caught the sun, the lion kite seemed to come to life, roaring at me, glowering with tawny intensity, making me clap my hands in delight.

'Come on then,' Nana said. 'Let's go and fly our kite.'

I helped him to his feet, and he led me out to the empty field that abutted the farmhouse, a deserted, dead piece of land overgrown with lank weeds and dense undergrowth. It was separated from the farm by a low wall that was falling apart, broken and breached in several places where the mortar holding the slate had flaked away and many of the stones had collapsed into untidy heaps.

Nana first carefully assisted me over this low obstacle and then clambered over it himself, struggling to straddle this narrow divide with an ungainly grunt while holding the kite carefully above his head.

Once we had reached the middle of the field, he pulled the ball of twine from his pocket and proceeded to tie one end to the kite securely, knotting the rope in a sheepshank before handing it to me with a small smile.

'Here you are, puttar,' he said. 'You get to take it for its maiden flight.'

Reverently, I took the kite from him, holding it as delicately as I could, scared that I would tear the fragile paper and ruin it before it had the chance to take to the air.

'Now run,' Nana said. 'Run as fast as you can.'

I was never an athletic child, far too fond of bacon and laddoos to ever challenge Daley Thompson, but I made a game show of it, sprinting away across the field, pushing myself to the very limit of my speed. And then, just as my knees were about to give way beneath me, I threw the kite up into the sky with all my strength.

It hung there limply for the longest moment before a flickering breath of wind seized it. Majestically, with an almost elegant languor, the lion kite rose into the air above me, much to my delight.

'Look, Nana,' I squealed. 'It flies. It really flies.'

Higher and higher the kite rose, dancing and skipping across the sky. Nana struggled with the mooring string as it was pulled taut in his grasp. Manoeuvring the kite with a deft, practised flick of his wrist, he shuffled over to me.

'Quickly,' he said, offering the string to me.

I took it, nervous, almost losing it as a flurry of wind whipped at the kite, but I held on with all my strength. It was surprisingly difficult. The kite battled me, restless to get away, to break free of this flimsy restraint and soar to the heavens, but I fought to tame it, hanging on as if my life depended on it.

'There,' Nana said, 'now you are flying the kite.'

I grinned, but before I could even enjoy the sensation of kite-flying for a whole minute, another, more powerful squall snatched at the lion kite, tearing its string from my grip and lifting it up, up, up, like a feather caught in a tornado.

'Quick, Nana,' I shouted. 'Catch it before it gets away.'

Hurriedly, my grandfather broke into a slow shambling run, chasing the runaway kite. I dashed after him, scampering madly across the field. We almost managed to catch up with it, but Nana tripped over a clump of sod and pitched forward, falling to the ground with an unceremonious thump.

For a moment, he sprawled there, utterly shocked, but then, once he had managed to collect his wits, he sat up with a groan, the shock fading to be replaced by a bright flush of embarrassment.

'Are you hurt?' I asked, reaching down to help him to his feet.

Nana didn't answer. Instead, he looked up at me dazedly, as if he wasn't quite sure where he was.

At that instant, he looked so comical, sitting there with such a vivid expression of puzzlement on his face that I could not help but burst into laughter.

And then, for the first time since Mrs Gandhi had died, my grandfather began to laugh as well, a low giggle to begin with, which then deepened into a rich, unrestrained gale of laughter. I flopped down on the ground next to him. We guffawed in a symphony, like a pair of madmen. At that moment, he looked just like the old Nana. As I glanced at him sidelong, it was like I could see the little boy in his eyes again, that joyful little child he must once have been.

Together, we gazed up at the kite as it cavorted away, flapping across the sky in a mad pirouette, getting further and further from us. But then, all of a sudden, a harsh din shattered the serenity, a loud tak-tak-tak, which I mistook to be the din of exploding firecrackers.

Astonished, I spun in the direction of this staccato salvo of sound, searching the horizon for the sight of flashing rockets or spinning firewheels hanging in the sky like shiny comets, but before I could see a thing, Nana seized me and pulled me close to him, shielding me protectively with his body.

'What are you doing?' I grumbled, trying to pull free from his grip, but he was surprisingly strong. With the most unexpected agility, he vaulted to his feet and began to scurry towards the shelter of the farmhouse, dragging me along after him, his eyes darting around us cautiously.

Just then, a fresh encore of cracks rasped through the air. High above us, the kite wavered and dipped before flopping down to the ground with a loud snap of splintering wood.

'Nana, wait,' I said. Wrestling free from his grasp, I ran back to pick up the lion kite. Much to my dismay, it was ruined beyond repair. There was a row of holes across its surface, puckered gashes through which I could poke my little finger.

Just as I gathered up these tattered remnants, Nana grabbed me frantically and heaved me off my feet, carrying me the rest of the way to the meagre shelter of the wall. Pushing me down behind it, he sank down next to me, gasping and trying to gather his breath.

'What happened to the kite, Nana?' I asked him sourly, holding it up for him to see. 'Was it killer moths or birds or meteorites?'

With one hesitant hand, Nana reached out to touch the neat row of holes that had sundered the kite almost in half.

'We should go back inside now, puttar,' he whispered, shaking his head.

'It is almost time for curfew.'

5

Later that night, just after 1 a.m., we were awakened by a strident knocking on the front door.

By the time I got out of bed and put on my dressing gown and came down to the sitting room, I found Nana and Nani already standing there, at the base of the staircase, watching the door worriedly.

Nani looked exhausted, her eyes bleary with fear. Much to my dismay, Nana seemed scared as well, confused, as if he was entirely unsure of whether to answer the door or not.

'Who can it be—so late?' Nani whispered.

'I don't know,' Nana replied as a fresh paroxysm of thumping rattled the door, almost battering it off its hinges.

'Who is it, and what do you want?' he asked querulously, shuffling forward.

'It is I, Gobind Singh ji,' A voice answered urgently. 'Opinderjit Singh, your most faithful friend.'

Sighing with relief, Nana hurried to unlock the door, opening it to reveal a familiar figure standing at the threshold.

Opinderjit Singh, or OPS as everyone called him, was Nana's oldest friend—a huge, shambling mountain of a man with a shaggy beard that came almost to his chest and shoulders that were as wide as a brick wall. They made an odd couple—this gargantuan Sikh who rarely spoke and my short, prematurely balding grandfather, who rarely knew a moment of true silence—but somehow, they had a beautiful, almost symbiotic friendship that had endured for almost half a century.

It was OPS who had introduced Nana to my grandmother, and as a result, he was very much a part of our family and a very frequent visitor to the farm. For a large man, he was impossibly sweet-natured, gentle and soft-spoken, with a deep booming laugh and a love of terrible jokes that nobody but he seemed to find amusing. And he had the funniest habit, I remember, of constantly nodding his head from left to right as he walked, as if he agreed with everyone and everything around him.

He had a grandson, Ranjit or Randeep, who was a little older than me. We all called him Rat, because he so resembled a rodent, with his thin nose and shifty eyes and protuberant teeth. Rat was perhaps the naughtiest child I had ever met, not evil-natured, but the sort of irrepressible scamp who couldn't help but get into trouble, even when he was trying his very best to behave.

Whenever he came over to visit with his grandfather, I became the particular object of his wicked sense of humour. Rat delighted in tormenting and playing tricks on me. Once, he put salt in my Gold Spot and stole my G.I. Joes, and another time, he pulled my hair so hard that a thick tuft came out in his hands and we got into a fist fight, which he would have won easily if his father had not stopped us and rescued me from an imminent beating.

I remember that moment so vividly. OPS had walked into the room and seen us scuffling on the floor and had lifted his son off me with one massive hand as if he weighed nothing at all. He had taken Rat out onto the verandah and given him a stern talking-to, after which, as a gesture of apology, he had come back and offered me two rainbow-striped bullseye candies to eat, pulling them out from his pocket like a magician producing a rabbit from a hat.

That's what I recall best about him. He always had a never-ending supply of bullseyes in his pockets and a vast smile on his face.

But that night, as OPS stood there, he looked like a different person, so distraught that he was almost on the verge of panic.

When Nana ushered him into the house with open arms, he did not smile, not once. His ordinarily impeccable appearance was slovenly, his turban unkempt, his beard matted and wild and his eyes bloodshot. His shirt hung half-open, missing two of its buttons, and his trousers were filthy, streaked at the knees with mud. And much to my amusement, I saw that his shoes were mismatched. He was wearing one brown loafer and one black Oxford with its lace undone, which flapped loosely with every step he took.

'What's wrong?' Nana exclaimed, taken aback by his agitated demeanour.

'They have taken my grandson,' OPS whispered.

'What?' Nana exclaimed, shocked. 'Why?'

'He threw a stone at a police car, so they have taken him in for questioning. Please, Gobind Singh ji, you have to help me. I beg you; come with me to the police station. You are an important man and your word still has some clout. You can save Ranjit from them. You can get him back. They will listen to you.'

'I think you will find that I have few friends left these days, Opinderjit,' Nana said sadly.

'Still, you are the only one I can come to, Gobind. I have no one else. You have to help me. For God's sake, you must!'

With that exclamation, OPS broke down. His giant shoulders heaved as he started to cry uncontrollably, holding his head in his hands. A steady torrent of tears welled from his eyes, streaming down his hirsute cheeks, gleaming in his beard like incandescent pearls.

I winced, unsure whether to be stunned or embarrassed. I wanted to look away, but I couldn't. There was something shamefully voyeuristic about watching a grown man cry, something fascinating and unnatural that refused to let me avert my eyes.

What was wrong with him? I thought when he began to keen, moaning with such visceral, heart-rending anguish that it made the hair on the back of my neck stand on end. Why was he crying like a girl? Had he gone mad? Had the whole world gone mad?

I waited for Nana to comfort him, to tell him not to worry and that everything would be fine, but my grandfather just stood there, motionless, his arms hanging by his side awkwardly.

Almost five minutes crept by before OPS managed to compose himself, before he calmed down enough to try and speak again.

'Help me, I beg you,' he said softly. His voice was desperate with supplication. 'They will kill him if you don't.'

'I … I can't,' Nana croaked, averting his eyes shamefacedly. 'I must think about my wife and grandson. Forgive me, my friend, but I cannot help you.'

When OPS heard the finality of those words, he let out a groan, a tragic exhalation of breath. The wan light of hope in his eyes flickered briefly and then was extinguished entirely.

He tottered forward, his features knotting with hard, cold rage. I thought he was going to punch Nana, but then, as quickly as it had manifested, his fury melted away, replaced by an austere resignation. Straightening his shoulders, he wiped his eyes clean with his sleeve, pausing to look at Nana stiffly one last time, his lips thin with distaste, before turning to depart.

My grandmother limped forward to stop him, to hold him back, but gently, he brushed aside her outstretched hand and strode away without uttering another word, slamming the door loudly behind him, so hard that the lintel shuddered and cracked in twain.

After he was gone, Nana just stood there, his shoulders slouched, his head bowed, too ashamed to meet my eyes.

'You should have gone with him,' Nani whispered.

'I couldn't. You know I couldn't.'

With a sigh, Nani shook her head, as if she understood what he meant, and leaned forward to take his hand in her own.

'I am sorry, Gobind,' she said, as if it was her fault that Nana had not gone with his friend.

Nana nodded but didn't say a word. Instead, he turned and shambled into his study, locking the door behind him. For the rest of the night, he did not sleep. I could hear him pacing back and forth like a caged lion.

The next morning when I woke up and came down for breakfast, I found him waiting in the kitchen, fully dressed to go out, clad neatly in his best Harris Tweed suit and a bright red bow tie, carrying his favourite elephant-headed cane.

'Where do you think you are off to, Gobind?' Nani asked, her face rigid with worry.

'I have to help OPS,' Nana replied. 'I have made up my mind. I shall go down to the district police station and have a word with the senior inspector there. I am sure he is a reasonable man and will let the boy go.'

'Are you certain you want to do this?' Nani said.

'I have no choice, Jaan. If I don't help him, what kind of man would I be?'

With that declaration, he hugged Nani with a broad smile.

'Don't you worry,' he insisted, kissing her gently on her cheek. 'I will be back in time for lunch.'

'I will make all your favourites,' she said, forcing herself to smile, even though I could see that she was terrified.

After Nana left, Nani spent the rest of the day worrying about him.

I could tell that she was anxious because she refused to sit down for even a minute. Instead, she flitted restlessly from one room to the next like an impatient hummingbird, frowning and mumbling to herself, a soft litany of Punjabi that I couldn't understand.

Finally, when she ran out of tables to clean and shelves to dust, she shuffled into the kitchen and began to cook.

I watched her with silent bemusement. I had never seen Nani quite this energetic, this agitated, before. Ordinarily, she moved slowly and carefully, crippled almost to clumsiness by her arthritis, but now, she was like a veritable whirlwind, hustling and bustling in and out of the kitchen, kneading and baking and chopping vegetables. She even forced me to help out, putting me to work, peeling potatoes and shucking peas, which I did reluctantly, grumbling all the time that this wasn't proper work for a man.

For hours Nani hunched over the hot stove, sweating and slaving. A cornucopia of delicacies emerged, platter after steaming platter—paneer makhanwala and sarson da saag, mutton biryani and mint and honey raita, pindi key choley and round aloo tikkis that hissed when I poked them with a fork, a medley of parathas, mooli and aloo and gobi and more, all lathered with thick clotted home-made white butter, and finally the pièce de résistance, an enormous chocolate cake, as large as my head, covered with gleaming icing.

Soon the cottage was filled with the delightful aroma of freshly cooked food, and as I saw the heavily laden plates piling up on the dinner table, my stomach growled and my mouth began to water.

'Nani,' I said, eyeing the chocolate cake appreciatively, 'can I have a piece of cake please?'

When she heard this request, my grandmother glowered at me angrily. Her eyes blazed with barely repressed ferocity, which surprised me because she was ordinarily very quiet, docile to the point of being benign.

'No,' she snapped adamantly. 'We are going to wait. Not one bite before your grandfather comes back. Is that understood?'

'Yes, Nani,' I whispered, miserably stealing one last glance at the cake as anticipation soured to disappointment in my mouth.

'I'll wait for Nana to come home.'

6

We waited all day.

The sun rose to its zenith and began to wane. The afternoon wilted towards evening, but still, Nana had not returned.

Silently, Nani stood by the front window, keeping a patient vigil. Meanwhile, in the dining room, all the wonderful dishes she had prepared in anticipation of my grandfather's return cooled and began to congeal into a sodden mess, assailed by a storm of flies and midges, but still, Nani refused to give me permission to taste a single morsel.

Finally, as the first shadowy blush of dusk began to descend, Nani decided that she was done waiting.

'Enough is enough,' she declared with an air of absolute finality. Clucking her tongue purposefully against her false teeth, she shuffled off to her bedroom to change. A few moments later, as if by magic, she emerged fully dressed, clad in a pair of pale grey slacks and a dark blue sweater. I goggled at her, barely able to recognise her. I had never seen Nani in trousers before. Ordinarily, she dressed in drab salwars and shapeless kurtas, but now, with her hair pulled back into a business-like bun and a chiffon scarf knotted around her head, she seemed so exotic, so glamorous, as elegant as Deborah Kerr.

As I stared at her, Nani put on her outside spectacles, huge, steel-rimmed bifocals, which made her eyes seem twice their normal size, and also her outside dentures, a row of shiny white teeth, which changed her appearance completely, making her look younger, more forceful somehow.

When she was ready to leave, she paused and frowned at me, a confused look on her face, as if she wasn't quite sure what to do with me.

'You are a man now, my son,' she whispered, caressing the top of my head. 'You have to be strong. I am going to leave you alone for some time because your Nana needs me.'

Nani was not much taller than me—just over five foot two. For such a tiny woman, at that moment she seemed larger than life, not delicate at all, but somehow powerful as if she was made of more than just skin and bone.

Her expression was so determined, I felt my heart twist as I looked at her. Suddenly, I was afraid, worried for her safety, and I knew I could not let her go alone.

'No, Nani,' I reached for her hand, 'don't leave me here. Please, take me with you.'

When she heard that appeal, she frowned, gazing at me critically, struggling to make up her mind.

Finally, with a reluctant nod, she said, 'Very well, you can come along, but only if you promise to obey me and do exactly what I tell you to do.'

'I promise, Nani. I will do whatever you say.'

She marched out of the farmhouse and I trotted after her. Purposefully, Nani strode out to the garage and unlocked the door. Inside, half-covered by a blue tarpaulin, I saw Nana's old Ambassador, which he rarely drove since his eyesight had started to go.

It was a real piece of junk, that car. Once it had been bright red, but now it was more a dingy orange, half-eaten by rust, with a front bumper held together only by fencing wire and prayers. The tires were almost bald and the brakes groaned like they were dying, but Nana kept the motor pristine and the car ran serviceably enough, although it had a tendency to shudder and groan at high speeds as if it was trying to shake itself apart.

Nani ordered me to hold open the door while she tried to start the car, but it refused to turn over, making a dull clicking sound each time she turned the key in the ignition. Wide-eyed, I watched as she clambered out of the driver's seat and lifted open the hood to check the spark plugs. I confess I was immensely impressed. Who would have thought Nani was so resourceful? After all, girls weren't supposed to know anything about cars, were they? But here my grandmother was checking the carburettor as confidently as a professional mechanic!

Frowning, Nani wiped an encrustation of grease off one of the battery leads with a rag and tightened it with a wrench, and then slammed the hood shut with a satisfied grunt. I smiled at her admiringly, but she didn't seem to notice as she slid back into the driver's seat and tried to start the engine once again.

It took a few attempts, her pumping at the accelerator angrily, before the car sputtered into life, coughing and rasping like a man with tuberculosis.

'Come along,' she said to me brusquely, pausing to push open the passenger door so that I could climb into the car. Hurriedly I leapt in, holding on for dear life as Nani reversed the car out of the shed with a reckless screech and made a quick three-point turn.

It was the most thrilling drive of my life. Nani drove like a racing driver at Le Mans, slipping and yawing across the road, taking every turn with mad abandon, the car shivering and juddering as she pushed it to its maximum speed.

Before I even had the time to figure out where she was headed, we had already arrived at our destination, which was the district police station. It was a dun, drab building near the outskirts of a nearby village, and looked more like a school than a police station. With a squeal of rubber, Nani skidded to a halt outside this unprepossessing structure. Outside, the world was cloaked in a particularly yellow twilight. A gauzy mist hung in the air, which was viscous with the promise of rain. In the distance, high over the plains of the Majha, a shiver of lightning jagged through the stolid sky, followed a heartbeat later by a deafening thunderclap as palpable as a slap to the face.

Securing the handbrake, Nani turned to me and said, 'Now, you listen, young man … whatever happens, you will stay in this car. If you dare leave this vehicle, I will give you a beating like you have only imagined in your worst nightmares. Do you understand?'

I nodded at her meekly, cowed by the intransigence of her tone.

With that ominous warning, Nani stepped out of the car and locked the door behind her. Then, while I watched with my face pressed up against the warm glass of the windshield, she turned and made a stately entrance into the police station, limping slightly because her arthritis was aching at her knees.

I hadn't intended to disobey her, but as I watched her go, abruptly, I was filled with an awful trepidation, a premonition that if I let her go in there alone, she would be lost to me forever.

Rolling down the window, I hurriedly wriggled out through it, tumbling to the ground with an ungainly thump.

'Nani,' I squealed, jumping to my feet and running after her, 'wait for me!'

She paused and looked down at me coldly, her eyes hard as flint.

'I thought I told you to stay in the car.'

'Please, Nani, I want to go with you. Please, please, don't leave me in the car.'

When she heard this entreaty, her fury abated. Brusquely, she took me by the hand and led me through the police station's verandah to the brightly lit antechamber within. Inside, we found ourselves in a large, somewhat dingy room. The walls were unpainted cement, stained wet by years of seepage, lined with battered wooden benches and a long row of Godrej cupboards that were overflowing with stacks of mouldy box files. Near the entrance, a plump khaki-uniformed havildar sat resting his elbows behind a metal table, yawning widely as he fanned himself with a yellow plastic fly-swatter. When he saw Nani, he lumbered to his feet hastily, moving to obstruct her path with one hand upraised, but she brushed past him with nonchalant disdain, as if he didn't exist, and barged straight into the senior inspector's cabin.

Mute, I trailed after her, staring around with immense curiosity. I had never been inside a police station before. Much to my irritation, it looked nothing like the eponymous police thanas I remembered from all the Hindi movies I had seen. For one thing, there were no swinging saloon doors at the entrance, creaking open and shut each time someone entered or left, and no holding cell full of hardened criminals banging their tin mugs against the bars as they protested their innocence.

Even the inspector's cabin was disappointing, little more than a pokey cubicle that resembled a clerk's office. There was only one small window in a corner, shuttered tight, giving the room a funereal feel. This sombre atmosphere was only added to by the spartan furnishings, a ramshackle writing desk piled high with a mess of manila files and government papers and two equally rickety wicker office chairs. From the wall, a garlanded photograph of Indira Gandhi glowered down at us, and above, an ancient ceiling fan turned tiredly, creaking with each rotation as it fought a losing battle to dispel the musty fugue of the room.

As for the inspector, he was even more of a disappointment. For one thing, he looked more like an accountant than a policeman—a short, sallow young man, not more than thirty, his squinty eyes hidden behind thick black-rimmed spectacles, with a careful moustache that lamentably did not quite join in the middle, thus giving his face a perpetually incomplete and rather lopsided look.

When we barged into his office, he was leaning back in his wingback chair with his feet propped atop his table, reading a newspaper, and the suddenness of our entrance almost made him lose his balance and topple over.

'Excuse me,' Nani said to him politely. 'I am sorry to disturb you, but I need help, please.'

For a moment, the inspector glared at her angrily, a sour expression of surprise flickering across his face. It was obvious he was annoyed by our unannounced intrusion, but then, folding the newspaper neatly, he smiled, an affected little smirk.

'How can I be of assistance, madam?'

'I am Sardar Gobind Singh's wife. He came to visit you earlier this morning and did not return home.'

At the mention of Nana's name, the inspector's smile vanished.

'I am afraid, madam,' he said briskly, 'that the person you are speaking of has been detained for questioning.'

That declaration made Nani flinch visibly. She shuddered, involuntarily clenching my hand so hard that I squealed with anguish.

'I … I don't understand.'

The inspector frowned. 'There is nothing to understand, madam. We have a few questions to ask your husband, and when we are done, we will be happy to release him.'

Just then, a cacophony of screams rent the air, making me jump. They seemed to be coming from the basement of the police station, a sinister concerto of pure terror as if an animal was being tortured. Nani shivered when she heard this morbid symphony and pulled me close to her, leaning on me for support.

'I demand that you release him at once,' she said, her voice querulous with barely repressed panic. 'You cannot hold him without an arrest warrant. He hasn't done anything wrong.'

The inspector's frown deepened into a scowl. At that moment, he was transformed from something insignificant into something monstrous. It was his eyes. They grew feral, blazing with lupine aggression that made me clutch Nani's hand even more tightly, cowering behind her, trying to hide.

'I would advise you, madam, to go back to your home if you know what is good for you. Do not force me to undertake a course of action that we will both regret.'

Despite the tangible menace in his voice, Nani refused to budge. Instead, she raised her birdlike chin to glare right back at the inspector.

'I am not leaving here,' she said resolutely, 'not without my husband.'

It made me so proud, looking up at her, so diminutive but still so brave, standing ramrod stiff as she faced down the policeman.

Much to my surprise, rather than losing his temper at this show of defiance, the inspector laughed, a short bark of derision.

'You rich Punjabis, you think we are all your servants, don't you, with your upper-class English and your family money? You think all you have to do is snap your fingers and we will all dance at your commands?'

Smiling snidely, he clapped his hands together. A moment later, a trio of policemen led by the havildar from the anteroom marched into the cabin.

'Take her away,' the inspector commanded dismissively with an absent flick of one wrist.

Immediately the policemen seized Nani by her arms, one flanking her on each side, while the third man, the havildar, grabbed me by the scruff of my neck so hard that I whimpered with pain.

'Don't you dare touch him,' Nani roared with outrage. 'He's just a boy. Leave him alone.'

In spite of her protestations, the policemen manhandled her out of the inspector's office. Nani tried to struggle, to resist, but she was no match for their collective brawn. They walked her unceremoniously through the police station and shoved her through the front door so roughly that she almost lost her balance, but I managed to wrestle free from the havildar's grasp and ran to steady her before she could topple to the ground and hurt herself.

'Go home, old woman,' the havildar cackled, 'otherwise we may have to keep you for questioning as well.'

The other policemen laughed when he made this threat as if the havildar had cracked a particularly hilarious joke. I glared at him. My hands bunched into fists, my knuckles whitening with rage. I would have attacked him, had not Nani placed one slim hand on my shoulder to restrain me.

Wordlessly, she gathered herself, straightening with an almost imperious dignity.

'Go sit in the car,' she said to me.

I started to argue, but something in her voice checked my objections and compelled me to obey her. Quietly, I retreated to the Ambassador with downcast eyes and climbed into the passenger seat, waiting for Nani to drive us back to the farm without Nana.

But Nani did not return to the car.

Instead, as I watched curiously, she walked up to the iron fence that bordered the police thana. She did not try to go back in. No, instead, she stood there, and with a soft sigh, raised her head and began to sing.

It was one of Nana's favourite songs, the quissa of Heer and Ranjha, as composed by Waris Shah. Appropriately enough, it was the heart-breaking story of two doomed lovers kept apart by fate and circumstance, and now, Nani sang Heer's words for my grandfather, hoping that her voice would reach him wherever he was, locked away in a cell somewhere deep within the bowels of the police station, and remind him that she loved him more than life itself.

Doli chardiyan mariyan Heer cheekan
Mainu lai chale babala lai chale ve
Ve mainu rakh lai babala Heer aakhe aiy
Doli kat kahar ni lai chale ve
Mera akhiya kadi na moda sahin
O din babul kithe gaye chale ve
Tera chatar chavanen rukh vang
Asi vang musafiran bai chale

As Heer sat in the palanquin, she wept
They are taking me away from you
Please keep me, don't let me go,
The bearers have me at their shoulders
You never said no to me, not ever

Where have those days gone?
I always enjoyed your love and protection
But now I am alone, a wanderer.

Nani had a beautiful voice—clear, lilting, full of passion and plaintive pathos—not an old woman's cracked caterwauling but rather a young girl's contralto, evoking the sound of the wind as it whispered through the cane and the scent of fresh mud in the fallow fields.

And as she sang, an incalculable sorrow seemed to well up inside me, an insurmountable wellspring of despair. I could hear the bottomless depth of her pain in her soaring voice. I could hear the threnody of all of Punjab's womenfolk, the collective lament of a thousand hearts breaking and the aching gasp of a million angry, unwept tears.

When the plaintive timbre of Nani's song rang through the air, most of the policemen stopped what they were doing and came out of the police station to watch her. They milled about until at last the inspector emerged and barked an order at them, commanding them to return to their posts.

One by one, they sidled away, shamefacedly avoiding Nani's eyes. She continued to sing until finally, only the inspector stood on the police station's verandah frowning at her, his sallow mouth twisted into a grimace.

'Stop this stupidity, madam,' he shouted, struggling to be heard above the resonance of her song. 'Stop it or I will be forced to have you arrested.'

But Nani refused to stop.

Without pause, her voice swelled louder and louder, echoing through the sky until it seemed to be the only sound in the world.

Even as the last light of day waned and darkness fell, she did not stop, not for a single breath, not even when abruptly, with a hiss and a crackle, the skies broke open and it began to drizzle, an insistent froth of rain that left her soaked to the skin.

Still, her mournful dirge persisted deep into the night, until at last, as the first gloaming of dawn crept across the sky, her voice began to waver and break and betray her.

One last time, her requiem rose to a crescendo, and then, with a hoarse gasp, Nani fell silent, unable to sing another word.

She looked ready to collapse. I jumped out of the car and ran to help her, but before I could get to her, Nani squealed with delight and pointed towards the door of the police station.

'Gobind,' she croaked, 'my Gobind.'

My eyes followed the direction of her out-thrust finger, and I laughed too, clapping my hands in delight.

They had let Nana go.

The burly havildar escorted him to the door and pushed him out brusquely without a word of explanation or apology.

Nana looked exhausted. I could see that he was in terrible pain, cradling his hands to his chest. His face was grey and ashen, and he had a florid bruise on his face, just beneath his right eye, a brilliantly plum-coloured discolouration, which caught my eye because it was shaped just like Pac-Man.

Barely able to stay upright, he stumbled towards us, hunched over like a cripple. With each step, he winced, swaying from side to side. When he saw Nani, he raised his arms, desperate to embrace her. But before he could reach her, his legs folded under him and he began to fall, unable to take his own weight.

Nani and I darted forward, each taking an arm and struggling to hold him upright. Slowly, we helped him to the car and hustled him into the back seat, where he collapsed in an untidy heap.

'My angel,' he whispered, smiling beatifically at Nani, 'you came for me.'

And then, with a groan, he fell into a faint.

'Get in,' Nani said to me, hastily slamming shut the door. 'We have to leave before they change their minds.'

While I scrabbled into the passenger seat, she got in the driver's side and started the car with some difficulty, wrestling to grip the keys with her arthritic fingers. This time, thankfully, the engine turned over immediately, and as soon as it began to grumble, Nani shoved her foot down on the accelerator and drove away from the police station as fast as she could.

When we got back home to the farm, it took all our collective strength to haul Nana out of the car. He was semi-conscious, drifting in and out of coherence, groaning and rambling feverishly, as Nani and I struggled to manhandle him upstairs to the bedroom.

Between the two of us, we managed to somehow help him to his bed, where he passed out unceremoniously without even bothering to remove his filthy clothes or even his shoes.

'Get him into his pyjamas,' Nani said, looking down at him worriedly with her hands on her hips. 'I will go make him a nice cup of tea.'

After she limped down to the kitchen, I was seized by an unexpectedly urgent bashfulness. I had never had to undress anyone but myself before. Inexplicably, the thought of removing Nana's clothes was embarrassing, even distasteful for me, as if by undressing him, I wouldn't just be stripping away his garments but also some vital measure of his personality, his very persona, to expose the naked truth beneath.

Nana was a mess. He had lost his cravat and blazer, and his shirt was torn, its front stained with what I realised was crusted blood. Reluctantly, I tried to unbutton it as delicately as I could manage, but Nana recoiled when I touched him, whispering deliriously.

'No, please, no more.'

'Don't worry, Nana,' I said soothingly, 'It's only me.'

Once I had undone his shirt, I turned my attention to his trousers, but before I could remove them, I realised I had to get rid of his shoes. Perplexingly, I noticed that he had only one shoe on, having misplaced the other somewhere along the way, and that his socks were filthy, papery with dried blood just like his shirt.

As gently as I could, I started to peel them away, but Nana whimpered when I touched his feet as if I was hurting him. It was only when the socks came off, much to my surprise, that I saw the soles of his feet were black and blue, swollen to almost twice their size.

Abruptly, Nana came awake and started to sit up.

'Nana,' I said, trying to gently push him back down, 'you're ill. You have to rest.'

'It's nothing,' he grunted. 'I'll be fine tomorrow.'

Groaning, he tottered upright, wincing when his bruised feet touched the ground. I rushed to help him, but he pushed me away and began undoing his trousers, struggling with his belt buckle. Every movement he made was slow and exaggerated. Embarrassed, I turned away as he changed into his night pyjamas before sinking back into bed with a fervid whimper.

Nana, I wanted to say, what have they done to you? You look so old and tired, so broken and so utterly fragile. And I miss your beard. Without your beard, you aren't the same man I knew and loved and trusted. Without the beard, you are a stranger, and I don't know if I can bring myself to love you, because something about you scares me more than anything else has ever scared me before.

But I didn't say a word. Instead, when I noticed that Nana was shivering like he had a fever, I fetched a blanket and carefully covered him.

Perching at one corner of the bed, I took his hand in mine, hoping to reassure him. His fingers were clenched tightly into fists. I tried to unfold them, but he groaned with agony and snatched his hand away before I could.

'Nana,' I asked, 'what happened to your hands?'

He didn't answer me. Instead, he tried to smile, but it was as if he could not control the muscles of his face. For one long moment, his cheeks seemed to twitch and shudder and dance of their own volition, as if his face was made of wax and was slowly beginning to melt.

'Do you want to see some magic?' he murmured so softly that I could barely comprehend him.

Excited, I nodded in agreement, watching as he stretched one shivering hand towards the lamp that stood by the bedside table, an ugly spindly thing made of stained glass and cane.

And as his fingers touched the bulb, much to my disbelief, it came alive, flowering into luminescence, blazing with bright light for one incandescent instant before the glow wavered and began to fade away.

'How did you do that?' I exclaimed. 'The lamp isn't even plugged in. How did you make it glow like that?'

Nana smiled wanly when he heard the astonishment in my voice.

'It is old man's magic,' he said. 'You will understand it someday when you are an old man yourself, puttar.'

'Please, Nana, tell me how you did it,' I pestered, eager to know how the trick was done, but Nana refused to reveal the secret, shaking his head tiredly.

'Someday, when you are older,' he whispered, 'I will explain it to you. But now, puttar, please, I need to rest.'

7

The next morning, they found Rat's body hanging from a traffic light at the crossroads outside the nearby village.

The police had stripped him naked, tied his hands and bound his legs before beating him to death. I heard he had been whipped with a television antenna because his corpse was covered with livid, razor-thin scars.

It didn't make any sense to me. How could the police have killed him? Why would they? The police only killed bad guys. Rat was just a child, and I could not conceive of a reason why anyone would kill an innocent boy, even one as mischievous as him.

It was very confusing for me because, in every book I had ever read and every movie that I had seen, the police were the good guys and it was the terrorists who were bad. But now, to hear this, that someone I knew had died and so horribly? No, I decided it must have been the terrorists dressed as policemen who had done it. Yes, that made sense. That had to be the real reason why people were so scared of the police because they were really terrorists in disguise.

That night, I went to my first funeral.

Nana still hadn't recovered completely from his ordeal. His hands and limbs still shivered uncontrollably, and there were moments while talking when he would pause suddenly, stuck in mid-word as if something inside him had short-circuited. Worst of all, he had begun to drool involuntarily at the strangest times, a soft trickle of liquid that brimmed from his nose or his mouth without him realising it, while he was listening to the radio or reading the newspaper, as though he had no control over his body any longer.

Nonetheless, though he was in obvious pain, when he heard that Rat was dead, he insisted on getting out of bed in spite of Nani's vociferous objections.

I helped him get dressed as he put on his best suit, black Merino wool with a thin pinstripe and a waistcoat, which made him look a little like a gangster from Chicago. But then, when it came to knotting a tie, he began to struggle, unable to make the deft motions with his injured hands, no matter how much he tried.

Finally, he gave up and turned to Nani for help.

'Go and get ready,' he said to me as she began to loop the tie around his neck with a practised gesture of her wrists. 'You are coming with us too.'

'He's much too young, Gobind,' Nani protested, tying a Windsor knot perfectly with her gnarled fingers and pulling it tight angrily, making Nana choke and sputter.

'He is old enough to know what is happening here,' Nana whispered obdurately, loosening the knot so that he could breathe again. 'He must see. His generation, they have to learn from what has happened in Punjab or they will make the same mistakes again and again.'

Nani tried to argue with him, but no matter how much she objected, he remained adamant, refusing to be budged. And so, obediently, I went and dressed in my best white kurta and climbed into the Ambassador with my grandparents when they departed for Rat's wake.

I had been to OPS's home before, a sprawling eleven-acre estate an hour away from my grandparents' farm, which was located next to a tributary of the river Beas. The last time we visited, it had been deserted, but this time around, it was like a madhouse, a frenzy of people, talking and eating and drinking and clucking their tongues together in a deafening blizzard of sound.

Everywhere I turned, there were faces I didn't recognise, milling around, white-clad, sombre, their faces absurdly serious.

By the front door, a pair of professional mourners greeted us—two middle-aged women in spotless white salwar-kameezes who were wailing as loudly as they could and slapping their heads with their hands, putting on a fine show of grief. Across the room, clustered in one corner, a group of elderly matrons with their chunnis draped across their faces surrounded a lady I recognised as Rat's mother, a pretty, plum-cheeked woman who began to weep soundlessly when Nana and Nani went up to her to tell her how sorry they were for her loss.

I was the only child present and everyone looked at me strangely as if I was from another planet. It was uncomfortable to be at the receiving end of so many disapproving glances, and I waited until Nana and Nani began to talk to some people they knew before trying to sidle away.

That was when I saw the body.

It was surprisingly … unexpected. I had never seen a dead body before. It wasn't horrifying at all, not like I had imagined it would be, like one of the zombies from those campy old Ramsay Brothers's movies they showed on TV late at night—fetid, rank and mottled.

No, with his hair tied back in a neat knot and his mouth closed so that his massive teeth were hidden, Rat looked peaceful—almost serene. He lay on the ground swaddled in a clean sheet that was knotted under his chin. His face was very pale, almost blue, and he had cotton balls in his nose, which I thought made him look funny, but other than that, it was like he was asleep, except his chest wasn't moving.

I remember noticing that even though he was just fifteen, he already had a rather fine beard, not patchy at all, but full and lush, which had been lovingly combed and oiled. Morbidly, I found myself wondering if it would continue to grow even now that he was dead, curling around him until it swaddled his body like a hirsute cocoon.

Around him, the crowd of visitors ebbed and flowed, whispering and shaking their heads sadly as they pointedly avoided looking down at his still form. Amidst this tumult, a few feet away from his son's body, OPS sat on a chair near the centre of the room like a wax statue, unmoving except to nod faintly as grievers whispered past, mouthing their platitudes and offering their respects.

Strangely, he did not look large at all, but rather tiny, dwarfed by the crowd around him, as if he had somehow shrunk in size.

I watched as Nana sidled across the room and shambled up to him, unable to meet his friend's eyes.

'I am sorry,' he tried to say, awkward, stiff, but the words seemed to dry up in his mouth, and he just stood there, staring down at his friend lamely, unable to speak.

For a moment, they faced each other like adversaries. OPS angled his neck to glower up at Nana, his eyes darkening with a sudden flash of emotion, which I took to be hatred. But then, heaving a massive sigh, he swayed to his feet tiredly, his shoulders hunched like a broken man, and enveloped my Nana into a massive bear hug, nearly lifting him from his feet.

He held him for a long time, refusing to release him. Nana did not object even though I thought it was quite embarrassing—two grown men hugging each other in public like that, much to my disgust, because everyone knew hugging was for sissies and boys from Doon School.

I cannot quite recall how long it was, but it seemed like a lifetime before OPS unlocked his grasp and released Nana.

Holding him at arm's length, he said, 'Speak, Gobind. Do not let my son die silently. Speak for him so that he may know that he was loved and will be mourned by all of us.'

Frowning, Nana nodded. He turned and approached Rat's corpse, sinking down on his knees and leaning forward to kiss him gently on his cold, dead forehead.

Then, closing his eyes, in a voice that trembled not just for this fallen boy but for all of Punjab's dead sons, he began to recite the Mool Mantra, the holiest hymn of the Sikhs.

'*Ik onkaar satnaam kartaa purakh nirbhau nirvair akaal moorat ajoonee saibhun gur prasaad.*'

'The truth is one whose name is truth. Only the truth can give creation existence, without fear, without hatred. The truth is timeless and does not go through the cycle of birth and death. The truth is self-existent. By the Guru's grace, the truth is obtained.'

Nani went to stand by him. She put one hand on his shoulder, and then, tremulously she too began to intone the words in cadence with him, the gentle flutter of her voice mingling with his gruff tenor.

One by one, the crowd that had congregated for the funeral joined in, their voices mingling into a beatific thunder of despair that buffeted against me, a cataclysm of sweet, sad noise.

It went on for hours. After the Mool Mantra came the Japji Sahib, then a sermon, followed by a kirtan. And then when the bhaiji from the gurudwara grew tired, an old man with a blue turban took his place, reciting even more verses from the Granth from memory.

Very quickly, I began to get bored, but when I tried to pull at the hem of Nani's chunni and tell her I wanted to go home, she shot me a furious frown to warn me to quiet down and behave myself.

As for Nana, he barely said a word to me the whole afternoon. He spent most of his time standing next to OPS, positioned one brief step behind him with his hand resting delicately on the giant Sikh's shoulder as if to reassure him with his presence.

After a few hours of sitting and nodding listlessly at his visitors, OPS lumbered to his feet and went into the kitchen, where he took out a bottle of Old Monk rum and began to drink, downing glass after glass without bothering to dilute the spirit with water. Nana tried to persuade him to stop but OPS refused to listen, continuing to drink heavily.

'Keep an eye on him,' Nana told me. 'I will go and fetch his wife. Maybe she can talk some sense into the big oaf.'

After he was gone, OPS fixed me with one red-veined eye and said, 'You there, boy, come and have a drink with me.'

With an angry scowl, he held out his glass, offering it to me. At first, I started to refuse, but then I thought, why not? Tentatively, after making sure that Nana and Nani could not see me, I took it and tasted a tiny sip. It was the first time I tried alcohol of any kind. I was wholly unprepared for such an acrid flavour. The raw liquor burned my tongue, making me cough and sputter, and immediately, my eyes filled with a bitter flourish of tears.

As I sniffled, OPS mistook my sputtering as a lamentation for his son, thinking that I was weeping for his poor, dead Rat.

Unexpectedly, he enveloped me in a bear hug, lifting me half off the ground. 'You were my son's friend, and you loved him just as I did. Will you be my son now, henh?' he asked, almost desperate.

Unsure of how to reply, I just nodded warily.

'My boy!' he whispered, holding on to me desperately, choking back a sob. 'My poor, beautiful boy!'

He hugged me so hard that I could barely breathe. Frantic, I thrashed against the constriction of his arms, struggling to release myself from his rum-stinking grasp, but OPS was much too strong. He held on to me for dear life, cradling me close to his chest, as if I weighed nothing at all.

He only released me when my grandfather returned. I ran to Nana whimpering. He patted my head, an effortlessly paternal gesture that made OPS scowl at us as if he was offended by this display of intimacy.

'Go away. Both of you, leave me alone.'

Once again, he picked up the bottle of rum and guzzled the rest of it down in one single swallow before throwing it at a wall. It broke with a sharp shatter, and I jumped back before the shards could gash me.

'OP, calm down!' Nana said and stepped forward to shield me.

'I said, leave me alone!'

OPS shoved past us, stumbling back into the living room where he began to ramble incoherently, raving furiously at the people who had gathered to mourn his son.

'What are you fools here for? Go back to your houses, and leave me alone.'

Like a madman, he began to pull at his hair and beard, staggering out to the verandah to shout at the empty sky.

'You cowards,' he screamed. 'Why did you kill him? He was an innocent boy who hadn't even had time to kiss a girl, who hadn't even learned to love, to live. Why, God, why?'

Furiously, he balled his hands into fists and punched the stone wall so hard that I could hear his knuckles splintering, but he did not seem to notice.

'You want to kill someone? Come and kill me, you bastards. Do you hear me? Come and kill me if you dare.'

Once, twice, thrice, he slammed his fists into the wall, punching the brick as hard as he could. I winced as the tiny bones in his fingers snapped like kindling. It must have hurt terribly, but he didn't let out a sound, nothing but a staccato series of grunts like a boxer trying to knock his opponent down.

In the end, it took three men to restrain him, pull him away and haul him bodily back into the house, where he turned on Nana like a rabid dog.

'You … you could have stopped this,' he screeched, holding up one blister-knuckled hand to point at Nana accusingly. 'You are the reason my son is dead.'

Scowling, he advanced towards Nana, his face swollen with savage emotion.

'Fight me, you bastard.'

'No,' Nana whispered, refusing to retreat a single step even though OPS was a good foot taller than him, 'I am your friend.'

'Fight me, damn you,' OPS groaned one last time and swung one enormous fist listlessly before pitching forward in a dead faint, collapsing to the ground in an intoxicated stupor.

Together Nana and I managed to heft his dead weight into the living room and lay him on the sofa. Nana draped a razai over him, tucking him in gently as if he was a child. And then, in a gesture of wonderful, almost paternal tenderness, he leaned forward and kissed him on his forehead, right there, in front of everyone, much to my surprise.

'Sleep, my brother. Sleep, and God willing, we will all awaken to a better tomorrow.'

8

It was well after curfew by the time we were finally able to leave Rat's funeral.

As we sped away from OPS's farm, the ironic pallor of the evening had long since turned to darkness, a funereal, murky night, as if the stars had been snuffed out in the sky. Even the cicadas were voiceless for once, leaving the world eerie with silence. The only noise that could be heard was the distant cackle of a pie-dog yelping haplessly at the saturnine moon.

Nana drove slowly, careful to avoid the roadblocks because he did not want to encounter the police. Instead of the highway, he took a broken, pitted dirt road that wound its way through the fields. It was so rough and uneven that we bounced and jostled about until our backsides were utterly sore. Each time the Ambassador creaked over a rock or through a deep pothole, I was certain the old heap's suspension would snap in twain, but thankfully the car didn't let us down and kept trundling right along, rattling and groaning in complaint.

We were about halfway to the farm when I first noticed two tiny pinpricks of light a few kilometres behind us, dancing in the darkness like fireflies. Gradually, they grew larger, drawing closer and closer until they resolved into a pair of headlights, following in our tracks rapidly.

'Nana,' I said worriedly, 'there's a car behind us.'

At first, we were terrified because we thought it was the police chasing us down for violating the curfew, but then, as the lights zoomed ever nearer, I saw that the headlights belonged to a Maruti van hurtling along at breakneck speed, throwing up a cloud of dust and grit in its wake.

Nana sped up but the van matched this acceleration recklessly, rumbling and bouncing over the rough terrain until it managed to catch up to us, pulling up almost by our side. I peered out at it, trying to discern who was driving, but its windows were tinted and all I could see were three dim shadows.

Gritting his teeth, Nana slowed down the Ambassador and drifted to one side of the road to give the van enough room to pass, but rather than overtaking us, the van swerved to cut us off, veering into our path sharply without warning.

Nana hammered at the horn, a loud squawking of outrage, and stamped down on the brakes hastily. With a metal-rending, rubber-burning screech, the Ambassador juddered to an abrupt halt, skidding and almost fishtailing into the narrow ditch by the side of the dirt road.

I was thrown off the back seat and Nana snapped forward, hitting his head on the steering wheel so hard that his nose began to bleed. As for Nani, she shrieked loudly and her dentures flew out from her mouth at the shock of this sudden deceleration, thumping into the windshield with a wet thunk.

It took Nana a moment to recover his wits before he mopped at his nose with a handkerchief and asked groggily, 'Is everyone okay?'

'I'm fine,' I said weakly, climbing back up onto the seat. Nani shook her head as well, dusting off her dentures before slipping them back into place.

Once he was satisfied that we weren't hurt, Nana rolled down his window to shake a fist at the van, which had come to a stop a few metres ahead.

'You barbarians,' he shouted, cursing like a sailor. 'Where did you fools learn to drive?'

In reply, the van's doors slid open with a thunk, and three men poured out from the back.

I could not discern their faces, which were hidden behind thick woollen monkey caps pulled down over their chins. All I could see was their eyes and the guns in their hands, long Kalashnikovs with banana magazines, which they levelled at us menacingly.

When she saw the guns, Nani moaned, panicking. With unexpected strength, she reached back and pulled me to the front seat, cradling me close to her, shielding me with her body.

One of the masked men, a thin, hunched figure with an incongruously magenta balaclava that didn't quite fit because his bulging topknot was pulling it out of shape, stepped forward and motioned at us with a revolver.

'Get out of the car,' he shouted. His voice was garbled, muffled by his mask, a guttural grunt.

'Do as they say,' Nana told me softly, calmly holding up his hands in surrender. 'Don't worry, they won't hurt us.'

Slowly, careful not to make any sudden moves that might antagonise the hijackers, we opened the doors and got out of the car. Nana went first and then Nani, who grabbed my hand and refused to let go, trying to push me behind her as the gunmen spread out to surround us and told us to get to our knees.

My heart was racing. I felt like I was going to wet myself with fear, but at the same time, I can't quite describe it; I felt impossibly alive, more alive than I had ever felt before.

As we sank down on the ground—Nani whimpering because her arthritis made her knees as stiff as pine—the leader of the hijackers announced in a loud voice, 'We are appropriating this vehicle in the name of free Khalistan. Do not try and stop us or we will be forced to cause you harm, which is not what we desire.'

He held out one hand for the keys, which Nana passed to him reluctantly. For a moment, I thought he was going to argue with the man, try and wrestle his gun away from him and then shoot the others dhishkow, dhishow, dhishkapow—three quick shots like in a Hindi movie. But Nana didn't say a word, not even as the man leaned forward and grasped his chin roughly with one hand and tilted his face upwards so that he could squint at him closely.

For an interminable interlude, he looked Nana straight in the eye before lowering his gun and whispering, 'Gobind Singh ji, is that you?'

Whipping off his mask, the terrorist revealed a most unexpected face. I had imagined a hardened criminal with a sloping brow, but what confronted us was a young man's face, delicate, almost feminine, barely twenty-five with a scraggly beard and bad skin that was pockmarked with old acne. It was then that I noticed that he had a pair of startlingly green eyes that shone as bright as emeralds.

With an enormous grin, he bowed his head as if to pay homage to my grandfather.

'It is I, sir. Harpreet Singh, your ex-student.'

When he made this declaration, Nana squinted at him, wrinkling his nose, and then let out a little laugh of recognition.

'I remember you,' Nana exclaimed. 'Smart boy, always sat in the first row in class, wanted to be an army officer, yes?'

The boy laughed delightedly.

'Yes, sir. It is I, the very same.'

Nana shook his head sadly, his mouth hardening with disappointment.

'And this is what you have done with your life. You have made yourself a thief and a thug who waves guns at honest people.

'What a waste! Is this what you studied so hard for, son? Is this what you meant when you said you wanted to become a soldier and protect those who couldn't protect themselves?'

When he heard this litany of rebukes, the boy terrorist's expression faltered, his grin of welcome replaced by a scowl.

'I *am* a soldier, sir. I'm fighting in a righteous war, a war for freedom, for equality, so that the common man can have the same justice as the rich.'

'This is not a war,' Nana said with a snort. 'This is a travesty.'

The boy terrorist frowned indignantly.

'Do you remember, sir, what you taught us about the Russian Revolution?' he whispered coldly and started to recite:

They never fail who die
In a great cause: the block may soak their gore;
Their heads may sodden in the sun; their limbs
Be strung to city gates and castle walls—
But still their spirit walks abroad.
Though years
Elapse, and others share as dark a doom,
They but augment the deep and sweeping thoughts
Which overpower all others, and conduct
The world, at last, to freedom.

'That is Lord Byron, isn't it, sir? You read it in class to us once.'

'You remembered?' Nana said, his face shiny with delight.

'Of course, sir, I remember everything you taught me.'

Nana winced when the boy terrorist said those words. A shadow swept across his face, a spasm of sorrow.

'I don't understand. You were such a bright boy. Why are you wasting your life with this … this foolishness?'

'We were all bright boys once, sir, but now we bright boys cannot find jobs because of reservation quotas. We cannot take care of our wives and mothers because of the sahibs in Delhi who sell our water to Haryana and Rajasthan. We cannot choose our own leaders because of the state of Emergency. We have to watch silently as our land is taken and given away to Mussulmans; those same Mussulmans who raped our mothers during Partition. We cannot even speak our mother tongue or even worship our God in peace because the army invades our holiest shrines and forces us to speak Hindi.

'You once said, sir, that no one will fight for the oppressed but the oppressed themselves. We are not terrorists. We are revolutionaries, and Khalistan is our revolution.'

'The revolution you dream of is not ours,' Nana said sourly. 'You don't want to change the world; you want to blow it up.'

'Jean-Paul Sartre, sir?' the boy said with a small smile. 'I have heard you use that quotation before.'

'Very good,' Nana said, clapping his hands together in mock sarcasm. 'I can see that I taught you very well.'

'Oh, but you did, sir. You once said in class that a man must aspire to something higher than himself, that to find a purpose he must fasten himself to a noble cause. I have faith in my cause, sir, and I'm willing to give my life for it. It is easy to mouth words but actions are difficult, and as you taught us, freedom is never free. It always comes at a cost—the cost of suffering and hardship and self-sacrifice. That is what we are fighting for, sir, for a dream of freedom, an ideal of a better Punjab. What could be nobler than that?'

'There is no nobility in what you are doing, son. Surely you understand that? You are just children with guns, nothing more.'

As Nana uttered those words, the two other terrorists hissed with rage. Raising their weapons, they advanced menacingly toward us, but before violence erupted, Harpreet Singh stopped them with a wave of one hand.

'What happened to you, sir?' he said sadly. 'When did you stop believing?'

'Enough,' Nana snapped, 'I don't want to debate with you. Take the car and leave.'

Harpreet Singh flinched. His jaw clenched with fury. From where I was kneeling, I could see his hands, his knuckles, whitening as his grip on his revolver tightened. I whimpered, scared that he was going to hurt Nana.

My whining must have caught his attention because he turned to me and smiled benignly.

'Is this your grandson?' he asked.

Nana nodded. Harpreet Singh knelt next to me, offering me one hand to shake.

'Hello!'

With a shiver, I shrank from him, nestling into Nani's shoulder.

When he saw my obvious fear, Harpreet Singh laughed and held up his revolver.

'Do you know what this is?' he asked me.

When I saw the gun, I let go of Nani and turned back to him, overcome with curiosity. My palms couldn't help but itch as I looked at the revolver. There was something infinitely menacing about the gun, but also something tantalisingly beautiful, a shiny, enticing sheen to the stamped metal.

'Would you like to hold it?'

Reversing his grip, Harpreet Singh offered the gun to me, urging me to take it. I was about to do just that when Nana pushed aside my hand angrily.

'No,' he said, pulling me to him with such alacrity that I nearly lost my balance.

'Leave him alone. He is just a child.'

Harpreet Singh looked at him with a sneer, rising back to his feet.

'Go home, professor sahib,' he said harshly. 'Take your car and go hide in your comfortable farm and leave the fighting to us real men. We warriors will free Punjab, not you big talkers.'

With that pronouncement, he turned to his masked compatriots and exclaimed, 'Let them go.'

'But the car?' One of them objected.

'Leave it,' he said dismissively. 'We will find another.'

Silently we watched as the terrorists climbed back into the van. Harpreet Singh was the last to go. He paused before he got in and offered Nana a curt nod, as if to bid him adieu, before pulling down his mask so that his face was obscured once more, hidden behind a dark shroud of wool.

With a shrill squeal, the van sped away. Only when they had vanished well into the distance did we get to our feet and return to the Ambassador.

'Let's go home, Gobind,' Nani said tiredly, but Nana didn't start the car.

Instead, he gazed after the van for a long time, frowning and shaking his head, waiting until it was just a speck far, far away.

'Who was that, Nana?' I asked.

'A boy I knew once,' he replied sadly, fixing his eyes on the rough road ahead as he put the car in gear at last.

'A foolish little boy pretending to be a man.'

9

By the time we finally got back to the farm, I was so exhausted by the day's excitement that I had fallen asleep in the back seat of the Ambassador.

When we trundled to a stop, Nani tried to prod me awake, but I grumbled and refused to open my eyes. Finally, my grandfather had to pick me up and carry me up to my bedroom, grunting with the effort of managing my weight with his battered feet.

That night, I had the most peculiar dream.

I dreamt that I was a grown man, even taller than Nana and as broad as an oak, with a bushy beard of my own and long, silken hair that fell almost to my knees.

I was lost, starving and parched, wandering through a vast and boundless desert, stranded amidst the ever-changing dunes of sand with no idea of where I had come from and where I was going.

I heard a shriek behind me, a shrill voice calling out my name. Turning, I searched to see who it was, but all I could discern was a pall of darkness, growing in the distance like a storm front, slowly consuming everything around me. The sand dunes shifted and disappeared, drowning before an inky tide of black, and I found myself standing in a winding passageway with a hundred twists and turns like a maze.

That was when I saw him, a darkling that broke from the depths of the gloom and began to run away from me, fleeing as fast as his shadowy feet could carry him. I broke into a run myself, chasing after him, but no matter how quickly I hurried, how desperate and breathless my pursuit became, my quarry always managed to elude me, ducking away before I could see his face, before I could determine his identity.

Somehow, I compelled myself to run even faster. My heart began to thump like a kettle drum. I gasped for air, choking and coughing. And then at that moment, he stopped, turning to face me, swimming into shape from the shadows like a mirage coming slowly to life.

It was a boy, thin, almost fragile to behold. I could not see his face, which was hidden, crawling with darkness as if he were wearing a living mask.

'Why are you running away from me?' I asked breathlessly.

'Am I running away from you?' he said. 'Or are you running away from me?'

At that moment, abruptly, I was awakened by the sound of screams.

They seemed to be coming from outside, from the nearby village, which was about a kilometre away from the farm. I sat up, shivering. Hurriedly I wore my slippers and dashed downstairs to the living room, fearing the worst, convinced that Nana and Nani were in mortal danger.

I found Nana standing by one of the windows, staring out at the distance. Much to my astonishment, I saw that he had his old 12-bore shotgun in his hands, gripping it tightly, chewing on his lower lip, as a faltering monotony of distant gunshots resounded across the fields followed by a fresh crescendo of cries.

'What is happening, Nana?' I squealed, barely able to contain my panic. 'Have the Congress-wallahs come to kill us?'

'It's nothing, puttar,' he said brusquely. 'Just the jackals. Go back to bed.'

It was not a request but a command. The finality in his voice was unequivocal, making it clear that he would brook no arguments from me. Sulking, I realised I had no choice but to obey. I tramped reluctantly back up to my room but found myself unable to calm down.

I tried my best, but no matter how many sheep I counted, the sweet, soporific stupor of sleep evaded me. Instead, as I lay there, I found myself consumed by a nameless fear, a terror that engulfed me so completely that I felt like I couldn't breathe.

They were going to kill us, I thought with a shudder. They were going to kill us all just like they killed poor Rat.

For the rest of the night, my morbid imagination ran wild. I envisioned a hundred, no, a thousand ways that the police and the terrorists would kill me, an endless soliloquy of solemn deaths.

I was shot down in the street, the machine-gun bullets slapping into my chest, tearing through me, mangling my bones and flesh and making me dance like a marionette on a string.

I was blown up by a bomb, a massive explosion followed by a moment of absolute agony, and then my limbs and blood raining down in a gory monsoon.

I imagined myself burnt and beaten and stabbed and hung, choking to death on my own tongue, gasping for air. Why, I even imagined exploding after stepping on a landmine, being blown to a gruesome pulp like something from a war movie.

When the sun finally rose and Nani shouted for me to get up and have a bath before all the hot water in the boiler was used up, I heaved a sigh of relief and sat up with a yawn, glad the night was past.

It was a tired, sallow morning. The sky was overcast, wispy with a humid, acrid fog that hung listlessly in the air.

My mood improved slightly when the phone rang just after eight. It was a trunk call from my mother all the way from Bombay. It had taken her the better part of a week to get through to us and she was near panic. Nani listened to her scolding patiently, trying to explain that we were all okay, but she insisted that she wanted to speak to me.

'Hello,' she said when I took the phone, 'are you safe, my love?'

Just the sound of her voice, so filled with worry, was enough to make me burst into tears.

'I'm scared, Mummy,' I gasped, choking back a sob. 'I want to come home *now*.'

'Soon, my wren,' she whispered. 'When things calm down, you can all come down to Bombay on the first flight, okay? But for now, you have to be a brave little boy. Be brave for your Nani. She needs you to take care of her.'

Somehow, this comment, albeit a platitude, was infinitely reassuring. That, and the sound of my mother's voice, scratchy and tinny as if it were a bad gramophone recording, went a long way towards dispelling the inchoate panic that had gripped me all through the night, leaving in its place a determination, the conviction that no matter what happened, I would endeavour to be as brave as a lion and make my mother proud.

Sadly, this promise to myself was destined to be tested less than half an hour later.

Just as we were settling down for breakfast on the verandah, the police arrived.

A convoy of three Jeeps screeched up with sirens blaring and rattled to a stop in front of the farmhouse.

The latter two discharged a cadre of Punjab Police havildars, who brandished their rifles at the ready and fanned out to surround the verandah.

From the lead vehicle, the same ferret-faced inspector who had treated Nani so crudely at the police thana stepped out, dusting his trousers fastidiously.

Smiling widely, he lifted one hand to wave at Nana and me, and marched up to the verandah, pausing for a moment by the steps to wipe his forehead with a starched white handkerchief.

'Ah, the nightingale with the beautiful voice,' he said, half bowing to Nani. 'How lovely to see you again!'

Nana scowled at the inspector, folding his arms across his chest.

'What do you want here?' he said stiffly, his voice sharp with antipathy.

The inspector raised one eyebrow and smiled at him slightly, but his eyes were as hard as obsidian.

'I have a few questions I would like to ask you.'

Without waiting for Nana to invite him, he sat down in a cane chair and picked up Nani's glass of lemonade from which he took a small sip, smacking his lips appreciatively.

'This is excellent,' he declared, raising the glass in a mock toast. 'My compliments to the chef, madam. On a day like this, it is like nectar from heaven.'

'Why are you harassing us?' Nani said, trying to remain composed, but I could sense her rising panic as the inspector leered at her, flashing his yellow teeth like a wolf.

Putting down the glass, he snapped his fingers and one of the havildars stepped forward and handed him a buff manila file.

From inside this folder, the inspector extracted a loose sheaf of photographs and fanned them across the table, inviting us to take a look.

I nearly threw up when I saw them. They were all pictures of dead men, young Sikhs all of them, battered and bruised and bullet-riddled, their turbans torn and their hair matted, their clothes drenched with blood. They were splayed across the ground in a macabre row like a child's broken dolls. And next to them, I saw the inspector and his policemen standing in a line, holding up their guns and laughing like hunters posing next to their gruesome trophies after a grand battue.

'There was an encounter near here early this morning,' the inspector said coldly. 'These dissidents were killed trying to resist security forces.'

'What does that have to do with us?'

'Do you recognise any of these men?'

Again, he waved the photographs at Nana, urging him to look at them, but Nana refused to give him the satisfaction.

'No,' he said, staring back at the inspector levelly. His jaw clenched with barely contained rage. 'I don't.'

The inspector clucked his tongue and shook his head as if he was appalled by Nana's lack of cooperation.

He turned to Nani next and brandished the photographs at her.

'What about you, nightingale? Have you seen these boys before?'

Nani blanched bone-white, barely sparing this gruesome array a glance before averting her eyes and shaking her head slightly with a mute expression of revulsion on her face.

Finally, the inspector turned to me, and said, 'What about you, little friend? Do you know this bad man?'

He held up a photograph in front of my face. I gasped, not only because I was sickened by this grisly sight but also because, to my dismay, I recognised the dead man's face.

It was him, Nana's ex-student, the same boy terrorist we had run into the night before, the leader of the gang that had stopped us and tried to take our car.

My mouth filled with the sour taste of bile. The corpse was almost unrecognisable with a ragged bullet-hole above one eye and a misshapen purpling face, but it was him. I was certain of it. It was the eyes, those same jaded eyes, wide open now in death, staring out at me, livid with the accusation that made me sure it was Harpreet Singh.

Before I could blurt out that fact, Nana snatched the photo away from the inspector and threw it to the ground.

'I told you,' he rasped, 'we don't know anything. Now go away and leave us to our breakfast!'

'Not quite yet, I'm afraid,' the inspector said, smiling widely.

From the folder, he fished out an official-looking sheet of yellow paper, which he shook in Nana's direction.

'As you can see, I have a warrant to search these premises. We have received information that you may be providing shelter to insurgents.'

He turned and nodded at his men.

'Search the house,' he ordered.

Obediently, the havildars spread out. One of them broke down the door, hefting his rifle like a battering ram, smashing the stock hard against the front door, which ricocheted open with a deafening crack.

We stood there on the verandah huddled together as the policemen shoved their way past us and began to thoroughly ransack the farmhouse.

Faced with such brutality, my vow to be brave wavered. I cowered against Nani, who hugged me close to her protectively, stroking my hair and telling me not to be scared.

The policemen were experts, obviously accustomed to searching houses. One of them rummaged through the cupboards and drawers, breaking open their locks and dumping their contents unceremoniously on the floor, while another pulled Nana's books off their shelves one by one and broke open the spines before tossing them away in an ungainly pile.

Next to me, Nana swayed slightly, his face ashen with rage, wincing slightly each time he heard the rasping sound of a page being torn, as though he had been struck by a physical blow.

As we watched, a thin havildar, not more than twenty years old, hauled Nana's typewriter out of his study.

No, not the typewriter, I groaned as the policeman threw it to the floor with all his strength. It smashed apart with a hard twang that made me flinch. Behind him, another cop made a slow circuit of the living room, tapping a cane against the floors to listen for hollow sounds that would indicate a hidden cavity or a secret trapdoor, while yet another, a fat-faced havildar with a protuberant belly that was barely contained by his Sam Browne belt, carefully and systematically shattered every single windowpane in the house with a lathi while grinning at us wickedly to expose brown, paan-stained teeth.

Meanwhile, the inspector settled back, and with a sigh lit up a cigarette.

'This is wonderful weather we are having, isn't it?' he said blandly. 'Do you think it will rain? It feels like rain.'

He waffled on like that, chain-smoking cigarette after cigarette while bantering inanely. Hatefully, I glared at him, wanting to step forward and choke him. Shut up, I wanted to scream—shut up, shut up, shut up.

'Why are you doing this?' Nana asked him sadly. 'Why do you hate me? I have done nothing to you.'

In reply, the inspector smirked, a cruel twist of his lips.

'Let me tell you a little story, Mr Gobind Singh, famous poet and writer. I was born not twenty-five kilometres from here. My grandfather was a Jat, an immigrant from Haryana, who came here as an indentured farmer, and my father was a farmer as well. They were, in the truest sense of the phrase, sons of the soil, simple hard-working peasants who had squandered their whole lives tilling the same acre of land for the same master for three generations. And for what? So that the government-owned collectives could buy their grain at a fixed price and resell it for enormous profits, of which they didn't see a single paisa?

'When Independence came, they thought they would become the owners of the land they so loved, which they had nurtured with their sweat and their tears, but no, even though the zamindars were banned in 1947, the system did not change. The name by which the landlords were known was altered but their faces remained the same, and a hundred thousand poor Jats like my father kept breaking their backs for nothing, for barely enough food to keep their children fed and clothed.

'But my father had one dream—to see me educated so that I would not end up like him. He saved money and sent me to school in Patiala, and then I was admitted to college, in Chandigarh, and he was so proud, ha! You should have seen his face that day. He looked like he was going to die of happiness.

'I was a good student, a hard worker like my father, but I wasn't sure about what I wanted to do after I graduated. But then one day, a famous Punjabi poet came to our class and gave us a lecture. He spoke about honour and told us stories about how great Punjab had been in the past and that its future was in our hands. And I listened to him with shining eyes, and that very day, I decided that I would protect that golden future by joining the police.

'But how could I, a humble Jat, get a commission in the police corps? I had no patron, no political connections, no pull, so for me, there was only one chance. I would have to bribe my way in.

'It costs twenty-five thousand rupees to get into the Punjab Police, Mr Singh,' he said with a florid sigh. 'Do you have any idea how much money that is for a poor man? No, of course, you don't. For you, it is a mere pittance, but for a farmer, it is a lifetime of back-breaking labour.

'But I had no choice. I had set my heart on joining the police force, and so I went to my father to ask him for the money—twenty-five thousand rupees, which he didn't have, but he didn't have the heart to say no to me.

'So he took a loan and gave a chit to his landlord, who was a rich sardar like you and your large friend, twenty-five thousand rupees against his rights to our land, all so that I could fulfil my dream and become a policeman.

'Of course, I didn't know any of this. I didn't ask where he got the money. No, I just took it and went off happily to the training academy, never knowing what my father had sacrificed for me.

'Three years later, when I was on my first posting, six Sikh thugs came to our farm and tried to force my father off our land, telling him that he had to pay back the money immediately or the farm was theirs. And when he resisted them, they burned our house to the ground and my father with it, all for twenty-five thousand measly rupees.'

He leaned forward, glowering at Nana with bitter, lifeless eyes.

'That is what your dream of Punjab was worth, old man. That is what it cost me.'

'I sympathise with you, inspector, and I'm sorry for your loss, I truly am. However, you do realise that you are part of the problem and not the solution,' Nana said gently, hectoring him. 'It isn't just the dissidents who are choking the life out of Punjab. You have to take some of the blame too. Hate begets more hate, and unless you stop this cycle—'

'Quiet!' the inspector roared. 'No more lectures! No more bhashans! This is not your world any more, old man. There is no place for words here, only bullets and guns. Remember that or I will have you taken in for questioning again.'

When he heard that threat, Nana fell silent. Grimacing, he turned away, resuming his morose vigil while the policemen continued their rampage through the cottage.

Finally, after two hours, when they still hadn't found anything incriminating, the inspector stubbed out one final cigarette and rose to his feet.

'That is enough, I think,' he declared, 'for now.'

He looked at Nana one last time, squinting malevolently. 'I hope you have learnt your lesson, old man. Do not poke your nose where it does not belong or something dreadful may happen to the nightingale or to your precious grandson, do you understand?'

With that threat, he spun and marched off to his Jeep, followed closely by the other policemen in a phalanx.

As their vehicles departed in a cloud of dust, I pushed Nani away and rushed into the house where the typewriter lay toppled on its side. Much to my despair, I saw it had been destroyed beyond repair.

The carriage lever had snapped, the ribbon mechanism splintered apart and most of the keys had broken off and lay scattered across the floor.

One by one, I gathered them up lovingly, that jumble of shattered letters, and tried to push each one back into its rightful place. But it did no good. No matter how desperately I pressed them down, they kept falling out, dropping to the stone floor with a series of soft, almost accusatory plinks.

As I looked down at that meagre pile of broken syllables, cradling them in my hand, it was as if I could feel something inside myself break as well, an incalculable splintering of innocence that was far too agonising for words to describe.

The police were not heroes, I thought. There were no heroes here—not in Punjab. There were only villains and victims, and it was the villains that were winning. It was the villains that were in control, in power, and we were all nothing more than victims unable to stop them from destroying our lives, as powerless as ants before a storm.

'Nana,' I wailed piteously. 'Look what they did to the typewriter.'

'Leave it,' my grandfather said coldly, surveying the wreck of his home.

Beside him, Nani limped into the kitchen and fetched a broom and a dustpan and returned to the verandah, where she hunched over to sweep up the remnants of the inspector's cigarette ash and his discarded cigarette butts.

'Don't you worry, my beloved.' Nana whispered to her as she shuffled past him, wincing as her arthritic knees ached. 'Everything will be fine. I promise.'

'No, Gobind,' she replied sadly. 'It will not. Nothing will ever be fine again.'

10

Two days later, Nani awoke with a stye in her eye. Her right eyelid was inflamed and yellow, so full of pus that it had swollen almost shut.

'This is an evil omen,' she said ominously, squinting at Nana. 'Enough is enough, Gobind. I think the time has come for us to leave Amritsar.'

First, Nani summoned Cookie and gave her a thousand rupees, and told her to take a few weeks off and go visit her aunt in Una. Cookie began to cry, insisting that she wanted to come with us to Bombay, but Nani refused gently, telling her that it would be hard enough to get three plane tickets, much less four.

Unfortunately, when she phoned the travel agent, he informed her that all flights out of Amritsar had been cancelled, that the planes had been grounded after receiving bomb threats from the separatists.

It quickly became apparent to us that the only way we were going to be able to leave the city was by train, and so, after we had eaten a light breakfast of leftover saag and roti, Nana and I were dispatched to the railway station, to acquire tickets somehow so that we could depart as soon as possible.

Because of the curfew, Nana was unable to hire us a taxi. As a result, he decided to drive to the station himself in the old Ambassador. At first, he wanted to go alone, but Nani had been quite adamant. She was the one who had insisted that he take me along.

'It will be much safer,' she said firmly. 'After all, who would think of detaining an old man and his grandson out for a morning drive…?'

Nana drove slowly, without any of his usual cheer or banter. He did not laugh or joke with me like he did normally, or even switch on the car radio and shake his head in cadence with the bhangra songs that were broadcast all day long.

Since his return from the police station, Nana had been sullen, almost haggard. He hunched over the wheel, his brow creased with worry. His eyes, normally bright with merriment, were cadaverous, surrounded by dark hollows, and every few minutes, his hands would begin to tremble as if he had no control over them any more.

As we approached the city, we had to stop more and more frequently because there were roadblocks every few kilometres along the highway. Ranks of heavy, metal barrels were arrayed across the road with a hulking green one and half-ton trucks parked behind them, ringed by groups of soldiers in crumpled khaki uniforms, who glared at us suspiciously when we passed by.

Excitedly, I stared out of the window at their shiny rifles and green helmets, but Nana didn't pay them any attention. His gaze remained fixed firmly forward. There was apprehension in the taut bowstring of his mouth, a nervousness that I had never quite noticed before, which had always been hidden from me by his moustache. His left eye twitched tensely, a tic that was as regular as the ticking of a watch. Also, much to my amusement, I saw that he had nicked himself in four separate places while shaving that morning, which he had patched with soggy wisps of tissue that fluttered listlessly in the mid-morning breeze, like a papery beard.

That morning, Amritsar was a ghost town, populated only by parked cars and closed doors. The still air was heavy with an almost unnatural silence, that eerie hush that can only exist immediately before or after the approach of death. Yes, that was it exactly. It felt like the city had died and all that remained was this pallid corpse that surrounded us, a cadaver of mortar and brick.

By the time we finally arrived at the station, it was almost two in the afternoon. Much to my shock, the platform was seething with a mass of people. All around us, absolute pandemonium reigned. The chaos was awful to perceive. I could sense the tension in the air—palpable, like a thick smog. The time for queues had long since ended. Now, an irate mob surrounded the ticket booking counter, screeching and shouting, pushing and shoving. It seemed as though everyone in Amritsar had woken up that morning with the same idea as my grandmother's—to escape the city somehow before the violence had a chance to intensify.

'Oh, God!' I heard Nana exclaim. 'It's like 1947 all over again.'

'Nana, what happened in 1947?' I asked curiously, but he did not answer my question.

Instead, he pushed his way through the teeming multitudes and made his way towards the stationmaster's office.

'He's an old friend,' he explained. I nodded and followed his lead without further argument, clutching his hand tightly. The throng of people scared me a little; the tumult of their proximity, the sour confluence of sweat and fear and rage, all mingled into one, made me feel queasy and ill.

'Wait here,' Nana commanded when we reached our destination. 'Don't move even one inch, okay?'

I nodded obediently. As he disappeared into the office, I pressed back against the wall, trying to avoid the crowd as they surged back and forth around me. Each time a train arrived, a mad rush of panic-stricken passengers dashed to clamber aboard, laden down with the accumulated debris of their lives, suitcases and trunks and canvas holdalls and cardboard boxes and, in one instance, even a coir gunny-sack filled to overflowing.

As I watched, an old woman carrying an enormous cuckoo clock stumbled. The clock slipped from her numb fingers and shattered into pieces with a resounding crash. Immediately, all the people around her froze worriedly, wondering if what they had heard was the sound of a bomb. But when all they perceived was the old woman whimpering as she wept and the strange, almost surreal cackle of the suddenly homeless cuckoo, the exodus resumed, even more urgently than before.

Nearby, a cake-wallah was prowling the periphery of the crowd, hawking pineapple cream pastries from a metal trunk. Not far away from him, a mithai-wallah poured orange spirals into his frying batter. They sizzled and hissed and spat. My mouth filled with saliva when I smelt the familiar scent of fresh jalebis cooking. My stomach growled with hunger, and immediately, I regretted having rushed through my breakfast.

About twenty minutes later, Nana emerged from the station master's office, clutching three tickets for the next Frontier Mail triumphantly.

When he saw that I was still standing exactly where he had ordered me to, he smiled down at me, pleased that I obeyed his instructions so precisely.

'Are you hungry?' he asked.

'Yes, Nana,' I nodded, so ravenous that my stomach felt knotted into a tight little ball.

'Very well,' he said, 'what do you say to a gola, eh?'

As soon as he said those words, I forgot my trepidation and let out a squeal of delight. Golas were ice candies—giant lollipops of crushed ice perched on a stick and dipped in fruit syrup, which melted slowly in your mouth and left the sweet taste of sugar lingering for hours and hours. I absolutely loved them. They were my favourite, better even than Toblerone or Hershey's Kisses.

Nana called out to a nearby hawker and indicated that we would have two golas, rose sherbert for me and khus khus for him. With a grin, he handed me mine, and immediately, I attacked it with immense enthusiasm, gulping and smacking my lips with brash enjoyment. Before I knew it, I had consumed nearly half in three bites so swift that my head began to ache. But when I looked up at Nana, I saw that he had not even started to eat his gola. He held it limply in one hand as if he had forgotten about it altogether. The ice had begun to melt and drip slowly to leave a dull green stain on the tan fabric of his slacks, but he did not seem to care at all. Instead, his gaze remained transfixed by the uproar on the platform. His face was so forlorn it worried me.

'What's wrong, Nana…?' I asked, losing interest in my gola momentarily.

'The trains,' he sighed. 'It is always the trains that are the harbingers of horror in Punjab.'

'I … I don't understand.'

'Once, a long time ago, when I was your age, I stood on this very platform, son, and watched these same trains bring in piles of corpses.'

His words choked in his throat. Abruptly, he whirled to face me. Without warning, he grabbed my arm and shook me like a rag doll.

'It is our fault, son,' he said sadly, 'don't you ever forget that.'

'In the future, a time will come where people will speak of 1984 dismissively and blame Bhindranwale and Mrs

Gandhi for what is happening here, but they are not the ones to blame. It is us, puttar, you and I, the watchers and the talkers, sitting on our sofas and hiding in our homes and running away when it is time to stand up and fight for what is ours. We are the ones who have killed Punjab. We were given paradise and we have turned it into jehannum.'

His fingers bit into the soft flesh of my bicep so vehemently that I moaned.

'Nana,' I whimpered faintly, 'please, you're hurting me.'

When he heard that, my grandfather's eyes widened with dismay. Sheepishly, he released his grip on my arm. Turning, he threw away his untouched gola. It landed on the pavement with a wet squish. Immediately, a pair of pie-dogs began to snarl and fight over this half-molten prize.

'Let's get going. Your Nani will be waiting for us,' Nana said gruffly and pushed headlong into the crowd. After hurriedly gulping down what remained of my own gola, I followed, licking my scarlet fingers and trotting after him as he hurried towards the exit.

As we returned to the car, his mood remained pensive, almost sullen. He didn't say a word when he started the Ambassador up with a hoarse growl, not one sentence as we inched our way out of the station and crept through the barren byways of Amritsar.

I was too meek to intrude upon the withdrawn solitude of his silence, even though I could sense that something was bothering him. Thankfully, his disposition started to improve little by little as we drew closer and closer to the outer boundaries of the city. I don't know precisely what it was that cheered him up. Perhaps it was because he felt safer now that our tickets were in his breast pocket or maybe, simply, he felt a little better because we were leaving Amritsar behind us and returning to the safe haven of the farm.

By the time we passed the bus depot and turned onto GT Road, he was almost his old, happy self once again.

Merrily, he began to drum his fingers on the dashboard and started to hum one of his songs softly beneath his breath, a lilting, melancholy Punjabi melody I didn't recognise, but the bass rumble of his voice made me glad somehow, almost comfortable. He sang:

Oh, my heart is wounded,
My soul is scarred,
But the melody of your voice heals me.
And cures all my pain.

Delighted, I couldn't help but smile when I heard this ballad. To hear Nana sing after all these days, it almost felt like everything was back to normal. Suddenly, it was like Mrs Gandhi was still alive and no riots had occurred and we were just out for another one of our Sunday 'geris', just Nana and I caught in a perfect moment, an arc-en-ciel of simple, joyful contentment.

Sadly, this bliss was doomed to be only temporary.

We had been driving for half an hour or so when we ran into a roadblock. It was located just outside the city limits, a few miles before the crossroads at which we turned off to head towards the farm. An ersatz barricade—a narrow line of oil barrels flanked by a makeshift bamboo barrier—had been erected across the road. Behind this temporary impediment, a cluster of CRPF jawans dawdled lazily, waving vehicles listlessly to the side of the highway so that they could check identification papers.

Nana clucked his tongue in irritation when he saw the blockade. Frowning, he slowed down the Ambassador, first to a crawl and then gradually to a dead halt. I leaned out of the window and peered at the line of cars that stood stationary before us—a slow, wriggling worm of hot metal and sun-glinting windshields that seemed endless, almost a kilometre and a half long.

Nana hammered at his horn, honking furiously, but even this repetitive cacophony had no effect whatsoever upon the forward motion of traffic. We remained stationary, hemmed in by hissing, sputtering automobiles. Almost forty minutes frittered by. We crept forward in inches, foot by tortuous foot, drawing closer and closer towards the checkpoint. All around us, the sun baked the flat earth of the fields, making it shimmer and glow, like beaten gold. It was very hot, almost oven-like, inside the closed confines of the car. I began to perspire profusely in a matter of minutes. My throat grew parched, my lips dry and sore—the cold comfort of the gola was quickly forgotten.

Frustrated, I carped at Nana, voicing my irritation, but he ignored my grumbling. Instead, he sat rigidly behind the wheel, uncomplaining, seemingly immune to the humidity, even though I could see the faint sheen of sweat glistening like dew on his upper lip.

That silenced me immediately; I sat back without another word. If he could bear the discomfort, I thought resolutely, then so could I. But it was not easy, not at all. I shut my eyes tight and tried to conjure up a mental vision of the ice candy I had eaten at the station, the memory of its frigid delight, but all that I accomplished was to make myself sweat twice as much and feel even more parched.

Once we were in close proximity to the barrier, one of the soldiers, a young, almost hairless boy, I remember, with an insolent scowl came up to the car and tapped the window with the long gleaming barrel of his rifle.

Wordlessly, Nana opened the door and climbed out. He exchanged a few words with the jawan, smiling and explaining and gesticulating, and then he delved into the secret breast pocket of his jacket and extracted a sheaf of neatly folded documents.

He handed these papers to the soldier with an authoritative nod. When the boy glanced through them, almost immediately his demeanour changed. He saluted Nana with a crisp snap of his arm and waved him straight through the blockade.

Nana clambered back into the Ambassador and carefully eased it out of the long static line of cars. He steered out onto the crest of the road and slowly began to weave his way past the roadblock. A pair of jawans oversaw our progress dourly from behind a blockhouse of sandbags. Their faces were grim and unreal, half-obscured by red scarves that made them seem strangely piratical, like dacoits from an old Hindi film.

To my delight, one of them lowered his bandanna and smiled at me broadly as we passed him, and waved his Sten gun in the air in mock threat, making me giggle with glee.

Just then, from somewhere behind us, a young Sikh boy on a scooter broke from the line of waiting vehicles and cut swiftly into our path. Nana stamped down reflexively on the brakes to avoid hitting him, bringing the car juddering to a stop with a shrill screech.

I don't know exactly what the boy's motivation to bolt was. Perhaps he had no licence or the scooter did not belong to him or maybe he was just scared, troubled by the sight of so many armed soldiers. Nevertheless, he revved the scooter and darted past us, its engine buzzing like a mosquito as he tried to skirt around the roadblock, but immediately, one of the soldiers dashed out from behind the sandbags and blocked his path, commanding him to halt.

Faced with this menacing ultimatum, the boy slowed and pulled his two-wheeler over to the side of the road.

As he rolled to a stop, I caught my first glimpse of his face. He was barely fourteen or fifteen. His cheeks were just beginning to rasp with the emergence of a foolish little beard, and his eyes, they were absolutely terrified.

At that moment, I felt awful precognition that something horrible was about to happen. One of the soldiers pulled the boy roughly from his scooter by the scruff of his neck, utterly unmoved by his strident protestations. The other jawan ordered him angrily to produce his licence, but the boy merely shrugged and shook his head. I guessed he was trying to say that he had no papers, that that he was just out for a joyride.

The soldier paused briefly, exchanging a knowing look with his comrade, and then asked another question. I couldn't quite hear what it was, but the boy scowled, and as an answer, spat furiously in the mud. That seemed to inflame the soldiers even more. Suddenly, without warning, the first jawan slapped the boy squarely on his cheek. The boy's eyes widened with shock. His fingers darted to his face, a flush of outrage flashing across his features.

By then, a small crowd had begun to cluster around the boy, a motley of khaki shapes, all heckling him. One of them shouted something at him in Punjabi. It had to be a racial slur of some sort because he reacted angrily. His hands cramped into fists, and he took one vehement step forward. Thankfully, he was smart enough to stop at that, checked by the loaded weapons the soldiers held pointed lazily in his direction. They all began to laugh loudly when they saw his hesitation, and then, abruptly, without warning, one of the jawans stepped forward and clubbed the boy hard in his midriff with a rifle butt.

He crumpled to the tarmac in an untidy heap. Incredulously, I watched as they began to beat him, less than ten feet away from me. Right there in plain sight, they rained down blows upon his supine form with their rifles and bamboo batons.

Stunned, I turned to Nana in panic, but he didn't say a word. One of the guards still standing by the barricade waved us on, and Nana pressed down on the accelerator silently with a leaden foot. Lurching, the Ambassador began to creep forward slowly.

'We have to stop, Nana,' I said urgently.

'No,' my grandfather whispered through clenched teeth. 'No, we can't.'

The final remnants of sugar evaporated from my mouth, replaced instead by the bitter antacid of disgust. I looked at him disbelievingly, but his face was grim with determination. I had seen this look before, so many, many times, the same stubborn scowl that had scarred his face whenever Nani had nagged him to shave his beard. Nana had made up his mind. No matter how much I begged, he would never listen to me.

Biting my lip, I turned and glared out of the window again. The boy had ceased screaming. Instead, he just lay there, rolled up into a tiny foetus, whimpering as each fresh onslaught landed. I think he saw me because he lifted his head slightly and looked straight into my eyes. For one fleeting second, his gaze locked unwaveringly into my own. His hair had unravelled. It hung around his face, streaming in the limp breeze. His sparse beard was caked with a thin filigree of blood. Desperately he raised one arm, beckoning at me, a thin stick limb that seemed too fragile to be real. The claret gash of his mouth flopped open and shut as if to beg for help, but no words emerged, only a soft mewling like the low moaning of an animal in agony. Spasmodically, he writhed as the soldiers continued to beat him until finally he lost consciousness and lay as still and silent as a corpse.

Nana did not even spare the poor boy a second glance. Instead, silently he just drove on. His lips were compressed into a taut line, and his cheeks burned crimson with shame. There was something in his eyes that alarmed me, something dark and nebulous, shiny and obsidian.

It was terror, I realised, barely able to believe what I was seeing. Nana was petrified.

'Please,' I whispered, on the verge of tears, 'Please … we have to go back and help him.'

'I said No!' Nana barked. His voice was furious, like the crack of a whip.

'What's wrong with you?' I groaned. 'Why … why are you acting like such a coward…?'

Desperately, I reached out and grabbed his shoulder, tugging at his arm, trying to wrestle it from the wheel. Without warning, Nana turned and struck out at me, a wild swipe with the back of his hand. It connected against my face, more with my head than my cheek, a dull thud of knuckle on bone.

A flurry of white dots starred across my vision. I fell back into my seat, stunned, barely able to believe that he had hit me. My forehead felt wet, a warm dribble slowly dripping down the side of my nose. Wincing, I raised my hand to touch my brow. My fingers came away covered with blood, seeping from a cut just above my right eye, a throbbing crescent where his ring had left a deep gash.

'I told you, damn you,' he yelled. 'I told you that we cannot stop. Why can't you understand that…?'

The outrage in his voice, that shrill twang of anger, was just too much for me to take. I did what any other child would have done. I burst into tears.

Just as quickly as it had erupted, Nana's fury abated. When the enormity of what he had just done dawned upon him, his face crumpled. For a moment, a rictus of regret flashed across his features, and he looked like he was about to burst into tears himself.

As soon as the barricade was behind us, he slowed the car to a crawl.

'I'm sorry, puttar,' he apologised. He tried to smile, but all that he could muster was a feeble shudder of his lips.

'Let me see.' Gently, he moved towards me, to check if I was all right.

Whimpering, I shrank back from him. When he saw me move away, his fingers clenched, wracked by grief. Reluctantly, he let his hand fall back, gripping the steering wheel so hard his knuckles turned white.

Sniffling, I averted my face, peering back out of the window. Behind us, I could see that the soldiers had returned to their posts, laughing and joking. One of them lit a beedi and inhaled the smoke deeply, sighing with satisfaction, as if nothing had happened at all. A few yards away from him, the boy's battered shape lay by the side of the road.

I cringed and closed my eyes, willing him to get up and move. But when I opened them again, he was still lying there, motionless, a twisted, broken shape.

I continued to stare out of the rear window, long after we had left the roadblock far, far behind. Only when we arrived back at the farm did I turn to glare at Nana. But he refused to look at me, to face the accusation in my eyes. Instead, he stared straight ahead at the narrow grey ribbon of the road as it dipped and turned.

Looking at him, I could barely recognise him. He seemed so tired and miserable—so old and worn and dilapidated. Somehow, until that precise second, I had never actually understood how human he was. My naiveté had always blinded me; a subtle haze of adulation had clouded my sight. I had always imagined my grandfather to be perfect—a heroic figure—wholly unable to have flaws or make mistakes, entirely incapable of experiencing anxiety or panic or any other weakness.

But now, without the grandiose mask of his beard to camouflage his face, it was almost as if for the first time, I could see Nana for what he really was.

When I look back now, it was at that moment, I think, that I stopped being a child, when it struck me, quite forcibly, that my grandfather was not special, not at all.

He was no hero.

He was just like everyone else.

A liar.

A coward.

A fake.

11

That was the last time I visited my grandparents. The very next year, my parents enrolled me in boarding school, and my trips to Amritsar came to an abrupt end.

In Sanawar, slowly but steadily, I started to forget about Nana. I rarely thought of him any more. Sometimes when I looked in the mirror and saw the scar that marred the bridge of my nose where he had hit me, I did think of him. The wound had healed to leave behind a vivid pink crescent of flesh shaped like an exploding star. It was my only real scar, but somehow I could not help but feel that it spoiled my face, making me look battered and older than I was, and it was all Nana's fault.

The truth is that I was much too busy to think of him. I had new passions, new interests and new preoccupations that consumed me. I made new friends, and I smoked my first cigarette, cowering behind the boy's bathrooms, coughing and giggling as we passed a Gold Flake butt around amongst us. I got drunk for the first time when four of us sneaked out to the nearby village and bought a quarter of cheap moonshine and gulped it down so quickly that it burnt our tongues and made us gag. Why, I even had my first girlfriend—a pinch-faced, flat-bottomed little thing called Meera, who never once let me kiss her.

Besides, by then I was an adolescent, locked firmly in Madame Puberty's embrace. My beard had finally grown out—a sparse moustache and goatee that did not quite join above my lip or on either side of my mouth, leaving me looking like a dogmatic billy goat instead of the manly man I had hoped to resemble. And as I grew older, those luminously innocent interludes I had spent at the farm with my grandparents had begun to fade, replaced instead by a fresh, more immediate set of memories—of cricket matches and house socials and board examinations and, most of all, of buxom young girls bulging out of their blue school sweaters.

In school, as regularly as clockwork, I continued to receive one letter from Nana every week without fail—two plain sheets of bond paper covered with his spidery handwriting, doling out wisdom and advice and always ending with an amusing anecdote gleaned from *Reader's Digest* with the sole intent of making me smile. I never replied to him—not once. More often than not, I bundled these epistles into a desk drawer without even bothering to read them because I had no time any more for Nana or his tall stories.

I didn't see him for almost ten years—until 1994.

That was the year I graduated from boarding school, and also the year India changed forever.

That summer, cable television beamed into a million homes for the first time with its steady saccharine diet of soap operas and music videos. A few months later, the Internet arrived, beep-beeping through dial-up modems at 64.4 kbps, bringing with it the promise of slow e-mail and even slower pornography. Even as I watched, the world was shrinking around me. The first clunky Ericsson mobile phones, which were more status symbols than conveniences, had just gone on the market, and Coca-Cola and Mcdonald's, those two most princely icons of American cultural imperialism, were just completing their triumphant ingress onto the shores of the subcontinent in spite of all of Mr Fernandes's left-wing whining.

When I looked around me, it was almost as though Bombay had metamorphosed overnight. The penny-pinching, fixed deposit and family planning era of the 1980s was past, and a new age had begun, a time where slogans such as liberalism, internationalism, brand equity and purchasing power prevailed. The thick, heady odour of optimism pervaded every square mile of Bombay's crowded streets, intoxicating the city's jaded inhabitants, enticing them to dream, hope and pray to the glittering neon gods of the middle class.

I turned eighteen that year, and I had no idea whatsoever of what I was going to do with my life. Somehow my father managed to convince me to join law school. He used his business connections to get me my first job as an article clerk in the law firm that handled most of his company's affairs. It was terrible, tedious work, and I was a terrible, tedious apprentice. I spent most of my time sitting in an extraordinarily tiny room in an extraordinarily uncomfortable metal chair, proofreading extraordinarily boring documents under the watchful eyes of an extraordinarily geriatric Parsi advocate who called me Percy since he couldn't be bothered to even remember my name.

That same summer, my Nani finally stopped walking, once and for all.

She passed away in her sleep, as silently as she had lived. The doctors said she succumbed to a stroke, but I like to think that she died painlessly; that hopefully, as the last breath escaped from her desiccated lips, all the lines and wrinkles that had marred her face were smoothed away until she was pretty and unblemished once more like a newborn child.

I was quite devastated by the suddenness of my grandmother's demise. I hadn't quite realised it, but I had loved Nani a great deal without ever understanding the true depth of my emotion. She had been kind and beautiful and sad, perhaps the only person I had ever known who truly deserved to be described as noble.

As for Nana, the shock of my grandmother's death affected him even more severely than it did me. When I saw him at her funeral, he seemed to have aged twenty years overnight. He had lost a great deal of weight, and his shoulders were stooped and sunken, robbed of their sturdy breadth. His sparse hair was uncombed, his clothes wrinkled and murky with sweat and grief. Even his beard, which had grown out once again until it was even bushier than I remembered, was untrimmed and unkempt like a great hedge speckled by flecks of dirt and fragments of forgotten food.

We stood opposite each other, on either side of Nani's bier, like nemeses, while the priests sang their ululating songs of lamentation. I made no move towards him, not a single nod of consolation, not one fond embrace. Instead, I watched silently as he set Nani's body aflame.

She burned surprisingly easily—the dry tinder of her flesh flaring alight, crackling and burning as if she were a creature of dry, brittle wood, not one of skin and bone. It took only a few minutes for her to be consumed wholly, and as the bitter stench of smouldering hair filled my nostrils, Nana turned to stare straight at me.

When his gaze met mine, he broke down. The stiff, dignified demeanour he had managed to maintain till then collapsed entirely, and he started to wail and moan melodramatically, pulling at his beard, slapping his bald skull with his ancient hands.

Uncomfortably, I stood there, more than a little embarrassed by this theatrical display of emotion. I found myself wondering if he really meant it or if this inundation of misery was merely a show, a tableau for the benefit of all the other mourners gathered around him.

Much to my dismay, Nana tottered towards me, groaning and shaking his head in grief. Reluctantly, at my father's prompting, I stepped forward and allowed him to lean on me. Then, much to my irritation, he engulfed me in his arms and held on to me so desperately that he almost choked me. The bristles of his beard rasped against my cheek, a feeling so familiar that it made me almost wistful, but somehow, I found myself unable to reciprocate the urgency of this embrace. I could barely even bear to look at him, not without experiencing a rush of anger that made me want to push him away.

After Nani's passing, I lost touch with him entirely. Once she was gone, Nana was never quite himself again, never the same blustering, talkative man that he had been while she was alive. It was almost as though Nani's death had extinguished something vital inside him, the animus that had burned so richly, which had always made him so curious and so very alive. The death of a loved one sours a man. It spoils him. No more did Nana boom with raucous laughter or tell loud jokes and slap the backs of his friends cheerfully. And he stopped telling stories altogether, those fantastic fables that had so captivated my imagination in my childhood.

He still wrote to me from time to time, but his letters were neither as punctual as they had been nor as lengthy. Nor, for that matter, did they contain the usual plethora of anecdotes. On the contrary, these communiqués were little more than notes, brief and impersonal, so succinct that they were almost sterile, so formal that I could not believe it was my grandfather who had actually authored them.

Then, finally, a few months after Nani's death, the letters stopped arriving altogether.

At first, it felt quite odd to not receive those familiar envelopes in the mail. Briefly, in spite of my antipathy, I was even worried that something had happened to Nana. But then, as one week became two and then four, I began to feel relieved that he had stopped writing. After all, at least now I didn't have to deal with the guilt of throwing his letters away without even bothering to open them.

Less than a year later, my application to SOAS was accepted, and I jumped at the opportunity to drop out of law school and finally escape from Bombay.

I think it was the fault of that peculiar wanderlust that so consumes twenty-year-olds—that insatiable longing for a fresh start. I think that was what compelled me to leave. The truth is that I was really quite anxious to break out of the quiet routine into which I had settled so comfortably—that bland pattern where I woke up each morning and went to college for an hour and then took a taxi to my feeble job and ate lunch at the Gymkhana and went clubbing on Fridays to the same dingy discotheques and tried to strike up inane conversations with prematurely haggard twenty-year-olds with golden highlights in their stringy hair and smokey grey contact lenses in their tired eyes.

Besides, I was sick to the bone of Bombay, so weary of its name-dropping, brand-conscious, film-star-worshipping soul. The more time I spent here, the more I came to realise that the city was exactly like one of the glossy film sets that dotted the Western Outdoor studio, opulent and magnificent on the surface but hollow within, a paste and gilt illusion held together by the spit of human cynicism and the baling wire of naiveté.

Being young and infected by tragically adolescent pragmatism, I chose to see London as my new beginning.

My ears still rang with Nana's enthusiastic reminiscences about his all too short stint there. As a child, he had often regaled me with joyous recollections of that singular year he had spent living there as a student just after the Second World War. I remembered every one of those stories so well—how he had shared a flat in Knightsbridge with a Czech émigré who had managed to survive Dachau; how he had spent countless hours wandering around the city by himself, drifting in and out of museums and libraries; how he had often visited jazz clubs in Soho and drunk glass after glass of Pimm's No.1; and finally, how once he had even had the good fortune to meet W.H. Auden himself on the Tube and ended up arguing with him about why the ghazal was superior to the sonnet.

Thanks to that eager litany of memories, I had grown to expect so much from London—an endless gamut of adventures, surprise after surprise, awakening after awakening, epiphany after damp epiphany.

Sadly, I was very wrong.

Instead of a constant flurry of excitement, I found myself surrounded by a cold, dead city, strange and frigid and grey, like an ageing dowager.

London was a disappointment. No, it was more than that. It was an unbelievably expensive disappointment.

It was always freezing in the dorm room they assigned me, and I found it impossible to stay warm, no matter how many layers of long johns and sweaters I wore. And I was lonely, lonelier than I have ever been, beset by that hapless isolation of a castaway who has been washed ashore on a desert island, desperate for any human connection.

Worst of all, everything seemed to make me homesick—the sight of Indian tourists taking photographs in Trafalgar Square, the rat-a-tat melody of Hindi film songs as they emanated from pirate cabs driven by Gujarati drivers, the guttural sound of Bengali being spoken by the Bangladeshi ladies who ran the neighbourhood laundry, even the spicy scent of garam masala wafting out from the Light of Asia restaurant at the corner of Bloomsbury. They all made me want to cry; it was so depressing that I felt I was going mad.

Much to my surprise, I found it particularly difficult to make friends.

I had always been rather an affable sort, and it had been easy for me to imagine I would fit right in London because of my innate Anglophilia, that same fervent adoration of everything British I had inherited from Nana. But much to my surprise, it did not take me long to find out that I was sorely mistaken.

It wasn't that the English students in my class were rude to me or that they were even standoffish. They were pleasant enough, convivial in a distant sort of way, and always eager to ask me silly questions about India, like 'How do you speak English so well?', 'Does your dad take an elephant to work?' and 'Do you really have cows wandering the streets?'

But, beneath this thin veneer of civility, there was something acutely offensive in the way they looked at me when they thought I wouldn't notice, a subtle hostility, a genteel suspicion, which made me feel awfully out of place.

I think the root cause was because I looked so different from them. Before I got to London, I had never realised how dark I was or rather, how brown. In India, I had been that indistinguishable shade called wheatish, but here, I was unavoidably East Asian to their anaemic eyes.

By then I had let my hair grow out until it hung well past my shoulders and my beard had flourished until it reached my chest, making me look like some demented heavy metal version of a Sikh. Unlike the other Indians in my class who tried their level best to fit in with their side partings, tab collar shirts and amorphous tan-beigeness, because of my ragged appearance, I remained an absolute outsider, an inexplicable oddity who resisted classification, and that made me all the more objectionable to their pale eyes.

When the whites looked at me, they saw just another foreigner. To them, it didn't matter that I enjoyed Marlowe and Shakespeare and knew every one of Byron's poems by heart. As far as most of them were concerned, I wasn't a person. I was a stereotype come to life—a raghead, a cab nigger, a cow kisser, a curry muncher, a diaper head, a Punjabi, a swami. A chasm of preconceptions separated us; an abyss so insurmountable that it made it impossible for us to form a bond of any real depth. They never mistreated me, no. Instead, they simply acted like I didn't exist, as though I was more shadow than man. Most of my attempts to try and get to know them were dismissed or courteously rebuffed. At first, I thought it was my fault. As a result, I worked harder than ever to be as friendly as possible. I made it a point to attend all the student mixers, even though more often than not I ended up standing in a corner by myself, feeling utterly out of place.

But then one afternoon, as I passed one of the boys from my international relations class and nodded hello to him, I overheard him mumble behind my retreating back.

'Bloody Pakis, why don't they go back to their damned jungles and stop stinking up our nice clean streets?'

I don't think he meant for me to hear him, but it was just loud enough to be audible. I paused dead in my tracks, turning furiously to glare at him with barely repressed consternation, but he didn't seem to care. Rather than apologising, he started to laugh, sniggering so vociferously that I was overcome with rage.

For one long moment, I wanted nothing more than to go back and pick an argument with him and to call out that he was a bigot and a racist prick. But this hot flush of ire faded just as quickly as it had appeared, leaving me so overwhelmed by embarrassment that I walked away, pretending like I had heard nothing at all.

That one episode left me feeling bruised like I had been beaten somehow, thrashed with a lead pipe. And the worst part was that it was a pain that was far more excruciating than if I had actually been assaulted physically. It turned into anguished self-loathing that seemed to grow and grow inside me, eating away at me like a sickness, until I couldn't bear to look at myself any more, ashamed at the sight of my face in the mirror.

From that day onwards, I decided to keep to myself and stop trying to make friends with the whites. No, instead, I spent most of my mornings reading dull papers in class under the watchful eyes of boring professors, and I spent most of my nights sitting in my dorm room by myself, drinking cheap vodka until I passed out.

My sole connection with the past, with the life I had left behind in Bombay, was my mother. She insisted on calling me every fortnight without fail, and it was from her that I heard that my grandfather had sold the farm and moved to Amritsar to stay with Uncle Sanjeev, her elder brother. It was from her that I found out that he was ill, that he had undergone bypass surgery for his heart and was now bedridden and could barely walk.

Strangely, I found that these revelations failed to stir me in the least. The truth was that I didn't really care, not beyond the polite pretensions I made on the phone.

I had lost interest in my grandfather. No, not just my grandfather. It was as though I had lost interest in that entire chapter of my life, like I wanted nothing more than to forget all that had happened and all that I had once been.

Still, from time to time, there would be sporadic moments of weakness when I would think of Nana. Late at night, as I lay awake in my bed unable to fall asleep, it was then that I would recall those placid days I had spent at his farm—how I had played hide and seek in the garden, how I had picked wild chestnuts from the bushes and threaded them through with shoelaces and fought duels with Rat and the other village boys, and how the tall gulmohar trees that ringed the bungalow had flowered with bright orange blossoms in the summer, making it seem as if they were aflame.

It was then that I would miss India the most. It was then that I would think longingly how good it would be to pack my bags and go back home—how very easy.

But no, I would say to myself in the very same breath, there was no returning to that life, for I had left it far behind. India was lost to me like a waking dream. I had been spoiled for it by that first taste of independence, of freedom and of autonomy.

This was my life now.

I wasn't Indian any more or Punjabi or even Sikh.

I was a nobody, a man without a country, without history, a refugee in the truest sense of the word.

A refugee from my past.

A refugee from myself.

12

There are three things I remember about that first year at the university.

The first was that something peculiar started to happen to my accent the moment I set foot in England. It was as if my tongue began to thicken, and for some inexplicable reason, my carefully cultivated public school diction began to disintegrate. In India, I had talked like a proper angrez, but here, I sounded like Apu from the Simpsons, rolling my vowels and stretching my consonants, all thank-you-come-again.

The second was that I began to have trouble sleeping. Part of it was because my neighbour was an exceedingly loud German called Ziggy, who delighted in listening to Sepultura all night long. But the real reason why I came to dread the silence of the night, I think, was loneliness. It was particularly bad just before dawn, in the early hours of twilight. That was when I felt it the most—a sense of solitude so absolute it made my joints ache and made it difficult for me to move.

The only thing, I found, that would assuage this sense of isolation was the harsh comfort of alcohol. That was why I think I started to drink—to forget, not just Bombay and my family, not just Nana and the events of 1984, but also because I harboured a faint hope that the booze would help me forget myself, that somehow I would awaken empty like an amnesiac.

Finally, the third thing I remember was that some English git in the housing office, in his infinite wisdom, decided to assign me a Pakistani roommate.

The room that I had been allotted, No. 47, was a double—two dirty minuscule carpeted bedrooms with cinder block walls, not more than ten feet by twelve, with barely enough space for a bed and a closet. They were separated by a small linoleum-tiled living space whose only furniture was a ratty old couch and a pitted, worn Formica table. There was no bathroom. Instead, I was forced to use a common toilet at the southern end of the corridor, a damp institutional loo with rows of stalls and a communal shower that always smelled of fungus and pee.

At the other end of the corridor, there was a common room with an ancient refrigerator and television that seemed to always be stuck on football. I rarely spent time there, preferring the privacy of my room to the loud boisterousness of the English boys.

For the first few months that I was in England, I had Room 47 all to myself, but then, just after Michaelmas, the Pakistani arrived.

His name was Tariq, a handsome boy from Lahore with a sense of superiority and entitlement that made me loathe him from the moment we set eyes on each other. He was the first Pakistani I had ever met. It's curious, isn't it, how we Indians seem to have to travel to London to meet Pakistanis? Even though they are our immediate neighbours, it is like we are separated from one another by a vast gulf, an insurmountable chasm of distrust, hostility and suspicion that can only be bridged on neutral ground.

I guess he was put in the same room as me because we were both East Asian, and with typical British superciliousness, some housing officer had imagined that would make us copacetic, without ever realising the extent of distrust between us. It had never even occurred to him that even though Tariq and I were coloured the same drab brown and hailed from the same subcontinent, it may well have been that we came from different planets.

From the moment I met Tariq, I disliked him, a sentiment that he reciprocated with cold, sneering disdain. I guess you could say that we fell in hate at first sight. Why did I despise him so much? It was probably because he fitted the epitome of a North Indian so effortlessly, far better than I did. It was like he was an extra in a Merchant-Ivory film come to life, perfect right down to his almond skin and carefully parted, slightly gilded hair. Everything about him made me feel impossibly gauche and jejune. While we were both Punjabi, Amritsar and Lahore being just a few miles apart, he represented everything that a Punjabi was supposed to be. Tariq was the sort of effortlessly aristocratic creature I had always wished I was, with a truly monumental nose, so aquiline that it resembled a Himalayan peak. As for me, to my regret, I was short and heavyset and rather hairy, with a tendency to perspire far too much, and my nose was an indiscernible lump, so large and amorphous that it seemed like some cruel God had plastered a potato to my face.

As for Tariq, I don't know why he decided to dislike me, but I can guess his motives. I think I scared him just like he dismayed me. My whole life I had been told a thousand negative things about Pakistanis—that they were untrustworthy and two-faced, cruel and duplicitous, that they were the ones responsible for Partition and that given the chance they would kill me out of spite just because I was a Sikh. I think that is what we are all brainwashed into believing in India, at some subliminal level, that Pakistanis are very different from us Indians, abnormal somehow, even monstrous. I guessed that Tariq had been told the very same stories, except with Indians cast as the villains, and I think that was why he needed to distrust me because he didn't quite know how to react to me, to not just meet an Indian for the first time, but have to live with him side by side.

That first week, I don't think we spoke more than two or three times, merely nodding at each other as we passed each morning like shadows intersecting. Part of it was my fault, I admit. Tariq had tried to be friendly at first, I will give him that, to say hello and introduce himself, but I had been so implacably suspicious of him that I couldn't bring myself to reciprocate those friendly overtures.

I couldn't help myself. My preconceptions were far too reassuring to give up, and it was easier for me to abhor him rather than try to get to know him. What else could I do? What could I say to him? He confused me, which is why I chose to keep my distance.

Tariq was studying economics, so we had only one class together, asian history, once every week on Thursday afternoons. It was ironic really—we were the only two Asians who had signed up for the course. All the others were a bunch of ghostlike upper-class whites with double-barrel surnames, descended mostly from Raj families, who genuinely believed that they knew more about India than I did because they had read Kipling and Edward Said.

Of course, they all loved Tariq, the girls in particular, because he looked so like Omar Sharif, except without the silly moustache. They ate up his whole brown sahib act—his pretentious old-world mannerisms and his mellifluous accent, which was much smoother than mine—with a spoon. It sickened me to see them tittering and laughing at his jokes while they looked at me with suspicion in their eyes. I couldn't understand it. Tariq and I were the same age, even the same colour, but to our classmates, he was much better at being Asian than me, a realisation that I found difficult to swallow.

I don't think I actually said a word in class once, not until one morning some three weeks after Tariq moved in, when our professor, a ruddy-faced old Scotsman with a penchant for tartan bow ties, started a discussion about the after-effects of colonialism.

'When it comes to the morality of British imperialism,' he pontificated rather pompously, 'there are two very opposing schools of thought.

'For the British, who saw their colonies from the point of view of the occupier, the coloniser, the evangeliser, they genuinely believed that they were on a divinely sanctioned mission, and that it was their Victorian Christian imperative to bring civilisation to those they perceived as savages.

'And to a certain degree, I think, they did succeed, for their influence, the sociocultural impact of the colonial era, is visible even today in the third world.

'However, there is an opposing point of view that has become more and more relevant in recent years.

'From the point of view of the colonised, one of the accusations which is frequently made against the imperialists is that in their frantic quest to build and sustain a grand empire, they sowed the seeds for many of the regional conflicts that rage across the world even now, a crop of bitter hatred that is being reaped to this day, decades after the end of the empire.

'Take Ireland, where Roman Catholics and Protestants still treat each other with distrust, or the Middle East, where the only real exports are terror and crude oil, and the spectre of militarised Islam hangs over the Western world like the sword of Damocles.

'And then, of course, there is Punjab, perhaps the most egregious of British creations, where India and Pakistan still remain locked in a pyrrhic battle, even though sixty years have passed since the grand debacle of Partition. Since 1947, these two neighbours have fought three wars and countless skirmishes, and although both nations speak similar languages and share common customs, even today the deep and abiding rivalry between Hindus and Muslims rages on unabated.'

He sighed, looking straight at me, his fat face bright with an empathy that made me blush.

'I was in India a few years ago,' he said, 'on a research trip, and I had the first-hand opportunity to see this festering hatred on display, during the bloodletting that wracked Bombay in the aftermath of the demolition of the Ayodhya mosque.

'Personally, I found it almost impossible to believe that such medieval barbarism was possible in our modern, supposedly enlightened times, but one of the people I spoke to while I was there, a very well-respected Indian historian, made a statement that still chafes at me.

'He insisted that it is simply not possible for Hindus and Muslims to live in peace because they have too much history, too much bloodshed in the name of religion to ever trust each other. The scarring, as he put it so aptly, runs much too deep to ever be fully healed.

'That is the question I would like to ask all of you today. Is that statement true? Is it really impossible for Hindus and Muslims to coexist harmoniously in India and Pakistan with such a shared history of conflict behind them? Or have we passed a point of no return?'

He looked around the classroom expectantly, waiting for an answer.

After a few minutes, Tariq put up his hand nervously.

With a smile, the professor called upon him to speak. 'Ah, our Pakistani gentleman wishes to say a few words. Come, let us listen.'

Shyly, Tariq stood up, clearing his throat. Everyone in the classroom turned to look at him, eager to hear what he had to say.

With a frown, he began to speak in a low monotone.

'As you know, I'm Muslim. I grew up in Lahore and from what I have witnessed, the average Pakistani bears no ill will towards India. My parents do business with Indians regularly, and everyone in Pakistan watches their films and television shows, and I genuinely believe that Indians and Pakistanis can live in peace.'

Much to my disgust, he had a rich and very likeable voice and not a hint of nervous stammer, as I had been secretly hoping.

'However,' he continued, 'I also believe that the rivalry between Hindus and Muslims is a complex problem that has many subtle levels. It is not about God versus God. It is about man versus man, individual versus individual, citizen against citizen.'

'Please,' the professor said, leaning forward, his brow knitting with interest, 'do go on.'

Tariq pursed his lips. 'In any society, there is bound to be some measure of friction between different racial, political and theological groups. After all, it is human nature to envy, to despair, to resent. The problem with India and Pakistan is this antagonism between Hindus and Muslims; It is only the glossy covering that disguises a much deeper malaise.'

'And what is that?'

'Rage, sir. That is the real problem. There are too many disenfranchised people in both countries, too many illiterate people, too many angry people, too many poor people, all looking for something to believe in, all desperate for some hope. And ultimately, there is nothing easier to exploit than hope, than faith. In India and Pakistan, that is what has happened to religion. It has become a tool by which the government and the clergy can control and exploit ordinary citizens and misdirect their despair, weaponise their frustration to serve their own devious agendas.'

Tariq sighed, a weary exhalation of breath.

'It is unfortunate,' he continued, 'but what is a very complex issue has become increasingly polarised. It doesn't matter what you believe personally. As far as the masses are concerned, there are only two sides. If you aren't Muslim, then to the Muslims, you are an enemy. If you aren't Hindu, then to the Hindus, you are a foe. There are no grey areas when it comes to religion. It is all just black and white.

'Regrettably, it is exactly this sort of pandering that has ruined relations between India and Pakistan. However, the key difference is that in Pakistan, this prejudice is visible, while in India, it hides behind the veil of popular democracy.

'It is sad really, but on a global stage, Pakistan is seen as the villain and India the victim, even though India is as intolerant a nation as Pakistan, if not more so. It is India where the seeds of bigotry are now coming to fruition with the growth of sectarian politics. It is India that is wracked by regional separatism. It is India that has a precarious human rights record and a flawed judiciary, where Hindus and Muslims are not even allowed to follow a unified civil code.

'That is what scares me as a Pakistani, I think—how shamelessly India is permitted to use Pakistan as a scapegoat to justify so many of their social failures, to validate their malfunctions as a republic and even as a secularity. As far as India is concerned, it is always Pakistan's fault. They call us a failed state, but what most people don't realise is that in many ways, India is a failed state as well, because it has never been able to reconcile its colonial identity with the problems of a postcolonial world. And that is the crux of the problem. There will never be peace between India and Pakistan, I believe, until India stands up and accepts its share of responsibility, its culpability. Then and only then we can start to forget the past, and the healing process can begin.'

In retrospect, I have to admit, it was a persuasive and well-considered argument, but at that moment, having to listen to his hectoring voice somehow made an impossible wrath swell inside me. I couldn't help but feel if he was talking to me personally, as if he was addressing me and not the class, because it was me that Tariq was staring at while he blathered on, his arrogant eyes boring into my own, adamant with antagonism.

Worst of all, his words, I think, must have struck a subconscious chord because I felt a worm of uneasy guilt uncoil deep inside me, a remorse, as I mulled over what he had just said. It sickened me to admit it, even if it was just to myself, but he was right, so very, very correct. The idea of India as Nehru had imagined it, where the mind was without fear and the head held high, had failed miserably. Contrary to the egalitarian utopia that our founding fathers had envisioned—that dream of freedom and equality for which they had fought and died—we had become a kakistocracy of the worst kind, where shit always floated to the top and the mediocre, the talentless and the corrupt were idolised. That was what India had turned into, not the great democratic experiment it had been intended to be, but a fool's paradise where the only real god was cold, hard currency.

But the real reason I was pushed over the edge was because of what Tariq said next.

'Take these stanzas,' he declared, 'written after the 1984 riots in Delhi by Sardar Gobind Singh, one of India's most recognised Punjabi poets:

> The poetry is gone,
> There are only whispers left.
> Let my tears soak into the soil
> And turn all five rivers to salt,
> For that is my home,
> A nation where men are wrought from stained mud,
> And that is why their clay knees are weak.
> The fires will always burn,
> The embers cannot be extinguished,
> The scars cannot be healed,
> And Punjab will always bleed.'

As he fell silent, I shuddered with outrage. It was the final humiliation. How dare he? I thought, how dare he quote my grandfather's words—that too straight at me?

Like a volcano, my rage boiled over when they began to applaud him, a smattering of acclaim at first, but then it grew into a thunderous ovation. Each overture of approbation, each slap of skin on skin, made me wince. In my mind, I heard the screams again, the jackals wailing outside Nana's farm, and I saw Rat's face and the Sikh boy who had been beaten by the police, lying broken by the side of the road. And superimposed over it all, I saw Tariq's glib face smirking down at me, so pleased by his foolish eloquence.

Before I knew it, I was on my feet.

'Enough,' I screeched. 'You are talking shit and you know it.'

'Is there a problem, Mr Singh?' the professor exclaimed, taken aback at this breach of etiquette. 'If you disagree with what Mr Hussein has said, why don't you try to articulate your disgruntlement with a little more clarity rather than subjecting us to an outburst of such unparalleled ruden—'

'Shut the fuck up,' I snapped, cutting him off mid-sentence, much to his surprise. 'You're a hypocrite. You are all fucking hypocrites.'

'What the hell do you know about Punjab?' I said, fuming. 'You come to India on your fucking research trips like scavengers picking over a dead body, but you don't see the truth. You only see what you want to see, what makes you feel good about yourselves. You English, you sit here and you talk with your plummy accents about postcolonialism and how good the Raj was for India. You chatter on and on about being civilised and how you gave us the railways and higher education and the rule of law but the truth is that the only gift that England gave to the subcontinent was the gift of hatred.

'You invaded and enslaved us for 400 years. You played the Muslims against the Hindus with your policy of divide and rule. You made us distrust each other so that you could control us, and you partitioned Punjab, all because of your colossal egos. You have made us what we are today and now you sit in judgment and pretend like nothing is your fault, and then this Pakistani prick comes here and feeds you his fucking propaganda and you have the temerity to applaud him.

'Well, I for one am not going to sit here and listen to any more of this rubbish.'

With that outburst, I stomped out of class. Nobody tried to stop me or said a single word as I left. Instead, they just sat there, watching me, their complacent faces bewildered, even pitying, gaping at me like I had taken leave of my senses.

It took a long time for me to cool down. As my rage dissipated, I found it replaced by embarrassment. Not only had I managed to make a fool of myself in front of my entire class, but the worst part was, even though I knew that most of what I had said was empty hyperbole, some small part of me still believed every word. Even though it irritated me to admit it, I *did* hate Tariq because he was Pakistani, because he was Muslim, which meant that deep down, beneath the tolerant person I liked to imagine myself to be, I was just as bigoted as everyone else.

That realisation was too much for me to swallow, at least while I was sober. So, naturally, I decided to get drunk. I spent the rest of the day drifting through the streets of London aimlessly, not quite sure where I was. Near Tottenham Court Road, I bought a quart of cheap gin from a Patel store and brown-bagged it, gulping it down so quickly that its acidic taste scalded my throat and I began to sweat even though it was a chilly, acerbic afternoon.

It wasn't long before I lost track of time. The day waned and ashen dusk began to descend, bringing with it a tepid sprinkling of rain. It wasn't long before I was soaked to the skin, shivering, but I couldn't bear the thought of going back to the dorm and having to look at Tariq's supercilious face. Instead, I wasted a couple of hours in Cecil Court, browsing through what seemed like an endless row of second-hand bookshops. I spent another hour in a used record shop in Charing Cross and ate dinner alone at a tiny cockroach-infested Korean place at the corner of Leicester Square.

As night fell, the streets became surprisingly quiescent and the intersections were denuded of traffic. As offices shut for the day, the lights in the buildings slowly winked out until I was surrounded by listless darkness, a suffocating, all-consuming gloom that clung to me like a shroud. It seemed to me that I was the only man alive, little more than a phantom roving through a ghost town. Much to my surprise, I realised that for once I didn't want to be alone. An inexplicable need for human contact seized me, a yearning to be surrounded by people, by their loud voices and their inane conversations so that I could lose myself in them like a chameleon.

As I drifted along near Trafalgar Square, I encountered a chattering horde of tourists, most of whom were Indians, laughing and snapping their cameras. They seemed so happy, so animated, that it made me a little envious. There was something about them, a strangely magnetic solace in their brownness, an affinity that called to me, that drew me towards them. Silently, I followed in their wake as they shuffled down the street, speeding up until I caught up with them. With a smile, I greeted them in Hindi, and they welcomed me into their midst, embracing me as if I was one of them. A woman in the crowd, a middle-aged housewife wearing a silk Kanjeevaram and a woollen shawl draped around her shoulders, solemnly offered me a bag full of Indian sweets. I took one even though I didn't really want it. Without a word, I trailed after them when they boarded an open-topped tour bus and found myself a seat near the back of the vehicle. While the bus slowly trundled through the desolate city streets, I sat there surrounded by these familiar brown faces, revelling in the sense of belonging and of homecoming. It amused me the way they oohed and aahed each time the tour guide pointed out something of significance. Here is the tower of London—Waaahhh! There is the Westminster Bridge—Haiiiii!

At first, it was immeasurably refreshing to be surrounded by my fellow Indians. It was like they camouflaged me like a stick insect blending in with a branch—that comfortable disguise of commonality, of race. For the first time in months, I didn't feel out of place or like an intruder. It was marvellous, at least briefly. But then, much too rapidly, I grew tired of them, especially when one of them, a plump man wearing a silly orange baseball cap, came and sat down next to me and began to ask me a lot of questions. 'Where you are from, what you do for living, how long you have been in London?'

Brusquely ignoring these polite inquiries, I hopped off the bus and found myself in the narrow lanes of Whitechapel not far from where Jack the Ripper had stalked his victims. It was getting late by then and I decided to finally head back to the dorm. Unfortunately, I ended up getting completely lost. I took one wrong turn and then another, and before I knew it, I had ended up in Wapping, standing somnolently by a wharf and looking down at the murky, listless surface of the Thames.

I don't quite know how I managed it, unless there is some immutable law of the universe that dictates that in the end all lost things wash up in Wapping sooner or later. In any case, I had never been this far east before, and a nagging instinct at the back of my neck told me to get the hell out of there as soon as possible before I ended up getting mugged or stabbed or worse.

Wandering back and forth through a confusing maze of derelict warehouses and dilapidated storage sheds, I was trying to find a familiar landmark by which to navigate back to my college when I ran into a trio of chavs. They were standing in an alley, leaning against a pile of empty crates, smoking and laughing while listening to some strain of impossibly tone-deaf electronic music on a ghetto blaster.

When they saw me, they stopped their gossiping and turned to stare as if I was from another planet.

'Well, well, what have we here, lads?' hissed a pinch-faced boy who could not have been more than nineteen, dressed in a bright red tracksuit and white Adidas Superstar sneakers.

His friend, a tall, skinny skater type with long, lank dreadlocks and a small rat-like goatee, wearing a tattered Tottenham jersey, frowned at me menacingly and shouted, 'Oy, you lost, Paki…?'

'I think he is, Kev,' the first boy replied. 'Come on, why don't we help him out?'

'I think we shall, Kevin, I think we shall.'

With that, the two of them shuffled forward to obstruct my path, but the third boy, a skinhead with a shiny metal nose ring, wearing a leather motorcycle jacket, hung back, watching me warily, a small grin playing across his skull-like face.

'Look,' I said, 'I'm not looking for any trouble.'

'Oh, yeah?' Kev the skater crooned. 'Well, you're plumb out of luck, Pakiboy, because trouble has surely found you, innit?'

'Heh,' Kevin the chav croaked, 'Good one, mate!'

The expressions of absolute malevolence on their teenage faces struck me as somehow contrived. There was something so clichéd about them, as if they were caricatures come to life, extras from *A Clockwork Orange*, trying hard to be tough, echoing dialogue that they had heard before from their fathers and brothers.

Kev the skater snapped his fingers at me impatiently.

'Give over your money, you wanker, or I'm going to have to get nasty.'

He leered at me with a studied B-movie tough-guy look on his face, so flimsy that it was like a paper mask. He seemed unreal to me, so silly, a little boy playing at being a man, trying his level best to seem threatening, to seem grown-up, that it was almost amusing.

'Is this a hate crime?' I sneered. 'Because if it is, I have to tell you, you are sorely mistaken. I'm not a Paki at all. I'm Indian. So I guess that makes me an Indie, doesn't it?'

'Are you taking the piss?' Kevin the chav stared at me, his face blushing red with anger.

'Shut up, and give over your money, you little shit,' Kev the skater growled.

His voice wavered with the barely repressed promise of violence. I shuddered, almost reaching for my wallet meekly. But then, before I could bring myself to hand it over to him, an amorphous rage gripped me. I can't explain it. It was like all the anger I had been suppressing since my arrival, my angst and loneliness, the resentment I felt for my classmates who treated me like I didn't exist, for my condescending professors who talked down to me, for Tariq and his fancy words, unexpectedly, this pent-up fount of emotion became an upheaval, bubbling to the surface like acid reflux.

'No,' I said nonchalantly, letting my hand drop away, 'I think not.'

'What'd you say?' Kev the skater snorted as if he could not believe my effrontery. 'What'd he say?'

'I said, no. I'm not going to give you my money.'

'Are you having a laugh?' Kevin the chav mumbled, perplexed.

I smiled, suddenly not nervous any more. Instead, I felt impossibly excited—my heart racing a thousand beats a minute and my body shivering with fresh adrenalin.

'I'll tell you what, boys. You want my money so bad, I'll fight you for it.'

I took my wallet out and proffered it to them.

'There's not much in there, just thirty pounds, but I'll fight any one of you for it. A straight fight, one against one. If I win, I walk away. If you win, you can keep the money. What do you say?'

'Is he fucking having me on?' Kev the skater said, looking at Kevin the chav in disbelief as if he couldn't quite understand what I was trying to say.

'I think he's a nutter,' Kevin the chav exclaimed, shaking his head. 'As barmy as me old uncle, who got hit by a lorry, he is.'

'You gone mental, you brown turd?' Kev the skater hissed, shaking one fist at me menacingly. 'You think this is a joke, yeah? You think we aren't going to beat the shite out of you?'

'Not at all,' I replied. 'I have never been more serious in my life. Come on, let's settle this like gentlemen. If you have the balls, of course. To the winner go the spoils.'

As I issued this challenge, the third boy shambled forward.

He was big, well over six feet tall, but whippet-thin, with a gaunt face that resembled a weasel, the same pointy nose and protuberant eyes.

'I'll fight him,' he said, speaking for the first time.

The other two, Kevin and Kev, nodded and moved out of his way hurriedly as if they were afraid of him.

Smiling, he took off his jacket to reveal that he was wearing a sleeveless tee shirt beneath that clung to his wiry physique like a second skin, revealing his lean, sinewy arms covered with a sallow patterning of tattoos.

'Let's go then,' I said.

Before he could react, without warning, I got in the first punch, a quick jab to his mouth that snapped his head back.

It barely fazed him, even though a trickle of blood dripped slowly from his split lip. He smiled at me, shaking his head. I swung my other hand with all my strength, aiming for his jaw, but he was too quick and skipped away. And then, in the blink of an eye, before I knew it, a flurry of blows drove me back, thudding into me from every side.

He was good, that skinhead, quick and very fit. Each time I tried to hit back, he swayed away like a dancer. I put everything I had into a vast right hook, but he dropped his head. My fist ricocheted off the hard bone of his skull with a knuckle-crunching crack. I wailed, cradling my fingers. That was when he surprised me by stepping forward and head butting me, his forehead crunching into my nose so hard that I saw bright stars.

Groggily, I wobbled, trying to keep my balance, and he snapped out a quick little kick, some kind of weird cockney taekwondo move that connected squarely with my shoulder and knocked me sideways.

Great, I thought, trying not to collapse, just my luck, I pick a fight and end up scuffling with the East End's answer to Chuck Norris.

With a feral smile, he raised one hand to hammer down at me, but I got lucky. Blindly, I kicked out and connected squarely with his groin, making him double over, yelping with anguish.

Gleefully, I laughed, because much to my disbelief, for about a minute I was actually winning. It didn't last of course. It took him just a few seconds to recover, and then he came after me, his face purple with rage, clouting me with a solid jarring roundhouse that sent me tumbling to my knees.

'Get him, Kev-O,' Kev the skater cackled.

'Yeah, knock his sodding Paki block off,' Kevin the chav chimed in, spitting at me.

Drunkenly, I staggered to my feet, just in time to hit Kev-O's fist with my face. After that, it was all pretty much him beating me up, grunting with effort as he inundated me with a storm of carefully placed punches.

I stood there swaying as each fresh blow landed until at last Kev-O the skinhead paused momentarily to gather his breath. I took advantage of this lull and crumpled to the ground once more, tucking my knees into my chest and rolling into a ball.

While I lay there, they all began to kick me, all three of them, setting upon me with vicious eagerness, thumping their boots into my ribs repeatedly. They beat me mercilessly, with an eager, almost animal brutality. The pain was excruciating, but each cry that escaped my lips, each desperate whimper, I was glad for it. I can't explain it. It was exhilarating, that pain, awful but still inexplicably galvanic. It wasn't masochism. It was more than that—like I had found a revelation in the pain, a meaning I had never found in anything before. It made me feel alive, more alive than I had felt for a single instant since I arrived in London.

Finally, after a few minutes, I think I tired them out because they decided to stop their relentless assault.

'That's enough,' Kev-O said. 'We don't want to kill the silly bastard.'

Briefly, Kev the skater and Kevin the chav ignored this command and managed to get in a couple more kicks, but then Kev-O stepped forward with a growl and pushed them away roughly.

'Enough,' he snapped, and then, to my shock, he knelt beside me and offered me one hand.

'You okay, mate?'

'I'll live,' I groaned.

'You feel better now?' He smiled, exposing an array of gold-capped teeth.

'Actually,' I gasped, 'I do.'

He laughed and reached down to haul me to my feet. I tottered upright, reeling with dizziness. He held my arm tightly, keeping me upright. It took a few moments for my balance to stabilise before I felt capable of standing on my own. At a snail's pace, wincing with each step, I started to limp away, but Kev the skater and Kevin the chav shuffled forward to block my path.

'Oy, what about the thirty quid?' Kevin the chav hissed.

Kev-O glowered at him.

'Forget it! Let him keep his money. He's earned it.'

Kevin the chav and Kev the skater did not look at all pleased by that declaration. Briefly, I thought they were going to disobey him, but then as Kev-O scowled at them, they nodded and moved aside, giving me enough space to leave.

Kev-O turned to me and nodded. 'Come on then, I'll buy you a pint.'

This invitation took us all by surprise, most of all me. I gazed at him, unsure of how to react. What was his game? One second he was beating the living daylights out of me and the next he wanted to buy me a beer. I shivered, filled with distrust. It just didn't make any sense.

As for his compatriots, they gaped at him as well, equally puzzled.

'You want we should come along, mate?' Kev the skater asked.

'Why don't the two of you bugger off, yeah?' Kev-O replied rudely.

With that declaration, he marched away, leaving behind his confused cronies. Silently, after hesitating briefly, I trailed after him, trying not to smirk when I saw the upset expressions on the faces of Kev the skater and Kevin the chav, hurt at being snubbed so brusquely by someone they so obviously idolised.

Kev-O led me to a decrepit building nearby, an old pub situated next to a row of ancient mews houses. Tramping up a flight of metal steps, he knocked on a rusty cast-iron door, which swung open with a creak. Slowly, I followed him with some difficulty, trying my best not to groan. It took all my strength to get up those stairs and through that door, each step sending a jagged shiver of pain juddering up my spine.

Once inside, I found myself in a dingy low-ceilinged room with grimy walls that were festooned with faded football banners and peeling posters slowly turning brown with age. The furniture looked like it had seen better days, the tables scarred and pitted, the chairs cracked and creaking. In one corner, an ancient television set blared out a football game, Spurs versus Arsenal in the central London derby.

At that late hour, the bar was full of dockworkers and stevedores stopping by for one last pint before they headed home for the night, laughing and joking and cheering each time a goal was almost scored. As I entered, a silence descended, all of them turning to glare up at me with open hostility as if I was intruding into a private club.

But then, when they saw I was with Kev-O, they returned to their glasses without a word. He shoved his way roughly through the crowd and approached the bar. I hobbled after him, straggling in his wake. Most of the patrons backed away from me as if I were a leper, much to my exasperation. But then it dawned upon me that they weren't retreating because I was Indian. No, it was because I looked like something straight out of a horror movie, with my mottled face and bloody shirt.

'Two pints of Guinness,' Kev-O said to the bartender, who frowned at me with an expression of pronounced distaste.

He served us reluctantly, hammering the glasses down with such hostility that a fifth of the beer slopped out on the warped, stained countertop with a splash.

Kev-O didn't seem to notice, or if he did, he didn't care. Picking up one glass, he handed me the other, shuffling nonchalantly to an empty table to sit down.

Still unsure why he wanted to have a drink with me, I trailed after him, accepting the chair he pushed out with one foot grudgingly. As I sat down, a sharp twist wracked through my back, making me wince. My face was sore and bruised, my left eye swelled half-shut and my nose so battered that I could barely breathe. My ribs felt cracked and one of my teeth rattled loosely in my mouth when I pushed against it with my tongue.

Kev-O, on the other hand, looked none the worse for wear after our little altercation. In mock salute, he raised his glass at me and then took a long draught, drinking half of its contents down in one gulp.

'You know, mate?' he grinned. 'You are one crazy bugger.'

I nodded and picked up my glass. Tentatively, I sipped at it, flinching as the bitter ale stung my split lip.

'So why are you here?' Kev-O asked.

This question took me by surprise.

'What do you mean?'

'Why are you here in bleeding Wapping? We don't see many of your kind this far east.'

His choice of words made me smile involuntarily, considering I was indeed bleeding in Wapping.

'I'm a student,' I explained, 'over at the university. I'm here on a scholarship actually.'

'Oh, la-di-dah!' He rolled his eyes. 'You're one of those lads with a plan, are you?'

It was meant as a joke, not intended to be cruel, but his words made me grimace. How easily he had read me! I did have a plan, a blueprint of sorts, for the life I wanted to have, all laid out in a neat progression—my degree first, followed by a job teaching at some university in the Midlands, then maybe marriage to a nice white girl, and then invest in some property and get a twenty-five-year mortgage and start vacationing in Spain once a year—but now, listed out like that, it all seemed so facile, so meaningless.

As that realisation struck me, I frowned at Kev-O sadly.

'I guess I'm lost,' I said softly, taking another sip of ale. 'I guess you could say that I'm trying to run away.'

Kev-O nodded in agreement.

'Yeah, that sounds about right.' He gave me an understanding, knowing look. 'We're all lost, one way or the other, aren't we?'

With that cryptic statement, he fell silent. A long moment passed. He looked down at his glass pensively, before saying, 'You want to hear a story then?'

'Why not?' I said recklessly, gulping down the rest of my Guinness. A warm glow began to spread through me, dulling the thumping ache in my ribs, and I leaned back with a contented groan.

Kev-O smiled his golden smile and waved a hand at the bartender, who bought us another pair of pints. Kev-O pushed one of the glasses towards me and picked up the other, guzzling it down in one long swallow. Then he sighed a voluminous exhalation, before beginning to speak in a low monotone.

'A long time ago,' he murmured, 'just after the Big One, an Irish boy with the reddest hair you ever did see came back from France and decided to settle in London rather than go home to County Clare.

'His head was chock-full of dreams, and for twelve long years, he worked his fingers to the bone in a factory until he had enough saved up to buy a small house and start a family.

'He had only one son, who inherited his red hair, but other than that, they could not have been more unalike. The son, you see, grew up ashamed of his father, ashamed of his foreign accent and the way the neighbours looked at him like he was a stranger and how they called him a bogtrotter behind his back.

'And that boy promised himself that someday he would change all that. He promised himself that he would never allow himself to end up like his father.

'He was an intelligent one, that lad, and his old man wanted him to have a future, so he put him through school and saved up every penny so that the lad could go to college.

'When the boy got to college, much to his surprise, he realised that he could pass for English because he was pale and tall and his hair was easily dyed, the bright red hidden away so that no one could guess that he was Irish.

'And do you know what he did? He changed his name, found himself a nice English girl, married her and started a small business. And slowly, as time passed, he forgot what it was to be Irish. His accent became pure London. Each week, he dyed his hair a dull, ratty brown, and soon he managed to forget everything his father had taught him about his motherland—about the music of the fairy folk, the whispering of the wind that was their voices and the poetry of the land itself.

'He had one son of his own, who was brought up to be entirely English and who never heard a word of Gaelic. Nor did he learn the stories of Ireland, not one. But strangely, the boy always suspected something was missing inside him, a vital piece of the puzzle. He always felt like he was different, like he was incomplete, but who would teach him what it meant to be Irish? His grandfather was dead and gone, and his father was too ashamed of his past to care, too eager to fit in, too afraid that his English friends would mock him if they knew the truth.

'As a result, the boy grew up with no idea of who he was or what he was supposed to be. He never quite managed to fit in at school, picking fights, until one day he broke another boy's arm. After that, it didn't make sense to go to school any more, so he dropped out, preferring to hang about with the lads down at the docklands, all of whom were as confused and angry as he was. While the rest of the boys his age dreamed of their future and made grand plans, he got into scraps and shaved his head because he was afraid of being a ginger, playing out the role his father had chosen for him.

'But what nobody realised was that deep down he had a dream too, the faint hope that maybe someday he could find out what it meant to be himself, the person he was in his blood, rather the person he was pretending to be for the world to see.'

Sadly, Kev-O looked at me, his eyes brimming with sorrow.

'What are you trying to say?' I asked.

'Think of it as a warning, mate. We can never forget who we are, whether it be Paddy or Paki. No matter how much it scares us, no matter how badly we want to fit in or forget, it's in our blood, and a man's blood, it can never be changed.'

With that pronouncement, he rose to his feet solemnly.

'Come on then, drink up! I'll give you a ride back to your dorm.'

He drove me back on his motorcycle, an old Norton Commando that was louder than an earthquake. Kev-O rode like a madman, racing along as fast as he could, swerving carelessly around cars, utterly uncaring of traffic lights and stop signs. I was terrified, holding on for dear life, but it was also the most exhilarating ride I had ever taken, not just because of how fast we were travelling but also because a delightful rush of fear—that tenuous thrill of my own mortality—gripped me each time we narrowly avoided an accident.

Outside the halls of residence, Kev-O came to a screeching halt. Weak-kneed, I got off the bike, wobbling slightly, my legs numb from the vibrations of the motorcycle and the pasting he had given me earlier.

'Thank you,' I said awkwardly, 'for the drink and the ride.'

Kev-O nodded. 'Take care of yourself, mate,' he said, 'and remember, stay the bloody hell out of Wapping.'

With that, he gunned the bike's engine and zoomed away. I gaped after him until he was just a speck in the distance, stricken by an immense sense of surreality. Was any of this actually happening, I found myself thinking, or had I drunk too much and imagined it all?

For the briefest of instants, I was sure that it was the latter, that I was lying in a gutter somewhere and Kev-O had been little more than an elaborate hallucination, but then, when I turned to go into the dorm, my back twinged with agony and I knew it was all real.

Wearily, I stumbled up the steps to my floor, dreading the sight of Tariq. Pausing outside the door to my room, dizzy with a combination of fatigue and too much Guinness, I steeled myself for the inevitable argument that was bound to occur after my abominable behaviour in class. I fumbled with my keys, struggling to find the right one. It took me a few minutes, but at last, I managed to get the door unlocked.

Inside, it was pitch-black. I flicked on the light, squinting as the solitary bulb burned into incandescence, blinding me for a second.

When my vision cleared, I saw what Tariq had done.

It must have taken him all day, hours of painstaking labour. I guessed that he must have gotten someone from the housing office to come help him, but somehow he had managed to put up a wall, a two-inch-thick plywood divide, that neatly bisected the room in half, segregating the living room in twain.

When I saw this barrier, I began to laugh.

Tariq had partitioned us—the great 'partition' of Room 47.

He had divided the room into two sovereign territories.

His tiny Pakistan.

My sombre India.

13

Of course, I wasn't the only Indian in my class. That is the one thing you can be certain of—that no matter where you go in the world, you will find at least five Indians have already beaten you there.

As fate would have it, there were exactly five other Indians in my class. A girl named Malini from Bangalore, attractive in an obvious sort of way, looked at me like I was trash when I tried to chat her up; two very quiet boys from Delhi and one from Gujarat, whom I couldn't quite understand because he didn't know much English.

And then there was Sikhboy.

He was a Bhapa from Birmingham, Baldev or Baljit or something like that, a broad-shouldered, barrel-chested bull of a boy who looked a lot like Hardy from Laurel and Hardy, except with a thick beard. He wasn't tall but he seemed larger than life because he had the most enormous head I had ever seen, as massive as a watermelon, and a penchant for brightly coloured turbans, red and yellow and purple, which he wore with matching Hawaiian shirts as though he were a Punjabi Jimmy Buffett.

We had no classes together because he was studying medicine at Imperial. As a result, I hadn't been able to exchange more than a few words with him, not until the day after my outburst when Sikhboy approached me during lunch in the cafeteria.

I admit I was taken aback by this overture. Until that point, we had done little more than share vague pleasantries when we passed each other in the corridors. But now, unexpectedly, he came and sat down at the same table as me, on the same side of the bench, so close that I could smell the overpowering odour of Old Spice aftershave radiating off him, which I thought was rather ironic since he was Sikh and didn't actually shave.

'I liked what you said,' he said warmly. His accent was odd, very Punjabi but with a slightly northern lilt, which made me smile. 'You know, about Pakistan. I want you to know that I agree with you completely. And I'm not the only one! There are a lot of us who hate what has happened to Punjab.'

As I contemplated those words, unsure of exactly how to respond, he smiled and asked, 'Do you have a pen?'

I nodded. Rummaging through my pockets I found a Bic, which I offered it to him. Taking it, Sikhboy picked up a paper napkin and scribbled something on its surface before folding it in half and waving it at me.

'Here, take this.'

Hesitantly, I accepted the napkin from him. It had an address on it, printed out in careful block letters, a location somewhere in Hounslow.

'What is this?' I asked, bewildered.

'We are having a small party tomorrow,' Sikhboy said, rising to his feet, 'just me and a few friends. We'd love for you to come.'

Grinning, he held out one hand for me to shake. I took it suspiciously, still unsure of why he was being so friendly. His palm was sweaty, and he let the handshake linger for a little too long, holding on firmly as if to test my strength, an overtly familiar gesture that made me grimace.

'Try and make it,' he whispered. 'It would be nice if you did. After all, we are all brothers, hain na?'

And then he lumbered away, leaving me sitting there, perplexed, unsure of exactly what had just happened.

I don't know why I decided to go to the party. It was temporary madness, I suspect, brought about by boredom, but the next evening, I shrugged into my best jacket and went in search of the address printed on Sikhboy's napkin.

I took a train down to Hounslow for the first time, which turned out to be a queer little microcosm of India, a pocket dimension, more like a suburb of Delhi than a borough of London.

I emerged from the Tube station and it was like I had stepped into another world, a very Punjabi fishbowl. If Brainiac had shrunk down a piece of North India and transported it overseas to resurrect it amidst the cold streets of England, it would be something like this, I imagine, an incongruous, colourful simulacrum of my homeland, but still somehow utterly artificial, like a theme park ride, much too nostalgic to be real.

Overcome by a bizarre sense of displacement, I wandered down the street, looking around me with incredulous eyes. Everywhere I turned, I was greeted by fragments of India—curry houses from which the scent of raw masala wafted, so pungent that it brought tears to my eyes, and rows of garish storefronts from which a barrage of deafeningly ethnic film music blared, selling everything from Madras sarees to shabby Rajasthani antiques. Why, there was even a cinema made to look like a paper mache Taj Mahal, its crumbling facade decorated with giant posters of Bollywood film stars.

And there were more Indian people on the streets, I think, than I had ever seen in India. Suited-booted banker types chattering away on their Motorolas, rubbing shoulders with matrons in sweater vests and salwar sets who were out for a matinee show, not to mention a huddle of surly teenagers who paused from listening to Fatboy Slim to look at me askance when I passed them, yelling, 'Oy, Pendu, get back on the boat.'

It took me almost an hour to find the address on the napkin. It turned out to be a small community centre half-hidden behind a brown brick building with tall minarets and a bulbous dome. It was a gurudwara, I realised much to my astonishment, when I saw the enormous Sikh Khanda emblazoned across its door, and above that a large sign that declared 'Hounslow Khalsa Sikh Temple, Wahe Guru, Welcome one and all'.

In front of this curious edifice, I paused, somehow mortified by how gaudy it looked. For a long moment, I stood there, gripped by an embarrassment so severe, so absolute, that I almost turned and left. Unfortunately, before I could make my escape, Sikhboy, who was standing at the door of the community centre and greeting guests as they arrived, noticed me and waved me over, beckoning that I should follow him indoors.

Half-heartedly, I trailed after him into the annexe behind the building, which turned out to be a rec room that had been decorated for a party. I was taken aback by how tacky it was, not just tawdry but woebegone 1980s prom tatty, with paper streamers on the walls and bright balloons floating back and forth. A temporary dance floor had been laid down atop the ancient basketball court, and a cacophony of bhangra music blared tinnily from a massive speaker in one corner. And above it all, a huge hand-painted banner declared 'Welcome to the Hounslow Sons of Punjab'.

Even the people around me were utter curiosities, a large crowd of young Sikhs all wearing kurtas and bright turbans and gold-trimmed sashes as if it were Baisakhi in a Punjabi village, not Tuesday afternoon in the very heart of London.

I shuddered, feeling entirely out of place. The embarrassment that had assailed me earlier returned once more, even more potent than before. Who were these people? I found myself wondering. Was there a factory somewhere in India that churned them out from identical moulds, a conveyor line that spat them out and exported them to colleges in England and America by the dozen to spread their Indianness like a virus?

As I looked at that herd of kids, laughing and dancing and having a good time, an unexpected repulsion coursed through me, a repugnance. It is difficult for me to explain, but for the first time, I did not feel proud of being Indian, of being Punjabi. On the contrary, what I felt was shame, a contrition so fervent that it was almost disgusting.

As if he sensed my discomfort, Sikhboy took my arm and hooked it into his own. He steered me through the crowd, introducing me around with an expansive smile. He seemed to know everyone there, but to me, they all looked much the same—an identical flock of Sikhboy clones, large and turbaned with frighteningly eager smiles. I failed to catch a single name. Instead, fixing a polite smile on my face, I shook each out-thrust hand mechanically, wondering how I could get the hell out of there.

But there was to be no escape. Before I could sidle away, Sikhboy guided me to a spot near the stage and asked me to wait there. I nodded, leaning against the wall as he climbed up on stage and picked up a microphone.

He stood there like a squat monolith until the crowd turned to face him. Smiling, he announced something in Punjabi, of which I couldn't understand a word, but it was greeted with a sporadic flutter of laughter. Then, much to my dismay, he began to dance, flailing his arms in the air like a windmill. Behind him, the speakers began to blare out a tinny pulsing thump of Punjabi music. The crowd cheered raucously and started to gyrate in synchrony with Sikhboy as if they had all been seized by collective dementia.

It was all too ridiculous, even for my finely tuned sense of the absurd. Unfortunately, that was only the beginning of the strangeness. After three more strident songs to which everyone danced maniacally, there was a brief lull during which we were forced to endure a series of pantomimed events up on stage. First, a team of teenaged Sikh boys did some carefully rehearsed acrobatics, tumbling and rolling and turning somersaults and backflips, and then a tall sardar, maybe forty years old, did a trick with a chain flail, whirling it about his head like a nunchuk. Next, a pair of burly bare-chested men mock-fought a duel, their swords clanging on each other's shields as they danced back and forth in a blinding display of martial prowess, which was greeted with deafening applause.

Deciding I had seen quite enough, I started to edge towards the door. Before I could take more than two steps though, Sikhboy returned, flanked by a pair of large frowning boys who hemmed me in on either side.

'Come,' he said commandingly. Before I could object, his compatriots gripped my arms, each grasping one bicep. They led me through the crowd to the back of the rec centre, guiding me down a short flight of steps into the basement.

At the bottom of the stairs, I found myself in a shadowy, dingy room. It smelled faintly of mildew, and in one corner, an old steam boiler hissed and clanked away. The rest of the room was filled with brown cardboard boxes and wooden crates piled precariously.

I squinted, struggling to see, because the space was dimly lit by just one naked lightbulb that hung from a strand of dangling wire.

In the indistinct twilight cast by this solitary illumination, I saw that a camp table had been set up amidst the piles of crates, around which three other sardars were gathered, sitting on metal chairs and playing cards silently.

When Sikhboy entered, they paused to welcome him, rising to their feet respectfully, but when they noticed my presence, their smiles faded, morphing instantly to looks of abject suspicion.

Sikhboy sat down at the head of the table and gazed up at me with a knowing smile.

'We want you to join us,' he said.

'I … I don't understand.'

'Please,' he said politely, 'sit down.'

The boys holding my arms let go. Uncomfortably, I pulled up one of the chairs, looking at Sikhboy, utterly confused.

'What's going on? Why have you brought me here?'

In reply, he leaned forward and whispered, 'We are the Sons of Khalistan, and we want you to become one of us.

'The world may have stopped believing in Khalistan, but we will never forget. It was the blood of our fathers and brothers that was shed in 1984, and we will not rest until we have thrown off the yoke of our oppressors.'

His voice soared as he warmed to this well-rehearsed diatribe, stentorian with practised eloquence.

'No matter the cost, we will fight to the death for a free Punjab. It is our birthright and we will not be denied.'

His acolytes all watched him adoringly, hanging on his every word. I cannot deny, it was seductive.

Sikhboy seemed so earnest and sincere that in spite of my innate scepticism, I found myself hypnotised by his passion.

'Will you join us, brother?' he said expansively. 'We are always on the look out for committed brethren who believe in a free Punjab.'

I was taken aback by this request, unsure of how to react—whether to be shocked or bemused. For an instant, as I gaped at Sikhboy and his Sikh boys, watching me with such fanatic intensity, trying their best to look all stern and revolutionary, I couldn't help but smile involuntarily, an incredulous, dumbfounded smirk. It was hilarious really, like something out of a badly written comic book. This was supposed to be some sort of secret society, I thought, and Sikhboy was the leader, the Rasputin pulling the puppet strings at which these silly children danced. And now he wanted me, of all people, someone who had never believed in anything, to become a part of his stalwart band. It was so utterly outrageous that I felt assailed by a spate of nervous laughter, a sudden cataclysm of absurdity that threatened to bubble out of me, even though I fought to suppress it.

Walk away, a voice inside me whispered warily. Walk away now and forget that you were ever here.

For one brief instant, I was tempted to pay attention to that warning, surrender to its cautionary counsel and turn and leave. But then I found myself thinking of Kev-O and what he had said to me that night in Wapping:

'No matter how badly we want to fit in or forget, it's in our blood, and a man's blood, it can never be changed.'

Watching Sikhboy, it struck me that perhaps I was wrong about him. Beneath the liminal threshold of skin and hair, maybe it was possible that we were much the same after all. Like fraternal twins, we seemed to be driven by the same things, the same compulsions. Hatred. Resentment. Regret. And most of all, fear, fear of losing control, of being reduced to nothing, of being alone. The only difference between us was that he had a cause, a dream he believed in. Maybe that was what I lacked. Maybe that was what I needed to surmount my innate embitterment. A cause like his, a conviction to sustain me, to give me some small semblance of purpose.

I think that was what prompted me to accept his offer. That and the way he held out his hand to me, his face shiny with a welcoming that I had never encountered before, a warm camaraderie that made up my mind for me.

'Yes,' I said, 'I will join you.'

'Good!'

As if they had been waiting for that cue, they surrounded me, that gaggle of bearded, turbaned boys, clapping my back eagerly, an inundation of goodwill so enthusiastic that it took me quite by surprise.

Sikhboy did not join in this elaborate expression of amity. Instead, his face grew fierce. From one of the capacious pockets of his kurta, he extracted a small Swiss army knife and unfolded it. It was just four inches long, but its blade was razor-sharp, gleaming wickedly as it caught the half-light, a menacingly silver glint.

I watched with grim fascination as Sikhboy lowered its sharp edge to his hand and cut a shallow groove in his palm, a thin gash from which a florid runnel of blood welled, so dark that it was almost ochre.

'Give me your hand,' he commanded.

Bewildered, I obeyed, unsure of what he meant to do. He seized it, and before I could object, slashed out with the knife to carve a matching cut on my own palm, a jagged little wound that began to weep red immediately.

The pain took me by surprise—a sharp sting that I wasn't prepared for.

'What the hell?' I tried to snatch my hand away, but Sikhboy was too strong for me, his grip like iron. I tried to struggle, but before I could break away, he pressed down his bleeding palm against mine in a parody of a handshake, until our blood intermingled.

'There,' he whispered, releasing his hold on my wrist. 'Now we are joined—brothers in blood.'

I looked down at my palm, somehow nauseated by the whole ceremony. It was clammy, stained with sticky blood. The cut Sikhboy had made ached dully, still seeping slightly. Half consciously, I wiped it against my jeans, where it left a bright smear. The sight of my own blood sickened me more than I could possibly have imagined. Unexpectedly, I felt a panic growing inside me. What had I done? I thought. What if Sikhboy had infected me? What if he had HIV or Hepatitis or something even worse, some sort of changeling disease with which he had contaminated me, and now slowly, I was doomed to turn into someone like him and his cronies, the sort of person that haunted basements and mouthed rhetoric without an ounce of self-consciousness?

Sikhboy didn't seem to notice my discomfort, nor did the other boys, who watched us silently, their faces rapt with zealous excitement.

'Now repeat after me,' he said. 'I swear that I will live and die for Punjab.'

His voice wavered, ecstatic with fervency. 'I will not rest until my motherland has been freed. I will fight with every breath for the nation of Khalistan. I will never betray my brothers. I will not bow before tyranny, not for profit or pleasure, and I shall never permit temptation to lead me astray from my chosen path.'

Listlessly, almost mechanically, I echoed these words, parroting each sentence half-heartedly.

When we were done with this childish litany, Sikhboy laughed and exclaimed, '*Bole so nihal, sat sri akal.*'

One by one the others chimed in, mouthing this slogan in cadence with him until they were all shouting at the top of their voices, so loud that my ears began to ring.

Beaming proudly, Sikhboy leaned forward and enveloped me in a bear hug. I shuddered, disgusted by his immediacy. He smelt of sweat and aftershave, and beneath it, something more sinister, that astringent scent of hate, of betrayal, which reminded me so much of my grandfather.

'Welcome, brother,' he declared.

'Now, at last, you are a true son of Khalistan.'

14

To tell the truth, I quite enjoyed being one of the Sons of Khalistan.

As anarchist groups go, we were pretty useless, poseurs of the worst kind, all talk and no action.

There were five of us. Sikhboy, who was the leader, and Tiger Bedi, a tall, slender boy from Glasgow whose parents owned a grocery store and who was studying management at Oxford Brookes. There was Pritam from LSE, who wore his hair in dreads and pretended he was black, and a short, dark boy from Colchester whose name I didn't know but everyone called him Happy, who was studying at King's College and was scared to death of girls. And last of all, there was me, the new boy, the only real Indian of the lot, as none of them had even set foot beyond their home counties, much less actually been to Punjab.

We didn't do much really. Sikhboy's uncle owned a balti restaurant in Southall. We met there every day after class. Sikhboy would make long harangues about all that was wrong with the world while we gobbled down whatever was leftover from the lunch service, gluey chicken tikka masala and cold naans that we didn't have to pay for. Like every bargain-basement Marx in the making, Sikhboy loved the sound of his own voice, going on for hours about Punjab and

Khalistan, spouting silly second-hand rhetoric that he had overheard from his grandparents and parents, pointlessly bombastic tirades about how Partition had ruined Punjab and the Muslims were our enemy, and that the only way the people of Punjab would be happy was if they broke away from the Indian republic and formed their own state.

He was utterly full of shit, of course. I knew that much of what he was saying was blatantly inaccurate, the immature hyperbole of an ignorant middle-class teenager who had never had to get his hands dirty. But I never interfered or interjected, not even when his ravings became patently racist. Instead, I listened to his ranting silently and pretended that I agreed with him because I was afraid that if I contradicted him, if I got into a semantic debate, he would expel me from his little group and I would end up alone again.

It was ironic, really, to think that I had come all the way to London to end up surrounded by sardars, but they were the only ones who welcomed me with open arms. To tell the truth, I felt quite at home around them, sitting in Sikhboy's basement in Hounslow, even though it was a seedy little hole with a tattered sofa and raggedy carpeting. The place always smelled of mould and dirty socks, but I liked it there. I enjoyed listening to the others as they chattered in Punjabi and sang old film songs. I enjoyed their bad jokes and their bawdy anecdotes, and their interminable boasting about the girls that they had slept with, even though most of these stories were patent lies.

I couldn't help myself. It was the first time I had ever had real friends, that I had found myself around people who treated me like part of the gang. There was something infinitely reassuring about Sikhboy and his mates, a sense of companionship that I was desperately hungry for. Even though deep down, I'm certain that some part of me hated them, despised what they stood for, another more urgent part needed them so badly, a dreadful necessity that I just could not deny.

Sikhboy had grand plans, as he often reminded us, but more often than not, most of the things we ended up doing were little more than pranks, harmless mischief really, nothing malicious or cruel, just the sort of testosterone-fuelled foolishness that boys get up to.

We made a lot of crank calls, mainly to this girl that Sikhboy had a crush on but was afraid to speak to. Once, during Ramadan, we tore down the posters for the local Muslim Union prayer meeting. Another time, we spent a week strutting about wearing matching saffron turbans like it was our uniform. On Saturdays, we lurked around Hyde Park distributing pamphlets, flimsy leaflets filled with spelling mistakes that Sikhboy had typed up on his computer and printed at home, proclaiming that Punjab deserved to be free.

There was this Pakistani dowager who owned a corner store near Pritam's house, who always spat when we walked by and refused to serve us because we were Indian. One evening, we threw eggs at her store window and ran away while she chased us with a broom, screaming and cursing in Urdu. Another time, Tiger told us that there was this pub down the street from his college where a bunch of white city types had abused him and called him a raghead. And so, early one Sunday morning, led by Sikhboy, we pissed all over the front door, all five of us, marking our territory as we shivered in the dawn chill.

The worst thing I did was paint graffiti on the wall of the local mosque. Sikhboy challenged me to do it, and I had no choice but to accept. One night, we all snuck out, and I got Happy to lift me up on his shoulders while I sprayed the slogan 'Sons of Khalistan Forever' in jagged red letters. I was so terrified we would get caught that my heart was in my mouth, but it went off without a hitch and ended up making me a sort of hero to the others, not the new boy any more but one of their own.

More often than not, it was just childish idiocy, but then, one evening, it went bad, really fucking bad.

We were sitting in Sikhboy's basement playing Tekken. He was raving on as usual about how Punjab had been ruined by the English and how the Mussulmans were winning, and that we spent too much time talking and not enough taking action.

'We need to do something now,' he said vehemently. 'Something big, something that will get us some attention.'

When he made this declaration, Pritam sat up. 'I know what we can do,' he said with a thin smile. 'Let's get the Pakistani.'

My ears pricked up. Were they talking about Tariq? Was he the one they were going to 'get'? I don't know why but the thought of them going after him made me quail with dismay.

'Who exactly do you mean?' I asked, my heart pounding.

'You know, your roommate. He always acts like he's something special, doing chamchagiri with the whites all the time. Let's find the bastard and hammer him.'

Even though he had never been anything but cold to me, I felt compelled to stand up for Tariq.

'Look, just leave him alone,' I said softly. 'He hasn't done anything.'

'Oh, hasn't he?' Sikhboy sneered with barely disguised hostility. 'He is a Pakistani, and they are the ones who raped our motherland. And have you forgotten what he said in your class about us Indians? The bastard deserves a good thrashing.'

What motherland are you talking about? I wanted to snap. Punjab isn't your home. You live in a goddamned two and a half split level in London. The closest you have been to Punjab is the gurudwara down the street, you fucking poseur. And you can afford to hide behind the cheap comfort of faux nationalism because you have options. You have parents who will support you. But I can't. I'm here on a scholarship, and I can't afford to screw everything up and end up getting kicked out of college. I can't afford to go back to India. I just can't.

But another part inside me, a cold, violent part I had not realised existed, to my surprise, was thrilled at the thought of getting even with Tariq, at paying him back for the way he had been acting, so disdainful and so superior.

'Well, are you with me? Let's find that Pakistani and teach him a lesson he won't forget.'

'Yes … Yes … Yes.'

All the others clamoured in approval, working themselves up into a frenzy. Even before I knew it, I found myself joining them, echoing their sadistic enthusiasm.

The five of us spent the next hour and a half searching for Tariq. He wasn't in the dorm or the student's lounge or at the learning centre. We checked in the cafeteria and the classroom annexe, and even lingered outside a nearby mosque, waiting to see if he emerged after the afternoon prayers, but there was no trace of him. It was as if he had disappeared, vanished clear off the face of the earth.

As time slithered by, my initial fervour began to wear off. Secretly, I was glad that we hadn't been able to find him. My ardour for revenge had cooled and turned to reticence. Deep down, I found myself hoping that maybe soon Sikhboy would grow weary of searching for him and we could just go back to his basement and abandon this temporary madness that had taken control of us.

But destiny, it seemed, had other plans.

In the end, we were headed to St. Pancras to catch a train back to Hounslow when Tiger Singh let out a whoop of delight.

'Look,' he squealed, pointing behind us, 'there he is.'

We all swivelled to stare in the direction of his upraised finger, just in time to spy Tariq come tottering out of the Senate House Library, struggling under the weight of a massive stack of books.

Sikhboy giggled when he saw him. 'Come on,' he said, indicating that we should follow his lead. Trotting across the road, he began to shadow Tariq. Like scavengers stalking their prey, the others fell in behind him, careful to keep a discreet distance so that they would not be spotted.

Tariq remained oblivious. He never even noticed us following him while he made his way back towards the dorm, trying his best not to drop any books.

I stayed at the back of the pack, overcome with shame. I wish I had been braver, that I had been bold enough to shout out a warning, but I was too afraid of crossing Sikhboy.

Patiently, we followed Tariq, biding our time until he was alone.

Our opportunity came at last, not far from King's Cross, when he turned to take a shortcut down a small alley between two buildings.

Immediately, Sikhboy dashed forward to overtake him and cut him off.

We fanned out to surround Tariq, careful to first ensure that there was no one around to see us or witness what we were about to do.

As we hemmed him in, he came to an unsteady halt. His face sagged with fear. He tried to bolt, to run, but before he could take more than a few steps, Sikhboy pushed him back roughly with a grunt, shoving so hard that the books tumbled from his arms, falling to the ground with a dull thump.

'What ... what do you want from me?' Tariq stammered. His eyes darted across our faces until they settled squarely upon mine, widening with recognition, with precognition, as if he knew what was about to come. I looked away, almost dizzy. I didn't want to play this game any more. All I wanted to do was go back to my room and pretend like I had never met the Sons of Khalistan.

Unfortunately, before I could slink away, Sikhboy reached out to clasp my shoulder.

'This is it, brother. At last, the time has come to strike a blow for Punjab.'

Turning back to Tariq, he smiled, a vicious grin that seemed to be made entirely of teeth.

'We are the Sons of Khalistan, you Pakistani piece of shit, and we are going to teach you a lesson you won't forget.'

Still smiling, he slapped Tariq as hard as he could, a short, swift blow that snapped his head to the left.

It took Tariq a moment to recover. To his credit, he didn't whimper, not one sound. Instead, he swivelled his neck back silently to glare at Sikhboy, his face livid with barely repressed contempt. It was almost heroic, this display of disdain. In a movie, it would have made a bully wilt and back off, but here, all it did was enrage Sikhboy even more. Without warning, he punched Tariq, battering a fist into his solar plexus and doubling him up, leaving him choking and sputtering for air.

'Don't ever fuck with the Sons of Khalistan,' he crowed.

This declaration seemed to set the other boys off. In the blink of an eye, they closed in on Tariq and began to beat him, pummelling and kicking at him with furious intensity.

As for me, I couldn't bring myself to join in this spate of violence, not even when Sikhboy turned to me and growled, 'Come on, what are you waiting for? Get him. Get the fucking Pakistani.'

But I couldn't. I stood there like a statue, unable to bring myself to move. It was like my body had ceased to obey me, as if my arms and legs had short-circuited and refused to accept the impulses transmitted to them by my brain.

Instead, I edged away furtively, unwilling to hit Tariq. As I watched them attacking him with such brutal fury, I was seized by a welter of self-loathing. It was my fault, I thought uncomfortably. I was the reason they were beating him. That realisation left me so nauseated I felt sick to the pit of my belly.

But then, for a flicker of a moment, our eyes met and Tariq managed to surprise me.

He smiled, a tired, pitying smirk, and then nodded his head slightly, as if to forgive me, before folding to the ground.

As his eyes locked into my own, I shuddered. He looked exactly like the Sikh boy at the crossroads, I thought, that poor child I had seen beaten half to death in 1984. I recognised the expression on his face. I knew it. I had felt it often enough, the same hopelessness, the same need, the same desperate entreaty.

Something swelled inside me, rising, gathering. My breath caught in my throat, and I knew then that I could not let them go through with it. If I allowed them to hurt Tariq, to attack him because he was Pakistani, because he was Muslim, I was enabling the hatred, the same hatred that I had seen in Punjab as a child and the same hatred that threatened to consume me now.

It was like I had been lost, but suddenly, at that moment, I knew exactly what I had to do.

I had a choice.

The only way to break the cycle was to choose not to hate, to choose to forgive.

If I did that, I could end it, here and now.

I could change.

That was when Sikhboy pulled out his knife.

It was the sight of that blade, that same shiny little Swiss knife with which he had slashed my palm before I took my blood oath to join the Sons of Khalistan, that finally broke the spell that had held me motionless.

'Cut him,' Tiger Singh snarled, his face glittering with bloodlust. 'Cut the Pakistani bastard. Cut the pig fucker good.'

Sikhboy paused, brandishing the knife, smiling cruelly as he raised it towards Tariq's face. But before he could touch him, I felt compelled to move, at last. Almost of its own volition, my hand darted out and seized his wrist, restraining him before he could use the knife.

My intervention took Sikhboy by surprise. He glared at me, his face suffusing red. He tried to wrench his hand free, but somehow, I can't explain it, even though he was taller than me and broader, I was too strong for him, as if I had found a hidden reserve of strength I had not known I possessed.

'What the fuck are you doing?' he snarled, so angry that his spittle flickered in my face like froth from a rabid dog's mouth.

It was at that instant, I think, that whatever illusion he had managed to cast over me, the magnetism that had convinced me to become one of his followers, was shattered.

Softly, I heard my voice say, 'Stop this.'

Letting go of his hand, I took one hesitant step forward and then another until I was standing in front of Tariq.

'Leave him alone,' I hissed at Sikhboy. 'Don't you dare hit him again.'

Angrily, he tried to push me aside, but I held my ground, refusing to back down.

'What is wrong with you?' he snarled. 'I thought you were one of us. I thought you were our brother.'

His mouth twisted into a scowl, but it wasn't just anger I saw warping across his features. It was betrayal, such utter disappointment that a frisson of remorse clawed at me, almost weakening my resolve.

'I'm sorry,' I said, 'I really am, but you know this is wrong.'

Even as I tried to make this half-hearted apology, one of the others, I think it was Happy, kicked out at me, catching me on my knee with a glancing blow that sent me sprawling flat on my backside. I winced, trying to ignore the sharp pang of pain that shivered up my spine. Mustering what little dignity I could, I got up slowly, steeling myself for an onslaught.

But Sikhboy did not move. Instead, he watched me wordlessly as I shuffled to stand in front of Tariq once again.

'Please,' I pleaded with him, 'you're better than this. You know you are.'

His face was taut with unbridled ferocity, an antagonism so palpable that I was certain that he was going to beat me to a pulp. I tried not to flinch as Sikhboy bunched one hand into a fist. For a long second, he stood there, but then his indignation seemed to wither and he let his hand fall back to his side.

'Go,' he murmured. 'Leave now before we change our mind.'

Wordlessly, I turned to Tariq. 'Come on, let's get out of here.' Tariq started to gather his books. I leaned over and helped him, gathering an armful as well. As quickly as we could, we hobbled away, leaving Sikhboy and the Sons of Khalistan standing there, staring after us, their faces incandescent with hostility.

Tariq could barely move, but I forced him to keep up with me, dragging him along bodily, half supporting his weight even though my leg was killing me. By the time we got back to the dorm, the adrenalin that had made me brave enough to confront Sikhboy had worn off, leaving me exhausted. It took the last vestiges of my strength to help Tariq stagger up the steps to Room 47. Once we were safely inside, I locked the door firmly behind me, a precaution in case Sikhboy and the Sons of Khalistan changed their minds and came looking for us again. Wearily, I sank down on the floor, watching Tariq, unsure of how to speak to him. Now that we were alone and the bravado that had seized me had passed, I was overcome with awkwardness. I didn't quite know how I was supposed to behave. I knew we couldn't go back to the silent impasse that had prevailed before, but at the same time, Tariq was still very much a stranger to me.

He seemed equally bewildered, offering me an inept nod of thanks, before disappearing past the partition into his side of the room. A few minutes passed before Tariq came back, having wiped his face clean of blood and changed into a nightsuit of all things, a matching pair of Marks and Sparks pyjamas that made me smirk.

I saw that he was holding a bottle of good Speyside malt, Glen-something or the other, and two teacups, one of which he offered me. Gratefully, I took it. He sank down opposite me, making sure he was still on his side of the room. Cracking open the bottle, he poured out a generous measure, first in my cup and then his own.

Without waiting for him, I guzzled it down in one long swig. Tariq smiled and took a small birdlike sip from his own cup.

'I thought Sikhs didn't drink,' he said, breaking the silence.

'I thought Muslims didn't drink either,' I retorted.

'We don't,' he replied, and raised his cup to me in salutation, before gulping down the remnants of its contents.

'Well,' I said, offering my cup up to him for a refill, 'I guess this makes us both hypocrites.'

Tariq laughed and poured me another large measure of whiskey, wincing slightly. He poured himself another shot as well, but he didn't drink it. Instead, he just held it, looking down at the amber liquid pensively.

'Do you ever miss it?' he asked. 'India, I mean?'

I looked away, staring out of the window. The hour of false twilight between afternoon and evening was just beginning, and the city was at its grimmest, unfriendly and hoary with frost. I could see the stark carcasses of the trees in the park behind the dorm, naked with autumn, their bare branches pointing up at the cinereous sky like accusatory fingers.

For a brief instant, as I looked at their macabre silhouettes, I was beset by an awful wistfulness. Suddenly, I found myself wishing that I had never come to London, that I was back home, not in Bombay, to my surprise, but in Amritsar, back at my grandparents' farm.

'When I was a child, we had a farm,' I said softly. 'There was a tree there, a tall poplar, in which my Nana, my grandfather, had built me a small machan, you know, one of those old hunting platforms like a treehouse.'

I smiled, losing myself in the simple pleasure of that memory.

'It was my lair, my hiding place, where I used to run and hide whenever I needed to be alone, when I was angry or confused or sad. And somehow, just sitting there, in that tree, it always calmed me down. It always made me feel safe, you know, like everything made sense.

'I don't miss India,' I said, 'but I miss that sense of home, that feeling of belonging. I just don't feel that here in London, not at all. Here, everyone stares at me like I'm an alien, you know what I mean?'

Tariq smiled slightly and nodded. 'I do,' he said. 'I know exactly what you mean.'

'What about you? Do you miss Pakistan?'

'There are times,' he replied with a faraway look, 'when the winter is ending and spring is about to begin, when Lahore is almost beautiful. There is this hopeful music in the air, you know, the sound of new birdsong, and the sky is humid with the promise of rain, but the rest of the time, it's just too hot to endure. Don't you hate the heat?'

I didn't answer. I don't know why, but a dread, a self-consciousness, filled my chest. I couldn't bring myself to look at him and to meet the penetrating candour of his eyes. Instead, I reached over and picked up the bottle and fumbled off its cap to fill my cup almost to the brim.

Tariq stared at me as I guzzled down the whiskey with almost frantic haste.

'Can I ask you something personal?' he said after a few minutes had passed.

'Sure,' I retorted nonchalantly, 'as long as you keep the whiskey coming.'

'Why did you help me?'

'I don't know,' I said with a shrug. 'It seemed like the right thing to do at the time.'

'I thought you hated me.'

'I don't hate you. I guess I just envy you a little. Okay, a lot. The way you manage to fit in with the whites so effortlessly. The way you get along with everyone. I wish I could do that.'

Tariq's eyes widened in astonishment. For a heartbeat, he looked shocked, and I thought I had made a grave faux pas, that I had offended him by saying something wrong, but then he started to chuckle, a low tympanum of nervous amusement.

'What's so funny?' I said tersely, assuming he was laughing at me.

'Oh, nothing,' he said. 'It's funny really that you should say you envy me, because the truth is that from the day I got here, I have been trying not to envy you.'

I looked at him in disbelief, taken aback by this revelation.

'Why on earth would you envy me?' I said sceptically.

He smiled widely. 'You know, how you aren't ashamed to be yourself. How it doesn't embarrass you when people pass snide comments or say rude things to you. I admire the way you manage to laugh it right off and the way you don't feel the need to play a role, to fit in with the whites like the rest of us do. Frankly, you make me feel like a fake.'

Somehow, that struck me as hilarious. Even before I knew it, I burst into laughter. Tariq looked at me like I had lost my mind. At first, his face remained stiff with bafflement, but then his lips began to twitch as well, until we were both cackling away together.

With each chuckle, the tension between us melted away little by little, dwindling towards nothingness. We laughed until we couldn't laugh any more, my stomach started to hurt and Tariq's eyes began to water.

Finally, it was Tariq who managed to compose himself first.

'You know,' he said, 'You aren't at all what I thought an Indian would look like.'

'Really? And what do you think Indians are supposed to look like?'

'Well, my grandfather said you are all short and fat and have bad breath and smell of garlic and onions.'

I rolled my eyes, feigning a mock affront.

'And I was told that all Pakistanis were psychos who would try to murder me in my sleep.'

Tariq grinned. 'And what do you think of us now?'

'Well,' I said, 'you're almost normal, but then I could be wrong. I don't know that much about you, do I?'

When he heard that, abruptly, his mood seemed to change. His smile faded, and he grew very serious as if I had struck a nerve.

'When I was a boy,' he said hesitantly, 'my grandfather would come over and take me to the madrassa on Fridays, and after we had learnt about the Hadith from the maulvi and prayed, he would tell me stories.'

Tariq shuddered, wracked by an immense melancholy.

'Every single time, he told me how he had lost his brother and sister during Partition after his mother and father had uprooted the family from Sangrur and marched westwards to Lahore. Along the way, they had run into a mob of furious Sikhs, who had beaten my grandfather's younger brother to death and took his sister, spiriting her away to India.

'She is still probably alive,' he said pensively, 'living somewhere in Indian Punjab, with her own family, her husband and sons and grandchildren, living out the life she was forced into. And when I think of that, it never ceases to make me wonder, does she remember Pakistan at all, and my grandfather, or has she forgotten all that? Has she discarded the past like a piece of old skin?'

He shook his head sadly.

'The day before I left Pakistan for London, my grandfather came to see me one last time. He bought me a scarf and told me he wanted to give me some advice. He told me that I would meet many Indians in

England, but warned me not to trust any of them. They are all heartless liars, he said, who would pretend to be my friends until I trusted them, and then they would find some way to betray me and cause me pain.

'And then he unbuttoned his shirt and showed me the ancient scars on his back, a jigsaw pattern of dead white skin, where he had been whipped as a child when the Sikhs had attacked his family during their migration from India to Pakistan.

'"Remember these wounds," he said to me. "These are not just the scars of an old man's suffering. They are evidence, living, breathing proof that Indians cannot be trusted."'

'Why are you telling me this?' I said, my old distrust of him rekindling even more intensely.

Tariq did not reply. Forlorn, he gazed at me for one long heartbeat, and then, before I could react, he leaned forward and kissed me.

It took me utterly by surprise—the soft glancing whisper of his lips on my mouth, brushing against my moustache with such shameful sensuality that I shuddered.

It seems laughable to me as I think of it now, even ironic, but that was my first real kiss. I hadn't even realised that Tariq was gay. The thought had never occurred to me. Still, regardless of my ignorance, it was one of the most perfect moments of human contact I had ever experienced, sexless, of course, but still somehow marvellously intimate, so poignant that it brought tears to my eyes.

Suddenly, it didn't matter any more that he was Pakistani and I was Indian. For one fleeting moment, we were exactly the same, he and I, just two scared, confused boys in a strange city, scarred deeply by the past.

But then an awful shame overpowered me, a heterosexual embarrassment when I realised I was kissing a man.

'What the hell are you doing?' I squawked, pushing him away, my voice shrill with outrage.

Tariq scrambled backwards, shamefaced. 'I'm sorry,' he said evasively, refusing to look me in the eye.

The contrition in his tone made my ire subside, and I nodded, accepting his apology without further argument.

'You know,' I quipped, 'for a bloody Pakistani, you're not too bad.'

That made Tariq laugh once more.

'Neither are you,' he retorted, 'for a stupid Indian.'

15

Two weeks later, Tariq dropped out of the university and went back to Pakistan.

After his departure, I felt even more alone than before. Sikhboy and his cronies were shunning me, and most of the white kids still looked at me askance after my little tantrum in class, like I was one step away from going mental.

They weren't so wrong. Increasingly, it felt to me like I was losing control, little by little, a creeping insanity that was starting to spread through me like poison. It began as mild misanthropy, a social distancing, as I found it increasingly difficult to interact with the other students around me and endure their chattering voices and inane banter. But then it started to grow into something more potent, an anthropophobia, as if somehow I was changing into something less human, a more basic organism that could only exist in seclusion.

Even though Tariq was gone, for some unfathomable reason, I couldn't bear to tear down the dividing barrier at the centre of our room. No, I left it as was, to commemorate Tariq, and to remind me that for a few brief moments, I had not felt entirely alone.

For a while, I thought about dropping out as well, packing my bags and going home to Bombay with my tail tucked between my legs, but somehow, the thought of Nana's supercilious eyes mocking me for failing where he had succeeded was too much to bear. After all, he had survived London, and anything my grandfather had done, I told myself, I could do better.

I stayed in college, but no matter how hard I tried to concentrate in class, I couldn't bring myself to care about what the professors were teaching. Somehow, their impersonal, faceless textbook version of history seemed so pointless, just words on a page, and I found myself wondering why I had to come to London at all and if it hadn't all been a wasteful mistake.

I began to drink too much, a fifth a day to begin with, but then a whole bottle each night, then two. And I was the worst kind of drunk, raging and ranting and trying to pick fights with everyone around me until my fellow students began to avoid me entirely, turning away as I stumbled down the dorm corridors, as if I was somehow contagious.

At first, it wasn't so bad that my studies suffered, but then I started missing lectures, one or two at first, until at last, I stopped going to class altogether. Instead, I started spending most of my time at the National Gallery, drifting through the endless rooms of art and gawking at the paintings like a silent ghost.

There was one picture in particular that I found myself captivated by—*Calais Pier* by Joseph Turner. There was something intoxicating about that one canvas—an endless depth that seduced me. It wasn't a particularly great piece, depicting a ship trying to make port during a hurricane, but puzzlingly, as I looked at it, at the waves raging furiously, buffeting against that unfortunate vessel, and the clouds above, Cimmerian, thunderous, impenetrable, it felt to me like I was being pulled beneath the surface, engulfed by the storm.

I can't explain it, but I felt an immediate affinity, a sense of belonging, to that hapless vessel. Just like me, it was rudderless, powerless, set adrift, without an ounce of control.

But then, as I spent more time in front of that tumultuous seascape, I noticed that at the centre of this elemental maelstrom, the artist had painted a single swathe of blue sky, peeking out from amidst the thunderheads, the eye of the storm, offering safe haven. It took me a while to realise it, but the painting wasn't about the storm at all, but rather about that tiny fragment of tranquillity, and I felt myself pulled towards it, towards its tenuously azure hope, like a lost mariner being drawn to a beacon.

Every morning I would walk the short distance from my halls of residence to Trafalgar Square and arrive just after the gallery opened. It cost me nothing to enter, and I would spend hours, sometimes even the whole day, sitting in front of that one painting, staring into its swirling depths silently, until deep inside me the beginnings of an inchoate heat began to swell. It is hard for me to describe the deeply sexual arousal that would send me scampering to the public bathroom on the second floor, where I would lock myself into a stall, unzip my trousers and masturbate hysterically.

I had never been a particularly sexual person, not through puberty when most of my classmates had been desperately intrigued by sex, not even when I first arrived in England and found myself thrust into the salacious hotbed of undergraduate life, where everyone was fucking someone or the other except me. Personally, I had always preferred the comfort of a good book, but now, unexpectedly, the more alone I felt, the more I found myself seized by an inexplicable chiromania so frantic that I could barely control myself.

The fecund thrust of my need for any human contact, any fleeting intimacy, was so overwhelming that I almost became a frotteur. Purposely, I started to take the Tube at rush hour, riding back and forth just so that I could enjoy the proximity of humanity, the closeness of sweating strangers packed as close as sardines, rubbing against me in an erotic parody of a mating dance. It was a delirium, a perversion I couldn't comprehend but which enslaved me. I thought I was alone in my madness until one afternoon I ended up making dry, desperate love to a middle-aged stockbroker in a wool skirt, grinding against her each time the train came jolting to a stop, surrounded by people who pretended not to see us. And all through this fleeting encounter, she refused to meet my eyes but held on to me with one hungry hand, pulling me to her like I was a lifeline and she was drowning.

I had always had little or no success with the opposite sex, but now my hunger grew inside me to such a degree that I felt I would burst. It became so bad that I couldn't help but jerk off three, sometimes four, times a day, clawing at myself like a teenager until all that I felt beneath my waist was a numb emptiness, a null, frustrated void that I just couldn't fill, no matter how much porn I watched. I even went to a prostitute, a drug-addled Jamaican streetwalker I picked up in an alley near Euston Road, who offered to shag me against a wall for ten pounds, but as she fumbled to undo my trousers, I was so overcome with disgust and self-loathing that I pushed her off me and ran away without doing anything.

At that stage, I was ready to give up on women altogether and become celibate.

Until I met Soraya.

Ah yes, Soraya. How could I forget about her? We met about three months after Tariq left, at a wine and cheese party in Chelsea, you know, one of those dreadfully kitsch art department affairs where everyone ends up drinking too much cheap Chardonnay and poking fun at the Americans and having little or no recollection the next day of exactly what happened the previous night.

We were the only two Indians in the room, so I guess that it was quite natural that we gravitated towards each other. Ordinarily, I would never have been brave enough to speak to someone like Soraya. After all, we could not have been more dissimilar. She was tall, slim and marvellously chic; I was short, heavyset and unavoidably pedantic. She was graceful, every movement like a note of music, while I was all elbows and knees, full of creaks, sighs and apologies. She was cultivated and self-assured, her head held high, her chin always challenging, and me, well, I was shy and nervous, uncommunicative, slouch shouldered and perennially self-conscious.

Nonetheless, in spite of this intrinsic opposition, I found myself drawn to her, and she to me. There was no logical reason to explain why we began to speak. To be honest, I'm still dazzled that Soraya chose to converse with me at all. After all, is it not one of the sad truths of life that attractive, leggy women in elegant silk dresses rarely have either the time or the inclination to speak with short, stocky men standing shyly in one corner looking at their feet?

When she came over and said hello, I had been much too scared to respond—no amusing bon mots, no flurry of badinage. Instead, I listened wordlessly, allowing her to chatter on. For seventeen long minutes, she babbled away and I did not interrupt her once. How is it that I remember the exact duration of time, you might wonder? It's because that is how long it takes for a man to realise that he desires a woman. Seventeen minutes exactly. For the first six minutes, he reels under the weight of his longing—his lust. For the next three minutes after that, once the lust wanes, he dreams, imagining a future, hopeful about the possibilities that await him. If he survives beyond that, for four minutes, he is overcome by fear, a myriad of inadequacies. Does she like me? Is she the one? Is she good enough? Am I good enough? Are we right for each other? Is this a mistake? Then after the fear comes a minute and a half of doubt, the most difficult ninety seconds for any man to endure, and another minute and a half of hesitation, as he struggles to convince his tongue to articulate the dialogue he hears so clearly in his mind.

And then finally, like sunrise after an endless night, the seventeenth minute, which is perhaps the most perfect instant that a man can know, better even than a climax, because that is the first moment he realises that he yearns for a woman, that first, perfectly crystalline, inkling of hope, after which every subsequent second in a relationship is little more than slow atrophy.

Please understand, I'm not talking about love. Love is for adolescents, for children who watch too many Julia Roberts movies and tell themselves that is what life is supposed to be. I'm talking about need, about visceral, primal longing, as uncontrollable as hunger.

It took me seventeen minutes to realise that I needed Soraya, that I wanted her more than anything I had ever wanted before, like an addict craving a fix.

Intently, I nodded my head as she told me that she had a master's degree in developmental economics and that she was studying international law in the hope that she would be able to work for the United Nations. The truth is I barely heard her words. I was more interested in the black bra strap peeking from one shoulder and the way her nose wrinkled when she laughed. I couldn't help myself. She was, well, for lack of a better word, exquisite. Pretty, but not overly so, not at all like the plastic imperviousness of a fashion model. No, what Soraya possessed was an almost-beauty, an imperfection. That was what made her so striking. Skin like terracotta; an unkempt, hopelessly curly mop of hair; a mischievous, almost pert little nose that wiggled when she smiled; eyes the precise grey of storms, so filled with life that they were mesmerising; full, clever lips shaped like sand dunes and a glorious, almost musical laugh. Taken in isolation, each of these features was pleasant enough but nothing special. But when they combined into the tapestry of her face, they endowed her with a sublime distinctiveness that was almost a work of art in itself.

Strangely enough, I saw that she had a small scar in the sensuous hollow above her upper lip—a sallow sliver of flesh that glistened darker than her dusky skin. It was almost a twin to my own, very nearly the same star shape, and I found myself wanting to kiss it, gently caress it with my tongue.

Politely, I smiled in sympathy as she explained that she had been in London for almost a year but had made so few friends, and that she missed India immensely, not just her family and the weather and school friends but, most of all, good old-fashioned Punjabi food, because the English, chee, they ate the most ridiculous rubbish—steak and kidney pies, fried fish and chips, not to mention black pudding, yuck!

And then, finally, she informed me that even though her parents lived in Delhi now, she had been born in Amritsar.

It was this unforeseen snippet of biographical information that grabbed my attention and made me bolder than normal.

'Do you ever feel ashamed,' I said, my first tentative words to her, 'to be Punjabi?'

Immediately, before I had even finished asking this question, I was overcome by an immense sense of folly. Soraya lapsed into stunned silence, gawking at me. I could see that she had no clue whatsoever what I was talking about. Suddenly, I wanted to kick myself because I was sure from the bewildered expression on her face that I had managed to scare her away.

But then, to my unmitigated relief, after an interminable pause, she burst into uproarious laughter.

'That's certainly the strangest chat-up line I've ever heard,' she said.

'I'm sorry,' I said sheepishly.

'Oh no, don't say that. It was an interesting question.' She smiled gently. 'What about you? Are you ashamed of being a Punjabi?'

'There are times when I am, yes,' I replied, fidgeting restlessly, unable to look her in the eye.

'Why?'

'It's difficult to explain.'

'Try me.'

Solemnly, she stared at me. I wilted before the candour of her gaze, before those sharp and crystalline eyes that bored into me like daggers. Bowing my head, I struggled to find the appropriate words so that what I was about to say would not sound entirely foolish.

'It's sad really, but most people have a misconceived idea that being Punjabi means this awful stereotype—that we are little more than Falstaffian, jocular, slightly mad-in-the-head gossipmongers. The truth unfortunately is that it's all an act, a mass delusion. In reality, all of us, collectively, we should be ashamed of what we have become.'

It astonished me how easily Nana's words poured from my mouth—those same exclamations that I had heard him make a thousand times during my childhood, with the same slightly outraged tone, the same inflexions even, as if I was little more than a recording of him, a jaded facsimile.

'For hundreds of years now, our people have suffered so much, faced such persecution, first from the Mughals and then the English. We endured Partition, the Haryana divide, the Khalistan troubles, so much horror and depredation that it has left us with a sense of collective guilt, I think, and an abiding shame. That is what being Punjabi really means—guilt and a sense of self-denial for what we have allowed the world to do to us. We have forgotten our nobility, our history, even our humanity, and allowed ourselves to become a cliché. And the worst part is, we are almost proud of it.'

With those words, I smiled ineptly, convinced that I had just managed to make an utter and complete fool of myself. Suddenly, I couldn't help but feel more than a little ridiculous.

'I'm Muslim, you know,' Soraya blurted out.

It was an unexpected announcement, to say the least. For a moment, I was uncertain how to react, unable to guess how she wanted me to react. And she did want me to react, I could tell that much, from the way she was glaring at me challengingly, waiting to see what I would say next.

The old, timid me would have turned tail and bolted, but then something quite unexpected happened. Inexplicably, when I looked at Soraya, I found myself reminded of Nani and what she had said to me all those years ago in the nascence of my youth. That memory somehow lent me absurd confidence. Everyone is entitled to at least one perfect moment in their lives, I think. In many ways, that was mine because for once I knew exactly what to do.

'I don't really care about that stuff,' I said, giving Soraya my best smile, all teeth and eyelids. 'Those are all just words. Hindu, Muslim, Christian, Sikh. It is of no importance. Frankly, all that matters to me is what a person feels in here.'

Reaching out, I gently tapped her chest, just above the soft declivity of her cleavage, with the forefinger of my right hand. It was a bold move and far too personal. This unexpected moment of physical contact made her stifle a gasp, recoiling slightly as if I had assaulted her. I held my breath. Had I gone too far? Was that too forward and too brash? Uncomfortably, I gazed at Soraya, expecting her to turn and retreat from me, certain that I had blown my chances. She eyed me seriously for a minute, almost desolately, but then to my relief, she started to giggle.

'Gosh,' she sputtered, 'you're just adorable, aren't you?'

Her tone was not mocking, but neither was it complimentary. She pronounced the word 'adorable' like it was a malaise.

'You say that like it is a bad thing…?' I carped, rather more offended than I should have been.

'Never mind,' she whispered, raising one taut brow at me, and then she touched me for the first time, just the mildest flicker of her forefingers on my arm, but it made me shiver with an almost electric delight.

'Will you get me another drink?' she asked, handing me her empty glass. Wordlessly, I fetched her a glass of tepid Prosecco, and as she sipped it, we chatted some more. I was careful to steer this tête-à-tête away from philosophical matters towards more trivial things. We discussed how cold and lonely it was in England, how strange the accents seemed sometimes and how incomprehensible to our subcontinental ears. We discovered that we were both secretly Hindi film fans (Her favourite was *Chashme Buddoor* and mine was *Kagaz ke Phool*) and that we both adored T.S. Eliot (she confessed to me rather shamefacedly that she had even pretended to be one of Eliot's practical cats as a child, Macavity, to be precise).

For hours we bantered on, exploring each other's verbs, but it was so idyllic and so effortless that it felt as though only a matter of minutes had elapsed. We seemed to become an island amidst the crowd, a nation of two. As I stood beside her, close enough to enjoy the sweet smell of her hair and skin, I found myself wishing, hoping, even praying that this one conversation would never end, that it would simply go on for ever and ever in an infinite loop, just the two of us standing there sipping wine and exchanging chit-chat for perpetuity.

Sadly, I knew that it could not last. As the clock struck one and gradually the other guests began to trickle away, my heart sank. Dread grasped at my chest with icy fingers, a solemn anxiety when I realised that my time with Soraya was almost at an end.

But then, just as I was about to bid her a mournful adieu, she surprised me by suggesting that I walk her back to her place.

I accepted this overture gladly. Though she lived just a few minutes away, in a rented one-bedroom near Holland Park, we took our time, sauntering along unhurriedly, not talking, just savouring the comfort of one another's closeness, step by marvellous step.

It was an unearthly night, so cold that every breath I exhaled turned to mist in a second, mingling with hers, mated into one fog-white cloud. Above us, a silver moon dangled in the sky. As we ambled along, it began to snow, a gentle blizzard of cold flakes tumbling from the sky, like confetti.

Surreptitiously, I watched Soraya out of the corner of my eye. If anything, she seemed even lovelier, her eyes sparkling with phosphorescence and her skin flushed, radiant from the chill. Much to my chagrin, she caught me looking at her, and I snatched my eyes away guiltily. She grinned, amused by the adolescence of this reaction, and then suddenly, without warning, she reached out and took my hand in hers.

There was something so perfect about that moment that I knew I should have been ecstatic just to be there, walking along with Soraya, to feel her cheek nuzzling into my shoulder and to have her hand clasped firmly in mine. Still, for some indelible reason, I felt a pang of panic because perfection, I knew all too well, was little more than finality in disguise.

'Tell me,' I said, in my most compellingly gallant whisper, 'do you think it is possible to fall in love with someone you barely know?'

'I can tell that you're really good at this,' she responded sarcastically.

'I know,' I grinned sheepishly. 'I'm sorry.'

'Why do you do that? Why do you keep apologising all the time?'

'I don't know. Just a habit.'

'It's a bad habit. Stop it! Stop saying sorry!'

'I'll try.' I started to take my hand away, but she refused to let go. Instead, she studied me almost evaluatively.

'You're a virgin, aren't you?' she said after a moment.

It was a very unexpected thing to say, catching me completely by surprise.

'What…?' I exclaimed, trying my best to conceal my embarrassment. 'Of course, not. What on earth would make you think that…?'

She smiled a glib, almost scornful stab of a grin, and stared at me so knowingly that I flinched, unable to bear the penetrating candour of her scrutiny.

Thankfully, she did not try to humiliate me further. Much to my relief, we did not exchange another word for the rest of the way, but then, when we did finally arrive outside her flat, she surprised me yet again.

'Would you like to come up for a while?' she asked, so calmly that it was almost matter-of-fact.

'Yes', I started to say, but the words caught in my throat, so I just nodded, following meekly as Soraya led me up to her room. My heart was thumping, racing with a mixture of nervousness and desire. Once we were inside, she locked the door behind us carefully. We stood awkwardly in the darkness; she refused to switch on the lights. I started to say something, but she silenced me with a wave of her hand. Instead, she ordered me to undress.

After hesitating momentarily, I obeyed, stripping off my sweater and shirt mutely, feeling almost foolish, shivering a little, less from the cold than from my self-consciousness.

'Now the trousers,' she commanded and I complied reluctantly, feeling more and more daft with every passing second.

Once I was naked, defenceless, she circled me like a predator eyeing its prey, inspecting me carefully, almost contemptuously.

And then, with a nod of approval, she shed her dress in one smooth rustle.

I gasped when I saw her. She was magnificent. In the dim light of the moon, she seemed to gleam, her body a sinuous shimmer of curves and shadows.

'You're beautiful,' I whispered.

She smiled, a flash of sharp white teeth.

'Yes,' she replied, 'I know.'

With surprisingly strong arms, she pushed me towards the bedroom. Leaning into me, she kissed me hard on my lips. Her mouth was cold and wet, and she bit my tongue with her small sharp teeth until I felt the metal tang of blood flood into my mouth, sour and ironic.

Wreathed by shadows, we made love for the first time. She smelled, curiously enough, like a man, of tobacco and sweat. It was the first time for me and I was nervous and unsure. My fingers were tentative when I caressed her body and my hands clumsy as I stroked her breasts and explored the flat angles of her belly, the proud flare of her hips and the eager thrust of her buttocks. Impatiently, she pushed me down on her bed and took over. I surrendered as her hands reached out for me, firm and confident, guiding me inside her. I groaned when she mounted me, and I felt her warmth thrusting against me, harder and harder and harder until I lost myself in the sinewy swell of her body writhing atop me.

Afterwards, when it was over, we lay next to each other, not quite touching, like two peas in a pod. There was no need for words; neither of us wanted to be the first to speak and dispel the reverie that enveloped us, that tender, tenuous warmth which is the aftermath of really good sex.

We just lay there staring at each other for what felt like an hour, two hours, five hours, until the first rays of dawn began to colour the dark sky. In this almost ecclesiastical twilight, Soraya seemed to be made entirely of glass. Her face was thin and fragile, stretched so taut over the skull shape of her jaw that I imagined I could detect the outline of muscle and bone beneath the translucence of her skin. Her face was slick with sweat; the scar on her lip glistened like a twist of mercury. Gently, I reached out and caressed it, tracing the ridged outline of this cicatrix with the ball of my thumb. Her eyes flared wide, but she didn't try to stop me.

'Did you know,' I said, 'that this little hollow above your lip is called the philtrum?'

'Really?'

'Yes.'

'That's kind of wonderful,' she said with a smile and caught hold of my hand to put my thumb in her mouth, sucking at it with such wantonness that I felt myself shudder.

'Can I ask you something?' I said softly.

'Why not…?'

'How did you get that scar?' I blurted out.

All of a sudden, her smile sagged. Soraya's face hardened, growing guarded. Immediately, I regretted having asked the question at all, but unfortunately, it was much too late to retract my words.

'When I was nine,' she said after an interminable pause, 'I fell once while skipping rope.'

At first, I thought that she was telling the truth, but when she averted her eyes from mine, I realised that she was lying.

'It happened a long time ago,' she shrugged, trying to grin, but all that she could manage was a brittle grimace. 'I was such a klutz back then.'

'You're lying to me,' I said blandly.

Her eyes widened with surprise, a brief flicker of shame.

'No, I'm not,' she stammered, almost too quickly. Her voice was thin and suspicious, full of guilt and exasperation.

'That's all right, Soraya,' I said. 'I understand. You don't have to tell me anything you don't want to.'

It felt so strange, almost wrong, to say her name. It was the first time either of us had uttered the other's name out loud. Straight away I wished I hadn't. I don't know why but it was almost as if saying her name had ended the lingering tenderness between us, that dreamlike intimacy that had followed our lovemaking.

I offered a smile, hoping that would placate her, but she refused to even look at me. Instead, gathering the bed sheets around her, she sat up, and then, for the first time, flicked on the lights.

I squinted, blinking uncontrollably as my eyes struggled to adjust to this abrupt transition from gloomy to bright. For the first time, I could see the room clearly. Illuminated, it was quite unlike what I had first perceived in shadow, very different from those dim impressions that I had registered while caught amidst the throes of passion. The walls, which I had thought to be stylishly pastel, were merely dull, plastered with peeling wallpaper. Gossamer cobwebs hung in the corners and a thick layer of dust covered every surface. Nearby, a crumpled pile of clothes lay untidily upon a wing chair, behind which two suitcases were propped up against an ancient dresser. Above this tattered chest of drawers, an oval mirror hung. Its smooth polished facade was cracked with a long vertical fracture that ran down its length, a splintered fissure of broken glass. I could see my reflection in its warped face. It seemed strangely distorted, misshapen, almost disfigured as if I was two distinct people, two very different halves that had been juxtaposed into one, the first being smooth and normal, the other broken and scarred.

Other than this funhouse trick of a mirror, the room was devoid of decoration. I frowned. I had expected something very different, something striking and stylish, carefully thought out and charming, like Soraya was. But all that greeted my eyes was a sense of austerity, like a nun's cell in an abbey.

Trying not to let my disappointment show, I watched Soraya cross to the dresser and rummage briefly through her handbag. From its faux leather recesses, she extracted a single Gitanes. Carefully, she broke off the filter tip and threw it aside. Then, she lit the butt eagerly, inhaling the acrid, bitter smoke hungrily before sighing with satisfaction.

After taking two more fervent puffs, she stubbed the cigarette out in a plastic ashtray shaped like a heart and returned to the bed. But instead of snuggling up to me, she sank into one corner of the duvet uneasily. I stretched out to embrace her, but she flinched, brushing away my eager arms. Instead, she pulled even further away, perching precariously at the very edge of the bed like a stork and folding her legs into herself neatly.

'When I was five years old, my mother and my father had this enormous fight one night.'

Her voice was little more than an apprehensive whisper, so low that it was almost inaudible.

'I don't know what it was about exactly. I think Dad had some problem or the other at work and was in a bad mood, but when he came home, the first thing he did was start to shout at my mother.

'I was in my room, fast asleep, but the sound of his angry voice woke me up, and I decided to sneak into my parents' room to see what was wrong.' She shivered, wrapping her arms around herself, before starting to rock gently back and forth. 'I still remember it so well. Dad was raving on and on about how my mother was useless and he should never have married her and how she couldn't even prepare a hot meal for her husband when he returned from a hard day at work. And my mother, well, she just sat there, crying and enduring his abuse silently.'

Her voice cracked and she paused, trying to compose herself. Apologetically, I tried to take her hand, but she snatched it away, frowning irately when she recognised the pity in my eyes.

'Look, you have to understand. My father was a good man. He really loved my mother and me and took good care of us. Ordinarily, he never shouted or screamed and never denied us anything. He always made sure we had everything we wanted or needed.' She winced. 'It was only that day. On that one day, he was not my father, the man I knew and loved. On that day, he was someone else.'

I tried to tell her I understood, but she did not deign to acknowledge this ineffectual gesture at all. Instead, she fought back a tear. If anything, Soraya was even more striking when she was forlorn. Her curls fluttered loosely in the dank breeze that wafted through the open blinds, and her eyes gleamed, bedecked by opaline poignancy.

A flutter of culpability shivered through me for having compelled her to share this most intimate of memories. But, at the same time, an exhilaration clenched in my throat, an almost voyeuristic thrill that made me sit up when she started to speak once again.

'Suddenly, without any warning, as I stood there and watched, my father started to hit my mother. I couldn't believe it. He slapped her once, twice, thrice, and she just stood there whimpering, not even trying to stop him. It was … it was awful.' Her lips quivered, distraught with the dreadfulness of that memory. 'I didn't know what to do. I just stood there, waiting for him to stop. But he didn't. He continued to beat my mother, even when I ran bawling into the room and caught hold of his arm, thinking that would calm him down. Instead, he turned suddenly, blind with rage, and swung out at me, almost without realising it. That was when his wedding ring caught me on the mouth and cut me.'

With those words, she sighed, a long, aching exhalation of breath. I thought, for one tremor of a moment, that she was going to break down completely. But instead, she wrinkled her eyes shut and struggled to compose herself.

'Anyway,' she whispered after a long, nearly unbearable pause, 'that is how I got this scar, okay? Now, are you happy…?'

Pouting, she waited for me to reply, to dispel the unnerving shroud that had settled over the room, but the enormity of her revelation had struck me dumb. I found myself entirely without words, with not an inkling of what to say, how to respond. Instead, I just stared at Soraya awkwardly. Suddenly, I couldn't help but regret having pressed her for the story behind her scar because that was precisely what had spoiled her for me. It was ironic really, as if the very thing that had made her seem so exotic to me just a few hours earlier now made her far too human for me to enjoy. Now, as I looked at her, Soraya was wholly too … too corporeal to abide. In the harsh white neon of the room's lights, she seemed so much more severe and so much more actual. I could see all too plainly the oily pores on her nose and the dark circles that ringed her eyes and the faint frown lines that webbed the corners of her mouth. I could smell the sour stench of her morning breath and see the gunk caking her eyelashes. In a flash, it occurred to me that I did not desire her any longer, just as a man does not yearn for that which he has seen and felt and tasted, for it is human nature to only crave that which is beyond you—that which is untouchable and empyrean.

'I … I'm so sorry,' I whispered gravely after what seemed like an eternity.

'That's okay,' she said, shaking her head wanly. 'You don't have to apologise.' She smiled at me fitfully. 'You want to know what is really strange though…?'

'What…?'

'I've never told anyone the truth about my scar before. You're the first.'

'Really…?' I replied, feigning surprise.

'Yes.'

'Well, madam,' I declared flirtatiously, 'I must warn you, now that I know your most personal secrets, I have a hold over you, and you will be forced to submit to my every whim.'

She laughed, but it was unnervingly empty as if she was just going through the motions to please me. Sitting up, I kissed her gently on her cheek, but she turned and pressed her lips against mine, devouring me almost hungrily. Her mouth was soft and sour and tasted of cigarettes.

Stroking my hair almost possessively with her fingers, she whispered, 'Now I want you to tell me something about yourself.'

'What do you want to know?' I turned on my side to face her, propping my head on my arm.

'Tell me a secret,' she said eagerly. 'Tell me something that nobody else knows.'

'I don't have any secrets,' I murmured evasively. 'My life is an open book.'

When I said those words, I thought I saw her flinch as if I had slapped her. Her smile melted away. In its place, an injured scowl appeared.

'Now who is the one who is lying?' she whispered sadly. Her face darkened with disappointment, and then, in a smooth flurry of linen and skin, she got up from the bed to vanish into the bathroom.

When she emerged ten minutes later, she was fully dressed, in a pair of faded Levi's and an ancient Van Halen tee shirt. Her hair was damp and pinned back with two butterfly clips; her bare face glistened healthy and pink, devoid of any ornament. As I looked at her, I couldn't help but grin because she looked so young like a schoolgirl.

'Where do you think you're off to…?' I inquired flippantly, trying to pretend as if nothing had happened, but Soraya did not reciprocate my facetious joie de vivre.

'I'm going to go out for a while,' she said acidly. 'When I come back, I expect you will have left.'

With that brief declaration, she turned and picked up her handbag, slinging it over her shoulder vehemently.

'Don't be silly, Soraya,' I growled. 'For God's sake, it's five in the morning.'

She did not pay any attention to my objections. Instead, she ignored me completely, pretending as if I did not exist, and picked up her keys before traipsing out of the bedroom in that purposeful manner that was so distinctively hers, with her head bowed forward and her shoulders thrust back, as if she was challenging the world to fight her.

She slammed the door behind her so hard that it jarred against its jamb with a crash and ricocheted halfway open once again. I flinched when I heard this thunderclap of noise.

'Wait,' I shouted after her, 'please, Soraya, don't go.'

The urgency in my voice must have gotten through to her because she paused. Grudgingly, Soraya shuffled back into the bedroom. I patted one of the brocade pillows on the bed and invited her to come and sit by me, but she refused with a dismissive sneer. Instead, she stood by the door and glared at me, her mouth set into a thin line and her arms folded defensively across her chest.

'What is it?' she said, deadpan.

Hesitantly, I began to talk. At first, it felt so unnatural, so difficult. But then, somehow, the more I spoke, the more impossible it became to stop, as if a dam had been breached inside me, and now a relentless deluge of words, a raging torrent of acrimonious memories, came flooding out. I told her everything—about Nana's grandiose beard, and how he decided to shave on the very same day that Mrs Gandhi was assassinated, and how we were sent to the station by Nani to fetch railway tickets, and how, on the way back, we watched that poor Sikh boy being beaten and were much too scared to stop, too frightened to help him.

By the end of it, I felt empty, drained. I looked to Soraya for sympathy, for validation, but she didn't say a word to me. Her face remained stern, swollen by what I assumed to be repulsion.

But then, for the third time that night, she surprised me.

Unexpectedly, she moved towards me. Leaning forward, she engulfed me in her arms, and I realised that it was compassion that scarred her sweet face, not disdain.

Sinking next to me, she cradled my head to her chest.

'It's all right,' she cooed, rocking me back and forth tenderly in a strangely maternal gesture. 'It's okay. I understand.'

'No,' I gulped, 'don't you see…? I'm a coward. A spineless wimp.'

'No,' she whispered sympathetically, 'you aren't.'

She sighed, and the mark on her lip shone like a beacon, a lodestone.

'You just have scars, that's all. We all do,' she murmured and kissed me gently on my brow. 'If we didn't, how else would we have proof that we have lived?'

16

Soraya and me; sadly, we were not destined to last. At first, yes, it was quite wonderful. For those first few months just after we met, we were inseparable, like beginnings are from endings and truths from lies.

We did all the things that couples were supposed to do. We went to watch *Cats* in the West End twice and took a train up to Wembley to catch *Umrao Jaan* in a cinema full of whistling Indians. I allowed her to drag me to a performance of *H.M.S. Pinafore,* and much to my unending astonishment, I absolutely loved it.

Every Saturday night, she cooked me dinner, and I woke early on Sunday so that I could go to a boulangerie in Brompton and get her freshly baked croissants. We ate lunch together every afternoon after class; she convinced me to convert from coffee to tea, and I persuaded her to change from non-vegetarian to vegetarian. We went shopping and Soraya forced me to buy a woollen dressing gown from Selfridges, and I tried to convince her to purchase red silk underwear at Victoria's Secret but she giggled and refused.

It was Soraya who got me to stop drinking. She tricked me into going to AA one day by lying that it was a film club. I was furious at first, but at the same time, intoxicated enough by her that I agreed to quit, if only because it made her smile and say that she loved me.

We took our first weekend trip together to Stratford-upon-Avon, where we visited the bard's birthplace and watched *A Midsummer's Night Dream*. Soraya wept profusely, but I found myself strangely unmoved, just a little disgusted by the hordes of tourists clicking away with their cameras. We went sailing on a Thames River barge, and I bought her a garnet bracelet to celebrate our six-month anniversary. We even adopted a pet together. Soraya wanted a cat while I preferred dogs, so in the end, we settled for a goldfish in a bowl. Predictably, we called it Wanda and it died a week and a half after we bought it, and I was the one stuck with flushing it down the toilet while Soraya cried and cried and cried.

In fact, when I look back, I think that was all Soraya did, cry and fuck me, both, ironically enough, with the same undeniable passion.

It was a passion that I couldn't quite understand—so relentless that it scared me sometimes. Beneath her carefree exterior, it was like there was something broken inside her, a vital cog that made her desperate for love.

As time passed, instead of cooling and subsiding, her hunger for me seemed to grow until it was almost a sickness. She made love to me with an anxiety that grew more and more frantic as if she was trying to consume me whole. And after we were done, she would cling to me like a limpet, holding on so tight that I could barely breathe.

She sought me out two, sometimes three, times a day, interrupting me in class so that we could fuck in the strangest, most unexpected places—the college library, the science lab, on the roof behind an air-conditioning duct, once even in a broom closet. It was desolate, impersonal lovemaking, monotonous, hurried, almost always without the prelude of small talk or foreplay, just me grinding against her as she winced and closed her eyes, shuddering each time I penetrated her.

It was exciting at first, like something from a dirty movie, but then, I don't know why, sleeping with Soraya began to make me feel dirty. I couldn't help but feel she was using me, as if I were little more than an object, a thing, to her. And the more intimate we became, the more I found myself coming to loathe and despise her for the very things that had attracted me to her—the sour milky smell of her skin, the musky taste of her lips and even the way she groaned when I kissed her, as if she were dying a tender little death.

About seven months after we began to see each other, I asked her to move in with me. She said yes, hugging me happily. And then she cried for about twenty minutes before telling me she loved me, but I couldn't bring myself to reciprocate, so I nodded and pretended that I was too choked up with emotion to answer.

Reluctantly, I moved out of Room 47.

It didn't take me as long as I had imagined to pack up my things, less than an hour. When I was done, I found I had barely a bagful of possessions—a small pile of clothes, a few books and CDs and one lone Manchester City baseball cap I didn't remember buying. When I was done bundling these meagre things into a duffel, it was as if no one had ever lived in the room at all. The only sign of occupation was Tariq's ersatz partition through the room, which I left for the next occupant to discover and wonder at its origin.

We found a small apartment, barely larger than a closet, in Battersea, but I couldn't afford anything more expensive. Soraya moved in. It took her almost two weeks. Much to my surprise, she had a lot of things for someone who didn't live in London—tables and duvets and chairs and lamps and a television set and, much to my surprise, a cast-iron bathtub that she installed with great delight in the all-too tiny bathroom.

For a while, it was really good. We painted the flat together, a dull pumpkin orange, and both of us drank too much Chianti and ended up having sex amidst the paint tins, leaving dull imprints of our bodies on the drying wall that we didn't have the heart to scrape off with turpentine. We went shopping in Portobello and bought chintz curtains and an old film poster of *Monty Python's Life of Brian*, and she surprised me on my birthday with a weekend trip to Blackpool, which was the strangest place I have ever seen, a cross between Las Vegas and a cheap Russian carnival.

But it wasn't enough. Much to my surprise, I found that I grew weary of her long before she grew tired of me. After all, I suppose that it is one of the unfortunate side effects of infatuation, isn't it? It always ends inevitably with abhorrence. As the relentless parade of time swept by, all of Soraya's little peccadilloes, those peculiarities that I had found so irresistible in the beginning, started to grate at my nerves one by one. The way she played with her hair constantly and how she always interrupted me when I was trying to read, the fact that she never wore matching socks and that she cracked her knuckles loudly, her queer habit of eating noodles with a spoon and how, in restaurants, rather than ordering an entrée of her own, she would always insist on taking little bird bites from my plate. It wasn't before long that I stopped finding these things endearing. On the contrary, Soraya's eccentricities began to rankle me until I was sick of her.

A couple of months after we moved in together, her parents came to visit.

I hired a Ford Fiesta and went out to Heathrow to meet them, thinking that I would make a good impression, but they disliked me from the moment they set eyes on me. They were extraordinarily typical specimens. Her father was a dour, plump man with a small pencil moustache and hairy, jug-handle ears who scowled at me disapprovingly when Soraya introduced us. Her mother reminded me of Moti, Nani's friend from Amritsar, a plump cliché shaped like a woman with a fixed plastic smile and a penchant for poly-cotton suits.

I think from the moment we met, they could see that I wasn't quite who I pretended to be, that deep inside me, there was a flaw I was trying to hide. I tried to be polite to them, smiling widely in welcome when we were introduced, but they kept looking at me oddly, like I was an interloper, intruding upon their happy little family unit. And then when Soraya revealed that she was living with me, her mother gasped, and her father, the same man who had hit her, I thought angrily, glared at me with open hostility, as if he was convinced that I just wasn't good enough for his only child.

That was, I think, the beginning of the end. That night, I took Soraya and her parents out to dinner. I had a grand evening planned. I had reserved a table at a nice little Italian trattoria in Soho, and I thought we would take them to a play after, but Soraya's father shrugged and shook his head and insisted that we go to an Indian restaurant instead.

We ended up finally at a curry joint in Richmond, one of those awful balti bistros that always made me feel like I had swallowed battery acid. But Soraya's parents loved it—from the cheap pasteboard and gilt décor to the tinny Talat Aziz ghazals playing in the background.

As the evening drew on, it made me sicker and sicker to be around them. I felt dreadfully out of place sitting there at the dinner table with them while they made small talk about places I had never been to and people I did not know. Soraya's parents left me entirely out of the conversation, acting as if I wasn't there at all. Personally, I couldn't help but be a little put out by their behaviour. How silly, I thought, how small-minded to come all the way to England and then end up in an Indian restaurant, eating the very same things they ate every night at home. Worst of all, everything about them was so overtly Indian, from their abrasive accents to their overloud voices. It made me feel awkward, even embarrassed, as the white people seated at the other tables looked at us with a mixture of amusement and curiosity.

People always talk about the moment they fall in love, but so few mention the moment they fall out of love.

For me, it was there, sitting at that table with Soraya and her family as they laughed and chattered away like some absurdly Punjabi caricature of a Norman Rockwell painting. When I watched them together, I found myself thinking, is this what Soraya dreams of? Is this what she imagines when she looks at me, that I will become her father while she slowly turns into her mother, and that we will live a quiet, boring life together, drowning, drowning, under the crushing weight of mundanity until there is nothing left of us but a pair of denuded shadows?

As though she could sense the disjointed discord of my thoughts, Soraya shot me a nervous glance. Smiling uncomfortably, she reached out to place one slim hand upon mine, as if to reassure herself that I was real and not just a man-shaped wraith. Her hand was unbearably cold, as frigid as death, and when she touched me, a sinking feeling crawled down my spine, making me shiver.

That was the precise moment, I think, when I realised that I did not love Soraya. It was then that I understood that we were doomed. She wanted so much, and I knew then that I had nothing left to give, no love, no warmth, nothing but the cold hard ferocity of my loathing.

To my credit though, our relationship lasted until we graduated almost a year later. I just didn't have the heart to end it before that. After all, Soraya was the most beautiful thing in my life, the purest thing, the only real hope I had to treasure, and after being with her, I could not bear the thought of being alone again.

In the end, I finished college with a very well-mannered second, far enough from the bottom of my class to think of myself as a scholar but not anywhere near enough to the top to get a good teaching offer. As for Soraya, well, she managed to get a job at the UN after all. She volunteered for a program to help teach indigent children in Third World countries how to read (so that they could fully appreciate the works of William Shakespeare as they starved to death, I imagine); and that very summer, she left to spend six long months in deepest, darkest Africa, which I think in this case was somewhere in the vicinity of the Sheraton Hotel in Addis Ababa.

We had our first and only fight the evening before her departure.

It was because of a silly enough reason, I confess. We were walking down Tottenham Court Road after an early supper, peeking into shop windows, when we encountered the strangest looking man. Hailing us, he asked for directions to Oxford Circus in broken English. He was Indian, that much I could tell from his accent. Most likely a tourist, I guessed, because he had an old-fashioned Minolta slung around his neck and a green plastic Harrods bag clutched in his hand. Other than that, he was clad in the most outlandish outfit that I had ever seen—a Union Jack striped tracksuit with the slogan 'I ♥ London' emblazoned across the chest.

Soraya tried to point him in the right direction. He listened to her very intently, his dark face glistening with a mixture of concentration and confusion, but it was obvious he couldn't comprehend a word she was saying.

Patiently, she repeated herself, this time enunciating each word carefully, first in Hindi and then in Punjabi. When the tourist heard the latter, he broke into a wide grin. Reaching out, he grabbed Soraya's hand and started to shake it effusively. This profusion of gratitude made her smile. Immediately, she launched into a dialogue with him, striking up a voluble conversation as if they were old friends.

I stood there as the two of them chattered away in Punjabi, growing more and more uncomfortable as they left me out of the conversation entirely, laughing and talking so loudly that a plump English matron wearing a bright pink Chanel jacket shot us a curious glance when she passed by, her eyes wary as if we were criminals.

Leaning forward, I placed one hand on Soraya's shoulder, trying to pry her away from the tourist, but she was enjoying herself too much. With a shrug, she asked me to wait. Crossly, I stuffed my hands back into my pockets and hunched over, trying to seem as unobtrusive as possible, but that only made me feel even more conspicuous and awkward.

As I stood there, waiting for her, I saw something very strange.

Nearby, a grey feathered pigeon landed on the pavement and began to peck at a discarded falafel wrapper noisily. I watched it hop back and forth, but then, unexpectedly, one of its wings got stuck to a lump of chewing gum that someone had spat out on the ground.

The poor bird struggled and squawked, trying to pull itself free, but all that its flailing managed to do was drive the chewing gum further into its own plumage until its back was a clotted, sticky mess and it could barely move its wings.

A moment later, another pigeon landed next to it, a fat white bird who looked over at the grey pigeon questioningly. The harassed grey turned to it and cooed desperately, bobbing its head back and forth in entreaty. In response, as I watched in astonishment, the second bird hopped onto the first one's back and delicately began to peck at the gum, trying to cut him free with its beak.

The hapless grey squawked with pain each time the white's beak pecked at him, but he had no choice. It was his only hope. At first, I thought the white pigeon would succeed in pecking its mate free, but instead, much to my dismay, it ended up becoming entangled as well, its feet adhering to the grey's back inextricably, glued together by the viscous adhesive of chewing gum.

It was tragic and still somehow laughable, the sight of those two birds bonded together as one. Desperately, the grey skittered along with the white on his back, both screeching so piteously that I stepped forward to help. But before I could reach them, the white spread his wings and began to beat them furiously, flapping them as hard as he could. To my disbelief, both the birds rose into the sky, taking flight slowly, a bizarre chimaera with two heads and four wings.

I watched, amazed, as they struggled into the air, but before they could get far, the white's wings gave out. Both birds fell back to the ground, landing in the middle of the road with a despairing caw. Gamely, the white flapped his wings again, even more frantically, trying to take off once more; the grey bobbing along beneath him, but he couldn't do it. No matter how much he tried, he could not break free from the ground, not with the weight of the grey mooring him to the earth.

And then, as he tried one final time, one final leap of faith, a passing lorry hit the birds dead on. With a thump, they ricocheted off the truck's grille, their mangled bodies thrown to the side of the road in a sticky, broken heap.

Sickened by this grisly sight, I averted my eyes.

Once more I tried to get Soraya's attention, but she was much too caught up in her discussion with the tourist and just fobbed me off again.

As I frowned at her, it struck me quite forcibly that we were the pigeons.

I was the grey and she was the white.

Somehow, we had become ensnared together, bound to each other by the chewing gum of despair. But unlike me, Soraya still had a chance to be happy, to find some meaning, some purpose in her life. The only thing standing in her way was me. Try as she might to flap her wings, to fly and break free of the past, I would always drag her down. As long as we were together, she would never be able to find any happiness, only regret.

That realisation made up my mind for me. Grasping her bicep, I pulled her away forcibly, literally wrenching her away from the Indian tourist, who gazed at me in surprise, taken aback by my ferity.

'I need to talk to you,' I snapped and started to drag her down the road roughly. At first, she did not resist, staggering along confusedly, her eyes wide with bewilderment at my churlishness, but then, grimacing, she tried to wrestle her arm free from my grasp.

'Let go of me, Himmat,' she snarled. 'You're hurting me.'

In spite of her objections, I refused to relinquish my grip on her arm, not even when she came juddering to a stop, resisting me with all her strength.

'I … said … stop!' she screeched so loudly that a pair of policemen walking by paused and gave me a dirty look.

Sheepishly, I let go of her. Soraya massaged her arm with a wounded look on her face and snapped, 'What is wrong with you? I was just talking to him.'

'Shut up,' I growled, surprising myself with my own vehemence. 'For once, why won't you just shut up?'

Shocked by this outburst, Soraya flinched, as if I had hit her.

'Why are you acting like this? Why are you being so unkind?'

Her eyes were full of accusation, and I shuddered, unable to meet her gaze. I think I'm going mad, I wanted to say. It's like I don't know who I am any more, like there is someone else inside me, an angry stranger, tearing at my skin, trying to get out. And I cannot stop thinking of that boy, that poor child I saw beaten at the crossroads. I see him everywhere, Soraya, staring at me, like I'm the one who killed him. I see him in you, when you look at me with those reproachful eyes of yours. I see him in me, each time I look in the mirror. No matter how hard I try, I cannot escape him.

'What happened?' she said softly. 'What's wrong?'

'It's nothing.'

'Something's changed,' she said flatly. 'You're being weird.'

The hurt in her voice made me shiver and almost change my mind.

'Come on,' she said, 'let's just forget it, okay? Let's just go home, huh?'

She tried to take my hand, but I recoiled from her, shying away from her touch.

'No,' I said sadly. 'I can't do this any more.'

'What's wrong with you today?' Soraya said, 'Why are you so angry?'

'I'm not angry,' I replied coldly. 'I'm tired, Soraya, of all this. I'm tired of you.'

The candour of this declaration took her by surprise. An expression of poignant disappointment flashed across her face, a look of stiff betrayal so perfect it could have belonged on the face of a master kabuki.

'You,' she hissed, '*you* have the gall to say that you are tired of *me*?'

Her voice was so strident that it made me cringe. For one moment, I thought she was going to claw my eyes out with her fingernails.

'How dare *you*, of all people, say that to me? God, if anyone has the right to be tired, it's me. I'm the one who is sick and tired of you, tired of your bullshit and your endless whining... You want to know what is wrong with you, Himmat.' Soraya's eyes flashed fire, so scathing that I could barely recognise her. 'You like to think you're so special, so smart and well-read and interesting. But the truth is that you're just a scared little boy who is too afraid to stop blaming everyone else for his shortcomings, who is too terrified to drop his guard for one minute and care for someone because it means having to change yourself. And you know what the really sad thing is? You will always be a scared little boy pretending to be a man until you learn to stop treating people like objects that you think you can just use and throw away whenever they are unable to live up to your stupid expectations. You will never be a real man until you stop believing that life isn't solely about you—until you learn to care about someone other than yourself. Until then, all that you will be is a sad, lonely little coward.'

The cold intensity of her words cut at me like the slash of a stiletto. What made it worse was that I knew she was right, that every single word she said, every accusation and every catechism, they were all completely true.

I'm sorry, Soraya, I wanted to say, please understand that I'm not doing this to be cruel. I'm doing this for your own good. I have to let you go. It's for the best because once you are rid of me, you can find someone better, someone who genuinely cares about you and will make you happy.

I should have said all those things, I know. I should have ended it properly, like a good guy. I should have been kinder and gentler, and given her more time, let her cry on my shoulder and consoled her, and told her it was my fault, not hers.

Instead, I turned and walked away.

I left Soraya standing there, all alone amidst the crowded street, without once stopping to look back.

17

I never saw Soraya again.

She left the next morning without even bothering to say goodbye. I found out later that she had been planning to break things off for weeks, long before we had our last spat, that she had been packing her things one by one and moving them out secretively, and I had been far too self-involved to notice her extricating herself from my life, fragment by insignificant fragment.

Three and a half months later, in Djibouti or Rwanda or Zaire or somewhere just as mosquito-infested, she encountered a Scandinavian, Lars or Ulrich or Sven or something equally blonde, and the two of them fell madly in love amidst the hordes of malarial children that they intended to rescue together.

She wrote to me only once, a Dear John postcard with a photo of a dogmatic zebra on its front, to inform me that she was getting married and how she was so very sorry and that I should try to understand that it wasn't my fault but fate that had pried us apart, and that now, finally, she understood what I had meant by destiny.

The same night I received that charming communiqué, I tried to kill myself.

Now, you have to realise that sounds a lot more dramatic than it actually was. When I say I tried to kill myself, I don't mean that I actually wanted to die. No, not at all. In all honesty, a lot of it, I think, was because I was lonely. I missed Soraya. It's hard to explain but the truth is that I hadn't spared her a second thought until I received her letter. But once I had read it, once I knew she had moved on, inexplicably I was stricken by the surety that I had made an immense mistake by letting her go. Strangely, from that moment onwards, the harder I tried to push her from my mind, the more I found myself thinking of her.

Everywhere I turned, I saw reminders of Soraya. There she was, by a parked car where once I had kissed her and fondled her breasts through the thick fabric of her coat, much to her outraged delight; there, on a bench where we had sat for hours and watched pigeons eat bread crumbs while I gently stroked her hair; there, in the shiny show window of a Debenhams where she had stopped to fix her hair and ended up buying a really smutty pair of black stockings; there, besides a Lebanese vendor where she had forced me to try shawarma for the first time and I had been sick for a week with diarrhoea.

Finally, I just couldn't bear this vivid diorama of memories any longer. Stumbling into a Tesco, I bought myself a bottle of Bushmills, a frozen chicken balti meal, a pair of hair clippers and a packet of Wilkinson razor blades, exactly like the ones Nani used to leave lying in ambush for Nana.

Dejected, I returned to my flat, which was too silent without Soraya, too empty without the clutter of her things and the clatter of her voice. Locking the door behind me, I cracked open the whiskey thirstily. In one throat-scalding gasp, I drank down a quarter of the bottle. It didn't take long to take effect. My senses swam and the world seemed to shift, everything going just a little out of focus as the alcohol soaked into my bloodstream.

By the time I finished the bottle, I was good and drunk. Picking up the clippers I had just bought, I tottered into the bathroom and shook my hair loose from my habitual ponytail. Soraya had always loved my hair. She used to oil and comb it for me every Sunday, and there were times when my hair would become knotted with hers when we made love, intertwined, as if we were becoming one person and I could not tell where she ended and I began.

For a long time, I stood poised in front of the bathroom mirror, and then I clicked on the hair clippers and slowly, almost ceremonially, began to shave my head. It was difficult at first. The clippers kept getting tangled in the denseness of my curls, but then, after I picked up a pair of scissors and roughly chopped away the undulating snake of my ponytail, it became much easier.

Angrily, uncaring of the pain as the clipper blades bit at my scalp, I scraped away every follicle, every hair on my head, even my beard, until the sink was overflowing with a mound of dark, lank strands and I was as bald as a newborn.

I had imagined that the act of shaving my head and beard would provide me with some small measure of expiation. I mean, it always worked that way in the movies, didn't it? Unfortunately, this time around, when I was done, I found the catharsis I had expected, even craved, was strangely lacking. I had thought that by shaving my head, I would symbolically be shearing away the past, cutting away Nana, Amritsar and India, hacking away Soraya, but instead, I ended up standing there, glaring at my visage in the mirror with a sense of rising embarrassment. Not only did my head have a funny misshapen angularity that made me look weird, but my scalp was also surprisingly pale, as necrotic as a new corpse.

Still half-drunk, I turned and shuffled back into the bedroom to collapse onto the bed. Much to my dismay, the pillow still smelt of Soraya and her warm musk. For a long time, I lay there, my scalp itching slightly. I found myself unable to stop thinking of her, lost in the aftermath of her scent.

Finally, I couldn't bear it any more. Tottering upright, I fetched the razor blades from the kitchen, where I had left them earlier. Carefully I unwrapped the shiny wrapper of the packet and took out one of the blades. Looking down at it, a shudder ran down my spine. It was difficult to believe that such a tiny, insignificant thing could be so fatal. The metal of the blade was cold in my hands, feather-light. Wickedly it glinted up at me, inviting, almost eager.

As I sat there, for the first time, I think, since we had broken up, it sank in that Soraya was really gone and that she was never coming back. And with her departure, I realised that one entire chapter of my life had come to an end. After all, that was what Soraya had been to me, wasn't it? An entire compendium of firsts. The first woman I had kissed, that I had made love to, shared my secrets with, fought, laughed and wept with. And now that she was gone, my quota of first experiences had been exhausted. Everything I would experience from this point hence, every subsequent relationship, every kiss, every smile, every argument, would all merely be a repetition, a litany of the already seen, the already heard and the already felt.

This realisation made up my mind for me. Taking the blade in my trembling fingers, I drew its narrow edge across the faint blue tracery of veins in my left wrist.

My skin parted like warm butter beneath the razor's hungry bite. The pain was surprisingly insignificant, almost negligible, more a pinch than the agony I had expected. Immediately, a vivid ribbon of red, thick and sticky, welled up from the shallow gash. In a matter of seconds, the blade was slippery with it, hard to grip.

Greeted by the zoetic sight of my own blood, I could not help but groan. For some indescribable reason, as I felt the warm trickle of liquid brim from my wrist and drip slowly down the ridges of my fingertips, a curious sensation of futility gripped me, an inexorable foolishness. I knew then that I could not go through with it—that there was no way I could make another, deeper slash. Nevertheless, I tried my level best to will myself to cut down. Clenching my teeth, I closed my eyes and tried to force my hand to slice the blade across my flesh, but I could not. No matter how many times I attempted it, I was unable to bring myself to press down hard enough to actually rend through my skin, and sever the arteries and cartilage beneath. All that I could manage was three weak, shallow incisions that dribbled mere crescents of blood, not at all that hot gush for which I was so hopeful.

Finally, I gave up. Chucking the blade into the dustbin, I limped back into the bathroom. Turning on the tap, I thrust my arm under a cold torrent of water. Biting my lip as the cuts tingled and oozed, I waited patiently until the bleeding ceased. Then, after binding my arm with a napkin, I took a wet rag and cleaned up the diffuse flurry of blood that had speckled the white porcelain of the sink.

When that was done, I returned to the bedroom and changed my dank and bloody bed sheets and put on a clean white shirt with long sleeves, starched and fresh from the laundry. What exactly happened after that I barely remember, except that I decided to go out and get good and hammered. I vaguely recall ending up in a bar in Charing Cross surrounded by a bunch of jubilant Arsenal fans drinking pint after pint of Grolsch. I also remember crying in a men's room and telling a fat, rather dumpy Greek girl who came over to flirt with me that she reminded me of my mother. I remember her slapping me, and vomiting all over someone's suede loafers, but other than those scattered details, the rest of that night is still a blur.

In either case, by midnight I had more than succeeded in achieving what I had set out to do. When the bar finally shut shop, thanks to a dozen pints of lager, Soraya's memory had started to dim in my mind, grow hazy and distant once again.

For some incomprehensible reason, I decided to walk home. However, I had barely made it halfway down Coventry Street when I spied the familiar red circle that marked the entrance to the Underground and decided to take the Tube instead.

Tottering unsteadily down an endless flight of steps, I bought a ticket from a machine and made my way to the platform. It was quite deserted, except for a pair of sleeping vagrants and a lonely wino who raised his brown-bagged bottle in a mock toast when he saw me, in appreciation of what he obviously recognised to be a kindred spirit. In one filthy corner, a solitary busker stood, playing 'Brazil' on his rusty saxophone. As I lurched past him, he looked up and nodded. I stopped and tossed a couple of coins into the battered trilby lying on the pavement in front of him. He did not pause to thank me. Instead, he continued to play his glum tune. Listlessly, each note echoed through the closed confines of the Underground, melancholy and elegiac, like the smell of scorched plastic.

I found an empty bench and settled down with a groan to wait for the next westbound. I think I must have dozed off for a while, because when I woke up, the busker with the sax was gone. Instead, his corner was now occupied by a trio of Asian teenagers—a husky young Muslim boy wearing a skull cap flanked by two girls, one who was wearing a green hijab and the other a blood-red churidar. The boy was singing a Hindi song I didn't recognise—something dreadful that was all grunts and pelvic thrusts and exclamations—while the girls danced around him, enacting a medley of carefully choreographed steps.

Yawning, I sat up. My head felt ripe and heavy, and my mouth tasted damp and rotten as if I had been chewing on sawdust. After stretching my back for a moment, I glanced at my watch impatiently. Almost half an hour had passed. Standing up, I crossed to the edge of the platform and craned my neck, staring into the dark mouth of the tunnel, but there was no sight of the train, not a glimmer.

Returning to the bench, I slumped back down with a sigh.

That was when it happened.

Behind me, the boy fell silent. Then, one of the girls stepped forward and began to sing with a wavering, reedy voice.

Much to my surprise, it was a song I recognised, the same tearful lament my Nani had sung all those years ago outside the police station in Amritsar.

Doli chardiyan mariyan Heer cheekan
Mainu lai chale babala lai chale ve
Ve mainu rakh lai babala Heer aakhe aiy
Doli kat kahar ni lai chale ve
Mera akhiya kadi na moda sahin

O din babul kithe gaye chale ve
Tera chatar chavanen rukh vang
Asi vang musafiran bai chale

As Heer sat in the palanquin, she wept
They are taking me away from you
Please keep me, don't let me go,
The bearers have me at their shoulders
You never said no to me, not ever
Where have those days gone?
I always enjoyed your love and protection
But now I am alone, a wanderer.

When I heard that familiar melody after all these years, a fervent pang of nostalgia assailed me. Unexpectedly, much of the pain I had repressed over the years, the horror of all that I had witnessed in 1984, came flooding back to the surface. It was almost too much to bear, so many half-forgotten engrams being resurrected, growing and deepening, from regret to sorrow to despair and then finally a melancholy so absolute that it made me want to scream.

And with it came a most unexpected realisation.

Soraya had been right about me.

I was scared.

Too scared to stop hating.

Too scared to change.

Most of all, I was too scared to forget.

18

After I graduated, my parents wanted me to come back to Bombay and surrender to the Indian middle-class dream, you know the cliché, find-a-nice girl-get-married-settle-down-hum-do-humare-do, all in one breath.

But I decided that I wanted to stay on in London, even though I knew I was disappointing them terribly. I told them I needed time to think. It wasn't so much that I was unsure about what I wanted from my life as much as the fact that I couldn't endure the thought of resuming the life I had left behind. Not that it wasn't a good life. My parents were decent, honest and hard-working people, and they had given me a good childhood, lacking no comfort or opportunity. And now they were offering me a simple, hard-working, nine-to-five life just like theirs.

That was the real reason I felt compelled to refuse. I couldn't bear the thought of returning to Bombay and surrendering to the fate that awaited me—that quotidian entropy of working the same job and going to the same club and meeting the same people every day until slowly I turned into my parents.

London had changed me far too much. In the few short years that I had spent there, I had become a true émigré, an immigrant not of body but of soul, of spirit and of self.

The truth was that I had stopped thinking of myself as an Indian. I can't explain it. It sounds insane, I know, to stop being what you are, but that was precisely what I had grown to love about London. It was a no man's land, where a man could reinvent himself, where he could become anyone he chooses to be, like a changeling, a protean searching for a form.

That was what I wanted more than anything else, a clean slate, a new beginning. I found myself a job painting houses for a city contractor who wasn't picky about work permits. It was exhausting blue-collar work, toiling away in the sun, and the wages were lousy, but I liked it because it was uncomplicated and I didn't have to think much while mixing paint or washing brushes or making cup after cup of over-sweetened tea.

Unfortunately, I was forced to give up the Battersea flat and move instead into something more fitting to my reduced financial circumstances. My new home was a rented one-bedroom in Camden, just a stone's throw away from King's Cross. It was a grimy, decrepit building filled with Turkish and African immigrants, and I told my landlord, an ancient Russian named Pavlov with teeth that were black from smoking cheap tobacco, that I was Lebanese and that I was trying to write a novel.

Much to my surprise, he believed me without offering a word of argument.

Curiously, I found that it wasn't particularly difficult to pretend to be Lebanese, actually a lot easier than being Indian. I watched *Lawrence of Arabia* at a seedy theatre in Holborn and began to try and speak with a trace of an accent like Alec Guinness playing Prince Faisal, stretching my r's a little until I sounded like an Irishman having a seizure, but everyone I met assumed that was how people from Lebanon talked. I took to buying a lot of hummus and couscous from this little bakery on Euston Road and handed it around to my acquaintances at work, telling them that I had cooked it especially for them, and they loved it, thanking me profusely and praising me when I told them it was my grandmother's secret recipe.

Strangely enough, I found that pretending to be Lebanese somehow made me more exotic to women, and it wasn't long before I found a new girlfriend for myself, a plump sour-faced Hungarian girl named Andrea, who was convinced that I was from Beirut and had been forced to leave during the troubles in the 1980s.

I liked Andrea. She wasn't pretty, on the heavy side with a big nose and uneven teeth, but there was a warmth about her that was almost maternal, a kindness that I found comforting. She treated me like I was a slightly unkempt pet, showing up once or twice a week with bowls of goulash, which she would feed me with great delight, and then let me make tepid love to her while going on and on about her job in the city, which she hated. She talked a lot, but I quickly became adept at pretending to listen because that was all that she really wanted, a willing audience for her complaints. In exchange, she took really good care of me, cleaning and sewing buttons on my shirts and cooking and cleaning for me, as if I was a child unable to fend for myself.

I did start work on a book, describing the things that I had seen in Punjab during 1984, but it quickly dissolved into one long pathetic adolescent whine, and I gave up after a measly forty-six pages.

Instead, I took to spending most of my free time on the Tube, riding back and forth on the trains all night after my shift finished at eight. The trains in London were not at all like the trains in Bombay. Taking a local train in India was a terrifying experience—a slow immersion into a sea of people until you were drowning in an ocean of noise and smell. But in London, crowded though the Tube was, there was something marvellously sterile about riding the trains, an isolation that appealed to me immensely. I found that there was no better place for me to lose myself.

On the Underground, I found myself in a strange new world, a London of the night when oddities emerged and strangenesses flowered.

In Soho, I ended up in the dirtiest, dingiest cabaret in England, where a peroxide blond burlesque performer who looked exactly like Barbara Windsor made love to a very bored python.

In Shoreditch, I found England's last carnival sideshow and saw a two-headed woman who kissed herself and winked at me, all at the same time.

In Covent Garden, I sampled absinthe for the first and last time and was nearly seduced by a very beautiful girl who was actually a very large Russian man in drag.

In Shepherd's Bush, I was befriended by a Nigerian dope dealer who taught me how to make crêpe Suzette and sold me a bag of psychedelic marijuana, which made me howl at the moon like a wolf when I smoked it.

In Clapham, I ended up amidst a celebration for Guy Fawkes and burnt off my eyebrows when a firecracker burst in my hand.

In Bolton, I took part in a bare-knuckle boxing match, and for a £200 purse, went three rounds with a fat Polish accountant who apologised profusely each time he punched me in the gut.

In Hackney, I got mugged by a very angry nine-year-old in an Aston Villa football jersey three sizes too big for him, who stole my watch and my trainers at knifepoint and left me to walk home barefoot.

In Camden, I climbed a fence and broke into Highgate Cemetery just before dawn, where I found Karl Marx's grave and placed a bouquet of calla lilies next to his frowning headstone.

At the South Bank Book Market, on a table piled high with yellowing books with cracked spines, I found seven copies of Nana's poetry, which I bought for forty pence apiece and then burned them later, making a merry little bonfire.

In Brixton, I went to an all-night rave and danced until I could not move, losing myself in a faceless, heaving sea of people, a giant amoeba of restless humanity, with a hundred shuffling feet and a thousand waving arms.

In Culford Road, I sat in a madhouse of a bar and listened to a bunch of awful poets rattle on about the state of the world at five in the morning until their words blurred into meaningless sound and I found that I couldn't understand what they were saying any more, as if language had ceased to exist.

In Spitalfields, I saw a ghost, a little Huguenot girl with flaxen hair, who laughed at me and clapped her hands when she saw my dismay.

I went mudlarking along the Thames riverbank and found a human hand, greying and rotten, lying in the mud like a gory piece of garbage.

In the drains below the city, I went potholing with a pack of urban spelunkers, and in Walthamstow, I lost a week's wages betting on a dogmatic looking greyhound named Punjab.

In Smithfield, I ate breakfast with the meatpackers, and in Vauxhall, I went roller skating at the last roller-disco rink in the world.

That became my world, the twilit, seamy shadow of the city when the normal was eclipsed by the liminal. And I revelled in it. I drank until I vomited and went in to work high as a kite, until it seemed to me that everything, reality, myself and the people around me, were moving in slow motion.

And then one night, as I came out of King's Cross, they arrested me.

I found a pair of blue-uniformed constables waiting at the end of the platform, near the ticket turnstile, where the escalators led up to ground level.

One of them, a tall ginger-haired sergeant, started visibly when he saw me. He nudged his compatriot in the ribs, and they steered forward to obstruct my path.

'Excuse me,' Ginger said courteously, with just a hint of very British menace in his voice, 'could you hold up for just a minute?'

From his vest, he pulled out a photograph, which he held up next to my face as if to verify my identity, before turning and giving his comrade a nod.

'It's him,' he said. 'He's shaved his head, he has, but it's him all right.'

'Excuse me,' I started to object, 'is there a problem?'

The second policeman, a plump Samoan or Fijian, I couldn't be sure, smiled benignly and clamped one callused hand around my arm.

'Come with us, please,' he said, over pronouncing each word carefully as if he thought I was a little child who didn't quite understand English.

It was all very, very civilised. Before I could react, the Samoan steered me along effortlessly, almost tugging me off my feet as if I weighed nothing at all. Together, he and Ginger marched me through the crowded station, smiling politely at the gaggle of bystanders who paused to watch us, looking and pointing at me curiously.

They escorted me briskly to a detention room on the second floor, a small windowless cell with a thick metal door.

Ginger punched a six-digit code into the door's electronic lock. It slid open with a cold hiss and he ushered me through. Inside, I was greeted by a glare of over-bright fluorescent lighting and cement walls painted in a dull institutional taupe. The only visible decoration was a framed portrait of Margaret Thatcher staring down at me disapprovingly from one wall.

Beneath Mrs Thatcher's glowering visage, I saw a metal table and two steel chairs, all bolted securely to the ground.

The Samoan pointed at one of these chairs, directing me towards it firmly.

'Sit yourself down,' he said.

Dazed, I obeyed and sank onto the hard seat of the chair, wincing because it was as cold as ice.

'Wait here,' Ginger said. 'Someone will be along to speak to you shortly.'

Then, before I could voice any protests, he seized my arm and shackled me to the table with a pair of grey plastic handcuffs, one manacle of which he clamped around my wrist and the other around the metal table leg with a curt snap.

'What do you think you're doing?' I exclaimed, trying to snatch away my wrist, but it was chained much too securely for me to move more than a few inches.

'Don't you worry,' Ginger said with a smile. 'We'll have this all cleared up in a jiffy, we will.'

With that, the two policemen turned and exited through the door, locking it securely behind them with a soft, almost final click.

I looked around me, trying to fight the unease rising inside my chest. It didn't make any sense. Why had they detained me? I hadn't done anything wrong. Maybe it was a mistake. Maybe they had mistaken me for someone else.

I noticed that there was a security camera, a cyclopean eye directly above the door, tracking my every movement. Half-raising my unshackled hand, I gave it a wave, wondering who was on the other side watching me and if they could hear me.

'Why am I here? What the hell is going on?'

There was no reply. I tried to get up, but my hand was so firmly cuffed that I found I could barely move. Angrily, I started to pound on the metal tabletop as hard as I could.

'Let me out,' I shouted. 'Do you hear me? Let me out of here now.'

I kept shouting, as loud as I could, until my throat was hoarse, but there was no response. Finally, I unlaced one of my Doc Martens and threw it at the camera. It missed, ricocheting off the wall with a thump. Shaking my head, I took off the other shoe and took careful aim this time before chucking it. To my satisfaction, it hit the camera squarely on its lens, knocking it awry with a thud that made me whoop triumphantly.

A few minutes passed and then Ginger finally opened the door. Scowling, he came in and fixed the camera, reaching up to turn it on its gimbal till it was pointed straight in my direction once more.

When he was done, he turned to me with a stern scowl.

'You had better behave, boy, or I will have to get unpleasant with you.'

With that warning, he left, taking my shoes with him.

I don't know how long I was made to wait in that awful featureless cage of a room, sitting barefoot and handcuffed to that cold table, but it felt like hours. After the first few minutes, time seemed to slow almost to a standstill, each tick of my watch becoming interminable, until every breath, every blink and every heartbeat seemed to last an eternity.

Finally, just when I was certain I couldn't take it any more, a policewoman, a pretty green-eyed girl in a carefully ironed uniform, opened the door and plonked a chipped white mug of lukewarm tea down on the table in front of me.

I tried to ask her what was the problem, why I was being held, but she merely replied that I should wait, that someone senior would come by shortly.

Another couple of hours passed before a plain-clothes detective finally came in to talk to me. He looked like he had stepped straight out of an episode of *The Bill*— a stocky middle-aged ex-prop, by the look of him, a little over fifty, dressed in a crumpled Argyll suit that had seen better days. He didn't introduce himself, so I decided to call him Sid because that's who he looked like, Sidney James from the old *Carry On* films, with that same balding head and wrinkled, big-nosed face.

Pulling out the other chair, he sat down opposite me. I waited for him to speak, but he didn't say a word. Instead, he sat there, leaning back and looking at me with a satisfied smirk on his face, as if he knew something that I didn't.

It became a contest, each of us waiting for the other to speak first. I was determined that it would be him. I glowered at him, gritting my teeth impatiently, but it didn't faze Sid one bit. He just sat there, watching me patiently.

'Why am I here?' I said at last. 'What gives you the right to hold me like this? I'm an Indian citizen. I insist you let me call the embassy.'

Ignoring my carping, Sid said, 'Did you know, Mr Singh, that London has the most surveillance cameras in the world? Orwell was right, it seems. Big Brother is always watching, at every street corner, every railway station, every traffic intersection. We have over four million cameras watching your every move—when you shit or cry and laugh; when you eat and dance and copulate. If there is one thing you can be sure of, it is that someone is watching you all the time, son, and it sure as sod is not the Holy Ghost.'

Behind him, the door slid open noiselessly and the Samoan policeman came back in. He was carrying another mug of tea and a red plastic folder, which he handed over to Sid before retreating.

Flicking it open, one by one, Sid spread out an array of grainy photographs across the metal table in a neat row.

'You should know,' he said, 'we have been keeping an eye on you for a while.'

Biting my lip, I studied that panoply of pictures, trying not to let my emotions betray me. They were all snapshots of me going about my life, oblivious to the fact that I was being photographed. There was one of me at work, wearing paint-splattered overalls, and another one of me stepping off a train drinking a cup of coffee. There was one of me entering the National Gallery and one of me outside my flat. There were dozens of them, so many that I shivered, suddenly nauseous.

'What … what is all this? You have no right to invade my privacy!'

Sid's smile wavered and then melted away, replaced by a scowl.

'Why do you go about telling people you're Lebanese when you have an Indian passport?'

'I … I don't understand.'

'And why are you working as a painter when you have a master's degree?' he asked next, a little louder, more forceful.

'Excuse me?' I said, perplexed.

Sid shook his head and clucked his tongue at me, mistaking my confusion for obtuseness, and placed one last photograph on the table.

It was a close-up of Sikhboy, taken, I guessed, while he was being arrested. His mouth was open mid-shout and his eyes wide with terror as a pair of black-masked soldiers hauled him bodily towards an unmarked panel van.

'It's no use denying it,' Sid said. His voice was taut with careful menace. 'If you and your friends are up to something, it would be best if you spill the beans right now.'

When he said that, it dawned on me what this was all about.

'Wait a minute! You … you think that I'm a terrorist, don't you? That I'm riding the Underground looking for targets?'

Just articulating that notion, it was too funny.

'That's the stupidest thing I have ever heard.' Doubling over, I burst into laughter. I couldn't help myself. It was like something from Kafka come to life.

Sid remained unamused, though. Very purposefully, he gathered all the photographs up and put them back into the folder. Then, taking a keyring from his pocket, he reached out and unlocked my hand.

Pursing his lips, he pushed the mug of tea towards me, an almost paternal gesture.

'If you aren't planning some sort of attack, then why do you ride the trains all hours of the night, eh, lad? What exactly is it that you are looking for?'

'That's none of your fucking business,' I snapped, massaging my wrist.

Rather than being put out by my rudeness, Sid gave me a kindly smile and whispered, 'Go on, son, let it out. You can trust me.'

The empathy in his voice made me pause. I don't know what it was that made me feel like he was telling the truth, that I could talk to him. He had an honest face and he seemed to care. There was something about him that almost reminded me of Nana, the laugh lines around his mouth and the deep wrinkles furrowing his forehead. It made me feel safe with him, so comfortable that suddenly, even before I knew it, I was pouring my heart out.

I told him the whole story, beginning with my grandfather and all that I had seen in Punjab as a boy. I told him about Tariq and Sikhboy and the Sons of Khalistan. I told him about Soraya and my attempt to kill myself. Why, I even told him how I was scared to go back to India, ashamed of what I had become.

All through this diatribe, Sid listened solemnly, his face emotionless as if he was made of wax.

When I was done, I fell silent. Uncomfortably, I waited for him to respond, to say something in consolation, but Sid just gazed at me stiffly, his eyes brimming with pity. Without a word, he rose and knocked on the door, a short, sharp rap with his knuckles, to which Ginger responded immediately. The two of them talked in a muted whisper for a minute or two, after which Sid came and sat back down in front of me.

'You can leave now,' he announced. 'We won't keep you here any longer.'

Behind him, the door opened and both Ginger and the Samoan came in. Ginger handed Sid a sheet of paper from his folder, which he signed before passing it over to me.

'These are your release orders. I will have my men escort you back to your flat. And on behalf of the Metropolitan Police, you have my most fulsome apologies.'

The Samoan stepped forward and offered me my Doc Martens. Taking them, I slipped them on, not sure whether to feel relieved or outraged.

While I was doing up the laces, Sid watched me thoughtfully, his face pensive, as though he was struggling to make a decision. When I was ready, I gathered up my backpack, but before I could make an exit, he stepped forward to obstruct my way.

'Can I give you an ounce of advice, son?' he murmured, placing one gentle hand on my shoulder, a very paternal gesture.

'Sure,' I said, taken aback by his unexpected intimacy. 'Why not?'

'Go home, where you belong. Go home, and forgive the old man.'

19

A fortnight later, my mother telephoned to tell me that Nana was dying.

She informed me that my grandfather had suffered another far more serious heart attack. This time, unfortunately, some complications did not allow a bypass, and the doctors had said that he did not have much time left.

'He wants to see you, Himmat,' she told me. 'You need to come back immediately.'

I have little or no recollection of the sequence of events after that telephone call. In my mind, it has all melted into an indistinct haze as if I was travelling on autopilot. I don't remember booking a ticket. I don't recall packing my clothes, calling a taxi or even locking the door of my flat when I left. All I can remember is arriving at Heathrow only to be told that my flight had been delayed because of heavy ground fog.

After I had checked in, I purchased a tepid cup of airport coffee and settled in for a dull wait. The lounge was quite crowded. I guessed that a number of flights must have been delayed, that a whole host of travellers had been doomed to endure the same fate as me. Outside, a bitter sleet fell, hissing on the tarmac like wet smoke. I remember reading once that time seems to pass more slowly when you're in a hurry. As I sat there in an uncomfortable plastic bucket chair, waiting for my flight to depart, it felt as if each second was stopping and glaring at me and having a laugh at my expense before finally ticking by.

An hour went by, then two. Finally, I was so bored out of my mind that I decided to go for a walk. For a while, I lurked around the duty-free shops, leching at a pair of attractive teenagers wearing tiny white tennis shorts and identical Bebe tee shirts. One of them had pink braces on her teeth and matching pink-tipped pigtails. For some reason, when she laughed, she reminded me so much of Soraya. She had the same proud neck, the same challenging intonation to her smile and the same tragedy in her eyes. When she saw me watching her, she giggled and stuck out her tongue at me. Suddenly, I felt like such a dirty old man.

Shamefaced, I turned and hurried away, making a beeline to a nearby WHSmith. I spent about twenty minutes browsing desultorily through the books at half-off. Much to my surprise, while I was leafing through a stack of old Graham Greene paperbacks, I found a slim volume of poetry half-hidden behind one of them, with my grandfather's face staring out at me mournfully from its back cover.

In a daze, I opened it to a page at random. It read:

There was a time when the wind used to sing to me.
But now, there are not enough words in the world
That can drown out the crack of a bullet,
Not enough adjectives
To silence the roar of the tanks.
There is no poetry left in Punjab
The stones are silent, the rivers have sunk
All that remains is the sound of screams
Of mothers crying for their sons

And the cackle of the demagogues
Who cry for more, always more
More hatred
More blood
I have become a refugee in my own home
A shadow that once had skin
Now, nothing remains of my history
But the memory of pain.

As I folded the book shut, delicately, almost reverently, my eyes fell across the dedication on the very first page.

It read, 'For my grandson Himmat, who has the heart of a lion.'

Much to my shame, I realised that at some point, I had begun to cry. I tried to wipe away my tears with the back of my hand, but that only made it worse.

I cannot find the words to describe how impossibly good it felt to cry. For the first time since 1984, I think, I broke down completely. A hot surge of sorrow brimmed from my eyes, an indignant inundation of shame and self-loathing. Like an overgrown child, I stood there in front of Section D through H, and I wept. I wept for Punjab and for my poor dead grandmother. I wept for Rat and OPS and for those poor boys who had tried to steal our car and been gunned down by the police. I wept for Soraya, for Tariq and for my Nani. But most of all, I wept for myself, for my lost innocence and for all the time that I had wasted hating, so much of my life squandered, lost forever.

I don't quite know how long I stood there, tears coursing down my cheeks, until the attendant who ran the shop, a slender bespectacled fellow, approached me warily as if I was a madman.

'Are you okay?' he asked, offering me a tissue from a box.

'I'm fine,' I replied.

'Grand! In that case, could you please leave? You're scaring the other customers.'

'Sure,' I said. I offered the book back to him, only to realise that my tears had left the pages spotted with dank patches.

'I'm sorry,' I apologised, 'I'll pay for it.'

'No worries,' he said, obviously eager to get rid of me. 'Just keep it. Nobody reads poetry any more anyway. It just doesn't sell.'

Another two, maybe three, hours drifted by before my flight was finally ready to depart.

Once we were in the air, I cadged a couple of tiny bottles of vodka off the stewardess and gulped them down hungrily. Then, reclining back, I closed my eyes.

As I dozed, a fitful slumber, I had the same familiar nightmare once again.

I was running, dashing along as fast as I could, with my heart pounding in my mouth. At first, I couldn't tell if I was chasing someone or the one being chased, but then I saw him, the wraith from my childhood, the dream boy, fleeing in the near distance, racing away, always away.

'Stop,' I wailed. 'Please, I beg you, stop.'

When he heard those words, much to my surprise, instead of disappearing like he always did, this time he slowed down. When I caught up with him, with an awful teeth-jarring creak, he turned to face me.

For the first time, I could see his face and I gasped, stunned.

It was me.

I was the boy in the dream.

I was the one who was running away.

As that realisation dawned upon me, I sat up. In spite of the frigid air percolating through the aeroplane cabin, I was soaked with sweat. Next to me, my neighbour, a plump Punjabi matron wearing too much make-up, was watching me, her corpulent face taut with a mixture of curiosity and disdain. Ruefully, I tried to apologise, but rather than engaging with me, she rose silently and moved to an empty seat two rows ahead.

I spent the rest of the flight shifting about uncomfortably, unable to go back to sleep. After what seemed like a lifetime had elapsed, the captain's tinny voice finally announced that we were about to land in New Delhi. When they allowed us to disembark, I was amongst the first people off the plane, shoving and jostling, as I made my way down the narrow, crowded aisle after pulling my duffel from the overhead compartment. I then spent an hour battling through customs and another forty minutes sweltering in the long queue at the immigration counter, sandwiched between a very chatty old auntyji and a short, fat man with a mullet, who I guessed was from Canada since he was wearing an oversized Toronto Maple Leafs hockey jersey.

When my turn finally came, an impeccably dressed Sikh with a carefully tied turban and a beard gleaming golden with pomade greeted me with a hospitable smile that made me dislike him immensely.

'Welcome to India,' he said. 'Might I ask, my good friend, what is the nature of your visit?'

'Family,' I said dully, refusing to elaborate, but I guess it wasn't necessary because he gave me a nod, as though to say that he understood perfectly.

'Of course! Welcome home,' he said and stamped my passport with a thump that made me wince.

Home, I thought wryly. After all the time I'd spent in England, I had imagined that I had changed in some essential way and stopped thinking of myself as Indian. But now, as the immigration sardarji smiled and handed me back my passport, I realised that deep down some small part of me was glad to be back.

Sadly, this sense of homecoming did not last. It was replaced very quickly by a glimmering of panic, a foreboding so palpable that the faded scar on the bridge of my nose began to tingle with trepidation.

I was sure that, thanks to the interminable delays, I must have missed my connecting flight to Amritsar. Actually, in a way, I was hoping that I would miss it, and somehow fate would conspire to rescue me from having to meet Nana, because the thought of coming face to face with him, after all these years, made me feel quite nauseous.

As it turned out, the connection was running an hour late. The plane, an ageing Dornier that was older than I was, had just landed and was in the process of being refuelled. While I waited for them to begin boarding, I found a payphone and called my mother.

Her voice was tired, cracking and hissing with fatigue, but somehow, she still managed to sound disapproving.

'Where are you?' she asked brusquely, without bothering with any pleasantries.

'In Delhi. I just got here.'

'When will you be in Amritsar?'

I sighed. 'I don't know, Mummy Ji,' I said. 'I'm tired. I'm thinking I'll just check into a hotel for the night and take a flight tomorrow morning.'

'Why must you be so selfish?' she snapped, without a hint of sympathy. 'Your grandfather doesn't have very long left, and he wants to see you before … before…'

Abruptly, her voice tapered off into silence, as if the connection had been cut off.

I groaned. What if I don't want to see him? I wanted to shout. Don't I have a choice here? Why does it always have to be about Nana and what he wants? Don't you realise what he did to me? Don't you realise what a liar and coward he is?

But somehow, I couldn't bring myself to say any of those things, not across the sterile barrier of a telephone.

Instead, in a cold dead voice, I whispered.

'I'll be there in a few hours.'

'Let's hope it's not too late,' she said and then cut me off.

I slammed down the phone so hard that its plastic casing cracked in my hands. Angrily, I wandered around the airport until I found a liquor store. Contemplating the racks of duty-free scotch, my stomach cramped with need, suddenly desperate for the unsubtle placation of another drink.

It took all my self-control to not buy a bottle and crack it open and gulp it down right there.

Thankfully, before I could give in to this impulse, a voice blared that the flight to Amritsar was finally ready to leave.

The plane was almost empty, just a scattering of Sikhs on their way to pay homage, I guessed. Thankfully, none of them spared me a second glance or tried to chat with me, and I found a seat near the back and passed out, exhausted by jet lag, already snoring as the plane lifted off the ground. I only woke when it banked on its final approach to Amritsar airport. With a yawn, I stretched and leaned forward to peer out of the oval window. For an instant, the clouds of smog parted, and I could see almost the whole city beneath me, laid out like ink on parchment. From up in the air, the buildings seemed so small, so neat, as if they were a diorama manufactured from a child's building blocks, not real structures of stone and steel.

In the distance, I thought I saw the golden gleam of the Harmandir Sahib, flickering as it caught the dying light of the evening, flaring incandescent like an ember. This sight should have made me smile, but instead, all I felt was anxiety.

A few moments later, the undercarriage touched down on the concrete with a bone-jarring thump. The aircraft lumbered towards the terminal. Immediately, all the passengers unbuckled their belts and scrambled to get their luggage out of the overhead compartments. This time, I stayed put, waiting until the plane emptied. It was only when the stewardess came and asked me if something was wrong that I reluctantly rose from my seat and made my way down the steps to the shuttle bus that would take me to the terminal.

In a mere matter of minutes, I was drenched with sweat. It had been bad in Delhi, but here the humidity was unbearable, almost hellish after England's frigid charm. I winced, my trepidation returning twofold.

The new arrivals terminal was brand new, sterile and surprisingly clean for India with no spit stains on the walls and no garbage mouldering in the corners. It was only temporary, I thought. It would only be a matter of time before all that changed and the spotless white floors became grimy with dirt, the dustbins began to overflow and the whole place started to stink of old piss and sweat. That was the one thing you could always be certain of. No matter how noble the intentions, in the end, India always won.

My apprehension only magnified the closer I drew to the exit. I had to physically force myself to leave the airport, and exert every ounce of my will, to keep my feet moving. Outside, it felt difficult to breathe. Despairingly, I decided to take a taxi and go straight to the hospital. Somehow, I could not bear the idea of going back to my uncle's sprawling house on Ranjit Avenue and having to confront my entire extended family, and being compelled to endure their persistently inquisitive inquiries, an endless flurry of questions about what had become of Soraya and if I had found a well-paying job and what my plans for the future were and when was I planning to settle down and get married?

It took me a long time to find a cab willing to chauffeur me to the hospital. Finally, after being refused by half a dozen indolent drivers napping in their vehicles, a tall, gaunt-faced Sikh with a silken white beard that reached almost to his waist agreed to take me. He was even more ancient than Nana, with narrow shoulders and a thin stork neck, dressed simply in an old-fashioned white uniform and a blue turban, his face so deeply lined that he seemed as wrinkled as a raisin. As for his car, it was older still, another ancient Ambassador, most of its white paint eaten away by rusty red spots, the once shiny leather interior now mottled and cracked. I settled into the capacious back seat, holding my duffel bag close to me as if it was a shield, and waited for the driver to start the car. But he remained immobile. Instead, he turned to look at me over his shoulder. His face was confused.

'Come on,' I said impatiently, 'let's get going.'

'No baggage, sahib,' he said curiously.

I could not help but smirk, amused by this inquiry.

'Oh, don't you worry,' I replied. 'There's plenty of baggage.'

Sadly, he failed to get the joke. Muttering to himself, he shook his head as if he thought I was nuts. Wrinkling his eyes shut, he offered a prayer to the automobile gods and then turned the key in the ignition. The car's engine coughed thrice and then hesitantly groaned to life, sputtering wearily.

With a massive smile, the driver gave me a thumbs up and disengaged the handbrake. The car wheezed into motion, picking up speed slowly even though he insisted on stamping down on the accelerator with all his weight, revving the ancient engine until it sounded like a hairdryer about to overheat.

By the time we got out of the airport and headed southwards towards the city, we were careening along at an even sixty miles an hour straight down an eight-lane highway. I was flung around in the backseat, holding on for dear life each time the car's antique suspension tackled a speed bump.

'Could you slow down please?' I asked worriedly.

In reply, the driver laughed and shook his head. 'This is the age of the fast, sahib. If you slow down, you will be left behind.'

Regardless of my request, he insisted on clattering along at the same breakneck speed, at least till we reached the outskirts of the city. Then the traffic forced him to slow down, which he did reluctantly, shaking a fist at each passing car, cursing and honking volubly.

The hospital was in the new part of Amritsar, quite far from the old city, bang amidst what had once been fertile farmland but was now a maze of concrete and steel. I sat back, gazing solemnly out of the taxi window at the panorama of half-familiar sights that flickered by. How strange it felt to be back here! It felt like just yesterday that I had driven down this very highway to buy tickets at the railway station with Nana. Back then, I had been so full of eagerness and ambition and optimism, but now … I just felt old, exhausted and somehow broken.

There were no roadblocks now, just an endless line of cars moving along inches at a time, so shiny and new that they seemed like toys, interspersed by carts drawn by rack-ribbed horses that seemed on the verge of collapse, and cycle rickshaws and two-wheelers that wove in and out of the traffic, and massive tourist buses belching noxious exhaust, and Tata trucks piled high with sacks of fresh produce headed for the vegetable mandis. The noise was deafening, a hundred car horns honking simultaneously in a raucous cacophony. It was such an assault on my senses that it made my forehead throb.

A dull breeze fanned against my face. Borne upon its fetid wings, I could smell that unique scent that was Punjab, a rich, ripe odour that I had almost managed to forget, that pungent stench of sugarcane and sweat and shit and despair, all bundled into one cloying fragrance.

As the car crept forward like a plump snail, I found myself thinking about Nana again, wondering what I would say when I saw him, what I could say. Predictably, I couldn't think of a single thing that didn't make me angry.

I tried to convince myself that nothing had changed between us, that when we met, he would smile at me and laugh and reach out to hug me, and that I would acquiesce readily, that I would go to him and embrace him like I still loved him, just like I had when I was a boy. But no matter how hard I tried to tell myself that was exactly how it would be, I knew that I was lying to myself.

Abruptly, we shuddered to a total stop, pausing at a traffic light, waiting for it to turn green.

'Too much traffic, sahib,' the taxi driver explained. 'Everyone has become rich on agricultural income and now has three-three cars.'

Annoyed, I leaned out of the window, trying to find a familiar landmark so that I could gauge where we were and how much longer it would be before we arrived at the hospital. But all that I saw was a massive shopping complex in the last stages of construction, an ugly glass-fronted building as immense as a beached whale, in front of which a huge billboard declared 'Welcome to the new Amritsar'.

I winced when I saw that ostentatious declaration. Almost twenty years had passed since my last visit, and during that time, I guessed, the problems of 1984 had been left long behind. Punjab, like the rest of India, was enjoying an era of newfound prosperity, and it was like the dreadful events that I had witnessed all those years ago had never happened at all, as if they had been purged from the state's collective memory, a carefully selective amnesia.

In the end, I thought with a cynical smile, capitalism had won. It always did. Just like the socialists, it was money that had defeated Khalistan. If there was one truth that could not be denied, it was that nothing could stand in the way of money, not ideals, not aspirations and certainly not something as tenuous as dreams. That was what had happened to the Khalistanis. It wasn't the army that had finished them, nor the clever machinations of the politicians in Delhi. Ultimately, they had been overcome by themselves, by their own avarice. After all the death and horror, all the speech-making and bloodshed, the war for Punjab had ended not with a grand explosion but with the slow, almost embarrassed clink of coins. The terrorists had laid down their guns and were now the power behind the throne, and their grand dream of an independent state had been long-forgotten, bought out by tax-free agricultural income and the promise of cheap retail, so easily exchanged for a new dream of middle-class prosperity and conspicuous consumption.

Unexpectedly, as I gazed around, a tremor of recognition trembled through me.

This was it, I realised with a gasp, the very same intersection where I had seen the boy beaten by the police.

Without the sandbagged roadblock and the police vans, it seemed benign, so different now that I had almost not recognised it. But after a moment, I saw it, not as it was now, but how it had been in 1984. I saw the unsmiling row of policemen, and I saw the Sikh boy on his scooter, retching by the side of the street, and I saw Nana, his face twisted into a scowl as he slapped me and sped away.

Horrified, overwhelmed by the weight of that realisation, I let out a groan.

I knew then that I could not go through with it.

I could not face Nana, not after what he had done.

'Stop the car,' I croaked. 'Turn around.'

The driver looked at me quizzically, a pair of inquiring eyes framed in the rear-view mirror.

'Are you sure, sahib? We are almost there, you know.'

'No, turn around. I have changed my mind.'

'Where do you want to go then? Back to the airport?'

Yes, I started to say, but before I could get the words out, in the distance, I saw it, a sparkle of gold, calling to me, like a lighthouse on a dark night.

'No,' I said. 'Take me to the Golden Temple instead.'

20

Even the old city had changed, almost beyond recognition.

Everywhere I turned, there were new buildings, ugly squat concrete blocks rising to the heavens like grasping fingers. And everyone I saw seemed to have a mobile phone, all ringing raucously, a million discordant ringtones pealing at the same time like the chirping of a giant aviary.

It surprised me how dirty everything seemed, how filthy and decrepit. In the glossy diorama of my memory, Amritsar had always been a magical place, but now, as I peered out at the narrow gullies festooned with a web of electrical cables and wires, I was struck by how dingy it really was. I saw piles of garbage rotting on the street corners and open sewers that made my nose wrinkle, and even a dog's corpse rotting in the middle of the street, surrounded by a swarm of buzzing flies.

The crowds were the only thing that was still exactly the same. I had forgotten how packed the narrow lanes around the Golden Temple were. Everywhere I turned, I saw a seething multitude of people, tall Sikhs with long beards and turbans carrying kirpans in their belts and pretty sardarnis with their gaily brocaded chunnis and long plaits.

The taxi driver finally gave up about four blocks from the temple complex. He brought the car trundling to a stop and shook his head, insisting that I would have to go the rest of the way on foot. I realised I had no choice, that he wasn't going to budge. Hefting my duffel, I paid him and got out of the car, but I had barely taken a step forward before it dawned on me that I didn't know which direction to take.

'Which way do I go?' I asked, turning back.

The taxi-wallah replied by letting out a booming laugh.

'This is Amritsar, friend. All roads lead to only one place.'

He was right. It took me a few minutes to detect it, but there was a subtle current amidst the teeming of the crowd, a steady stream of people, all headed towards the same destination. Silently, I joined this inexorable flow, letting them carry me forward like a piece of flotsam caught by the tide.

As we entered the arched front gate, the marbled floor was delightfully cool beneath my feet. A sombre Nirankari with a blue turban offered me a magenta silk rumala from a wicker basket, and a laughing girl showed me how to wrap it around my head and then tuck the corners behind my ears like a biker's bandanna.

Even though it was late in the day, there seemed to be no end to the line of devotees waiting patiently. They came on and on, their faces rapturous with anticipation, shuffling along in a never-ending queue. It was marvellously well-ordered. There was no arguing, no jostling, no fraying of tempers, no cutting in line. Solemnly, inch by inch, I let this throng carry me forward into the temple itself. Once inside, I found a deserted corner and sank down cross-legged on the durrie-carpeted floor, pausing to enjoy the singing of the bhaijis. I let out a sigh, overcome by a sense of belonging that I had all but forgotten. A beatific rapture engulfed me—a simple, almost effortless calm, a peace I had known as a child, but which had eluded me ever since.

I don't know how long I sat there, my eyes tightly shut as one hymn concluded and another began. It could have been an hour, maybe longer, I can't say, but it was indescribably fulfilling. The kirtan revitalised me. With each resounding crescendo, the hard carapace of my resentment, that rancid bitterness that had so consumed me for most of my adult life, was slowly stripped away.

Nobody disturbed me. Nobody asked me who I was, where I came from or why I was there. They left me to my own devices, and for the first time in years, I felt free, released from the fetters of my memories. It was so good not to have to think for once about London or Nana or Soraya. My mind was a blank, clean slate. It was exhilarating.

I could have sat there all day, but then a shadow fell across my face, interrupting my reverie.

'So,' a voice said, 'you have come back to us at last, puttar?'

I looked up to find an old man watching me, a gaunt Sikh with a wispy white beard that reached almost to his waist. He was so pale and insubstantial that he seemed almost ghostlike. It took me a heartbeat to recognise him. At first, I took him to be a stranger, but then, like a punch in the gut, I realised who it was.

It was Nana.

Somehow he had managed to find me.

His sudden appearance, seemingly hale and able to walk, here at the last place I expected to see him, left me dumbstruck. I did not think of objecting when he sank down next to me, sighing with pain. I watched sullenly but did not offer to help him. Thankfully, he kept his distance, staying just far enough so that there were two handbreadths between us. Nor, to my relief, did he try to embrace me.

'What are you doing here? Shouldn't you be in the hospital?'

'There are things we need to talk about, puttar,' he said, squinting at me so knowingly that I felt like a little boy again, wilting before the intensity of his gaze. 'Tell me, have you forgiven me yet?'

I did not answer this question. To be honest, I was afraid to reply. Nana's unexpected arrival had managed to dispel the spell the kirtan had cast over me, that wistful sense of harmony. Now, the rage I had thought forgotten came rushing back, three decades of bottled-up indignation, somehow magnified a hundredfold, so vitriolic that I was scared that if I tried to speak to him, I would end up making a scene.

'Why do you hate me so much, puttar? What did I ever do to you that was so unforgivable?'

This was just too much to take.

'Don't you remember?' I hissed. 'You let them beat that boy. You did nothing. You hit me when I tried to…'

My voice choked away, extinguished by the sheer weight of antagonism. Nana let me work my way through my tirade, unflinching, his face as still as a corpse.

'What choice did I have, my son?' he said gently. 'If I had intervened, they would have arrested us. I couldn't let that happen.' Frowning, he stretched out one sepulchral finger, pointing at me. 'I had to protect you. That was my priority.'

It was a perfectly reasonable explanation. I knew it was most likely true; I had known that for a very long time. But that is the thing about hatred, isn't it? It makes you deaf, and unwilling to accept anything except that which you want to hear. And all I heard were accusations. How dare he? How could he pretend like it was my fault? How could he have the gall to blame me for what he had done?

'You're a liar.' I squealed. My voice was shrill, cracking like a child throwing a tantrum. 'You lied about everything.'

Even as I made this outburst, my fury leached away, replaced by an abject embarrassment when a medley of heads swivelled to glare at me, their eyes gleaming with censure. Ashamed, I bowed my neck. Nana did not even seem to notice, as if they did not exist for him, as if he was past such mundane things as self-consciousness.

'I never told you about my father, did I?' he said. 'We come from one of the oldest and wealthiest families in Punjab. Before Partition, my ancestors owned most of the land in Pasrur, which is now in Pakistan.' He nodded. 'Do you know what a pargana is, puttar? It is the distance a man can walk in a day. A hundred years before my grandfather was born, Maharaja Ranjit Singh himself granted one of our ancestors twelve parganas to call our pinds, our villages.

'My father grew up living like a prince. Everything he desired was handed to him on a silver platter. But then when Partition came, like so many others, he was forced to leave it all behind.

'My grandfather, Sardar Kulwant Singh Bedi, refused to leave Pasrur. This is where I was born, he insisted, and this is where I will die. My father was the youngest son. He had six elder brothers, and they all decided they would remain in Pasrur as well. But my father was afraid of staying behind. He wanted to leave and come here to Amritsar.

'His brothers, of course, made fun of him. They called him a fool and a coward, but my father was convinced he was doing the right thing. In the end, he stole a car, an old Ford from his father's garage, and piled us all into it—my mother, my elder brother, my sister and me, of course—along with all our worldly possessions. I was eleven years old at the time. I don't remember much of what happened, but there was a terrible argument, much shouting and hulla-gulla, before we left. My grandfather was furious, but my father refused to change his mind.

'We left Pasrur seven weeks before Partition and drove eastwards to Pathankot. About an hour out, we saw a mob heading towards us, and my father changed course, veering south. For the rest of the day, we drove. My mother prayed the whole way, and my father refused to stop, not once, not even when we needed to go to the bathroom, until we got to Lahore safely.

'He had a friend there, an Irishman who was a major in the army who said he would escort us personally to the border. We were lucky, I guess. We made it across without any incident. I only realised exactly how lucky we were about two months later when my father found out that all his brothers and his father were dead. They had all been murdered by a mob, maybe even that same one we had so narrowly avoided, and now we were all that was left, the last of the Pasrur Bedis.

'Of course, I did not understand how much leaving them behind to die had hurt him until years later, when I decided to marry your Nani.'

He shuddered, a shiver of his shoulders that spoke volumes.

'When I informed him that I intended to marry a Muslim girl, he told me to leave and never come back. He said that I had broken his heart, that I had betrayed the memory of his father and brothers. They were only words, of course, but then words hurt more than knives sometimes, don't they?'

Nana shook his head, and in spite of my antipathy, I could not help but feel an inkling of empathy.

'I never saw him again. He wrote to me only once, one letter, the same year you came to see me for the last time—1984. It was such a terrible year in so many ways!

'In his letter, my father revealed that he was dying and said that he wanted to put things to rest between us. He told me he forgave me, that he wanted me to come back and see him one last time, that he needed to see me before he died.'

'What did you do?' I asked, even before I had realised it.

'I did nothing.' His shoulders slumped. 'I tore up the letter and never bothered to reply. I couldn't bring myself to do it. I never even went to his funeral, which took place two months later.'

He looked at me, his eyes grim with sorrow.

'That is my greatest regret, puttar. I was too weak to forgive him. I did not realise that everything he was, everything he did ... he was a victim of circumstance. He was what the world had made him. Nothing more, nothing less.

'I have lived with guilt my whole life, puttar. Guilt that I survived while others died, guilt that I could not live up to my father's expectations, guilt that I failed you, that I was not brave enough to stand up for that boy all those many years ago. But no guilt can ever come close to that pain I feel for not being strong enough to forgive my father.'

He let out a sigh, a forlorn threnody of breath.

'Guilt, puttar, is in our blood, in our very souls, here in Punjab, as intrinsic to our existence as suffering. For thousands of years, we have suffered. The Aryans, the Greeks, Aurangzeb, the English ... Jallianwala, Partition, Haryana and, of course, Blue Star. But still, we remain optimistic. Still, we remain indomitable. Do you know why?'

He gave me a sorrowful smile.

'It is because of what Nanak taught, puttar. Suffering is the ultimate test. It is the crucible in which the truth of a man's nature is tested. That is where real heroism comes from, not just for standing up for something but for having the strength to survive even when you are not strong enough to take a stand. That is what character is—to never let adversity break you, to never let suffering break you, because a man is not defined by happiness. He is defined by his regrets, son, but it is his choice if he chooses to let them cripple him or if he decides to be elevated by them. That, in many ways, is the only real choice any of us have.

'That is what makes us great, us Punjabis. It has taken a very long time and a hell of a lot of suffering, but like the Jews and the Irish, we have taught ourselves how to suffer with grace. We laugh and drink and sing and dance and pretend like we are fools, but it is all a lie. The truth is that we have become adept at hiding our pain, our collective sorrow, the amputation of our spirit. We have become experts at hiding how broken we are, how damaged.

'We are all liars, puttar. We lie to the world, to each other, but most of all to ourselves, just so that we can go on, day after meaningless day.'

His words stung at me, so reasonable they almost managed to beguile me.

Almost but not quite.

Instead of forgiveness, all Nana managed to spark off was even more rancour.

'Stop it,' I snapped. 'Just go … go away and leave me alone. I'm sick and tired of listening to your bullshit.'

My grandfather flinched as if I had hit him.

'You have not changed, puttar,' he whispered, shaking his head mournfully. 'I was hoping you would have grown up, but you are still a foolish little boy.'

I don't have to listen to this rubbish, I started to say, but he forestalled me by rising wearily to his feet.

'Goodbye, my boy!' he said. 'My time has come. When I'm gone, I want you to remember one thing. Whatever my flaws, whatever my shortcomings, I have always loved you.'

There was a finality in his voice. Patiently, he gazed down at me for what felt like an eternity, waiting for me to say something in return, that I loved him too, but I couldn't bring myself to even look at him. Instead, I stared resolutely downwards, at the carpet underfoot, clenching my jaw and studying the intricate patterning of its weave. It was stupid really, a puerile act of defiance. But what other way did I have to hurt him?

When I looked up again, Nana was gone. It was like he had vanished into thin air. Panic seized me. I don't know how to describe it other than to say that it was the certainty that I had made a mistake. I had to follow him. I couldn't just let him walk away. I had to stop him to tell him that I was a stubborn, pig-headed fool.

But I didn't.

Instead, I just sat there, unable to move.

21

It is nearing dark by the time I finally make it to the hospital.

The receptionist at the front desk is very kind. She tells me that Nana is up on the third floor and asks an orderly, a plump chaprasi, to show me the way. He beckons deferentially that I should follow him. I have to physically force my recalcitrant feet to waddle after him down a crowded corridor towards a bank of elevators. Inside the lift, I'm pushed up against a gurney being wheeled back from an operating room. On it, a young Sikh boy lies, barely conscious. I glance down at him, wondering what is wrong with him. His sweet, unlined face is stretched taut with pain, but when he sees the worry in my eyes, he smiles boyishly. Then slowly, quite purposefully, he winks at me as if to tell me that everything will be fine.

For a second, that simple gesture makes me feel immeasurably better. Unfortunately, it is an elusive comfort. When the elevator doors open and I step out to see a cluster of my relatives congregating outside the door of what is obviously Nana's room, my anxiety returns a hundredfold.

Uncle Sanjeev is the first to spot me. His eyes settle on my face, but he does not know me, not at first, until I raise one hand in wry salutation. Befuddled, his brow knots when he sees this gesture, trying to reconcile my shaven head and gaunt visage with his recollections of the chubby boy he had last seen some two decades previously. Finally, recognition seems to dawn. Uncle Sanjeev does not smile. He just gives a brisk nod before coming to greet me. He has not changed. He is still the same bear of a man who stinks of Denim aftershave and looks so much like Nana that it makes me grimace.

After a momentary hesitation, he throws open his arms, about to hug me. I quickly shake hands with him instead.

'Where were you?' he asks, almost accusing. 'We have been waiting for you all day.'

I bite my tongue and ignore the castigation in his voice.

'How is Nana?' I ask. 'Is he feeling any better?'

Uncle Sanjeev's face stiffens, purpling with sorrow.

'He's gone, puttar. He died this afternoon, just after one.'

He continues to waffle on, something about how it was quick and painless, but I cannot hear him. A thundering fills my ears. I'm dizzy, unable to catch my breath. Nana, gone. How can it be? I just saw him. He was with me at the Golden Temple, not two hours ago.

My legs buckle. Before I know it, I'm falling. Uncle Sanjeev surges forward and catches me. Bodily, he props me upright, wrapping one strong arm around my shoulders.

'It's okay, puttar,' he murmurs, mistaking my confusion for heartbreak. 'It's better this way. It was his time.'

'Can … can I see him please?'

'Of course.'

Refusing to relinquish his grip on my shoulder, he leads me into the hospital room. My relatives crowd around me, cousins and uncles and aunties of all shapes and sizes, all of whom want to meet the prodigal grandson. I fix a smile on my face and lapse into a sort of semi-consciousness, a strangely comforting ritual of lean forward, kiss on the cheek, clasp hands and shake, that I endure silently like an automaton.

The hospital room is surprisingly pink. The walls, the curtains and even the linoleum underfoot are so vivid that I think for a moment that I'm going insane. I guess that it is supposed to make the patients more comfortable, but somehow, all that this ... this pinkness serves to do is make me feel nauseous, almost ill.

Other than this violent bubblegum palette, the room is sparsely furnished. It has that familiar hospital smell—liniment and disinfectant and vomit and death all mixed into one noxious odour that makes me sniff. In one corner, a pair of squat chairs sit next to a side table covered with an array of wilting flower bouquets. On the other side is a large machine, some sort of ventilator, I imagine, and next to it, a metal hospital bed atop which my grandfather lies silently, so peaceful that at first, I think he is asleep, not dead.

I can barely recognise him. He is smaller in death than he ever was in life. They have bathed him and swaddled his body in a white sheet as tightly as a mummy until all that remains uncovered is his face, ashen and sunken cheeked, as if his bones have collapsed. There are balls of cotton in his nose. His beard, which was always so magnificent, looks like soggy cotton wool now, a bedraggled mess.

As I gaze down at him, a sudden rush of emotion gnaws at my chest. It is not rage, not the bitterness that has become so familiar to me over the years.

No, instead, I'm gripped by a paroxysm of pity.

Mutely, I find myself examining the fragile web of lines that surround his ancient eyes and the delicate embroidery of wrinkles that has slowly spread down across his cheeks like the slender veins on the surface of a leaf. For one futile moment, I try to count those lines, but there are far too many, so numerous, that I cannot tell where the wrinkles end and his skin begins.

Those are his scars, I think with a shudder, so many, many scars. Every one of those creases is a story inscribed in the ink of suffering and merriment. Every frown furrow is a sad, sour moment, every laugh line a sweet, fleeting second of joy.

At that moment, I finally begin to understand what Nana was trying to explain to me.

All this time, I was the one who was wrong.

Wrong about everything.

About him.

About myself.

But most of all, I was wrong about what it takes to be a man.

It does not take a beard or chest hair or muscles.

What it takes is honour.

Character.

And more than anything else, it takes compassion, the willingness to forgive.

All this time, I was the one who had been a coward, not Nana.

I was the one who had been too afraid, too weak to forgive him.

Too weak to forgive myself.

And until I learnt how to do that, to absolve and to accept, my journey into manhood would never be complete.

With that epiphany, the last vestiges of my hatred shrivel inside me and wither away, leaving me wonderfully empty, like a story waiting to be written, not one that had already been told.

Leaning forward, I kiss my grandfather gently on his cold cheek.

'You were never a coward, Nana,' I whisper.

'You were the bravest man I have ever known.'

ACKNOWLEDGEMENTS

In many ways, books are like journeys. Whether it is a joyous expedition or a painful one depends, more often than not, upon the fellow travellers you encounter along the way. I have been very fortunate to have made this long and somewhat difficult journey in the company of a number of people who have helped me nurture this book into existence. I wrote the first draft of what would ultimately become *The Anatomy of Loss* almost twenty-five years ago and had long since given up on ever seeing it in print, relegating it instead to a forgotten corner of my computer hard drive. And there it would have continued to languish if not for my wonderful wife, Masumeh. She was the one who convinced me to edit the manuscript down from 400-plus pages to its current avatar and held my hand through the ups and downs of finding the right publisher. In fact, we fell in love while editing the manuscript together, which, in my opinion, makes this as much her book as my own.

I am equally grateful to my mother, who found such pleasure in teaching me about Punjab and its myths and traditions. By reliving the stories and folk tales that her parents had once told her—those marvellous legends that are all that remain of an oral history long lost to us after the Partition of India—that is how I learnt what it means to be Punjabi. It is she and her parents, Charan Singh and Motia Chawla, who are the inspiration behind the Nana and Nani in this story, and I owe them a debt that no profusion of words, however eloquent, can ever repay.

I am indebted to Opinderjit and Neena Sandhu. Much of the setting for this book is based on their lovely farm outside Amritsar, and several of the incidents recounted are based on the apocryphal stories I overheard while eavesdropping on their conversations with my parents as a child. Their warmth, kindness and hospitality represent, in my opinion, all that is best about the people of Punjab.

I am grateful for Kanishka Gupta, my valiant companion in arms. This is our fourth book together, and he is so much more than my literary agent. He is my therapist, my agony aunt, my friend and, most of all, my brother. I can only hope we have the pleasure of charging at many more windmills together.

I have always believed that while writers may write books, it is editors who make them worth reading. In this instance, I have had the good fortune of working with Prerna Vohra, whom I cannot thank enough for her patience and expertise. Without her, this wouldn't be half the book it has turned out to be. I would also like to offer a heartfelt vote of thanks to Jaishree Ram Mohan for stepping in at the last moment and seeing this book to print, to Thanglenhao Haokip for his thorough and exacting copy-editing and to Devangana Dash for designing such a striking and magnificent cover.

Last but certainly not the least, I am truly thankful to Krishan Chopra for the enduring faith he has shown in this book. If not for his support, Himmat's story might never have been told.